Brontë Lovers

ANGELA PEARSE

Set in Black Chancery and Sabon.
Cover art by My Lan Khuc Valle.

ISBN 978-1-914531-85-9 Paperback (IS)
ISBN 978-1-914531-84-2 Paperback (KDP)

Author Note

This story includes references to depression and suicide and features on-page sexual content. If you are sensitive to these elements, please be mindful.

Chapter 1

It was an incident of no moment, no romance,
no interest in a sense; yet it marked with change
one single hour of a monotonous life.

(Charlotte Brontë, *Jane Eyre*)

As heritage steam trains go, the one that travels between Keighley and Haworth in West Yorkshire is a real beauty. Not that I know much about the mechanics. I'm excited by the shiny black paint, belching grey smoke and the *wump wump wump* as it chugs off down the tracks once we're inside it.

My boyfriend, Klint, is somewhat less excited even though steam machines of nineteenth-century Britain are the subject of his doctoral thesis. Still, he'd seemed pleased this morning when I announced I'd bought us tickets as a treat. I was also sure I'd caught a glimmer of interest in his eye as we boarded, though he'd tried to hide it in his usual stoic fashion. I know I'm to blame for his stand-offish behaviour, and I'm trying to make amends, but it's mentally draining.

After ten minutes of silence across the table, I nudge his ankle with my foot. 'Having fun?'

He glances up from his laptop, peering at me through his round glasses. For the life of me, I can't fathom why he's working when we're joyriding on a steam train. *Probably to punish me.*

'Sure. It's giving me time to write up yesterday's notes from Bradford,' he says.

I sigh to myself. 'But this is your thing—steam and trains. Isn't it getting your pistons pumping?' Truly, I hoped he'd be bouncing off the carriage walls.

'Yes, Lizzy, I'm having fun. And yes, my pistons are pumping,' he says dryly, returning to his notes. Maybe they are, but quietly. Wow, I thought if anything could light our flagging flame, this would be it. It seems I'm wrong. Yet again.

I give up on him as a lost cause for now and glance out the window. We're chugging along nicely; and soon, we'll be in Haworth, where we're staying for a few days. I've never been there, but I'm looking forward to it since it's the home of the infamous Brontë sisters. I'm even re-reading *Wuthering Heights* in the hope it will inspire a thesis topic of my own. I stare at Klint's thin absorbed face as he methodically types. Despite his outward lack of enthusiasm, he is fully into his subject. He lives and breathes steam.

Like a man-dragon, I think, resisting the urge to giggle.

We rent a small flat in Oxford near Balliol College, of which is Klint is a member, but we've been on a two-week research trip across the north of England visiting museums and archives in various industrial towns. Now Klint has a lead on some historical documents in Haworth that he wants to follow up on. Having recently quit my job in town and at a loose end, Klint suggested I tag along for the ride. He said it might be more interesting than staying alone in the flat, but personally, I think he's trying to keep me out of trouble. Bored, I gaze out the window again.

'Why don't you go to the Brontë Parsonage tomorrow?' Klint suggests, as if he knows I'm brooding.

I look back to find him contemplating me. 'Oh, I guess I could.'

'I assume, since you've been reading *Wuthering Heights* for the past couple of nights, that you're looking for the catalyst?'

By that, he means the deep intrigue of a subject necessary to undertake a three-year doctoral degree. But I'll require enough grit and determination to complete it as well. I'm not sure I have the stamina; my master's was difficult enough. Besides, I've been working for a year in a menial office job to pay off a student loan. I'm out of practice in the brain department. My knife has gone blunt, if you will.

'Hah, maybe. But I'm not expecting it,' I reply, feeling disgruntled. It *would* be nice to be engrossed in a subject like Klint, but at least I'm having a small break from reality before I look for another job to pay the bills.

'You never know, the spinster sisters might surprise you. Perhaps you could investigate why they created such roguish book boyfriends when there were perfectly suitable men in the village.'

I smile thinly. *Men in the village are never as exciting as book boyfriends.* 'Charlotte Brontë did actually marry one of those, to her detriment.'

I'm beginning to wish he would go back to his notes and stop trying to pressure me. You can't force these things to happen. Sometimes they just do, out of nowhere.

At Haworth station, we grab a taxi; and it winds through the narrow cobbled street of the village, which is set on the side of a hill. I get a brief impression out the window: a jumble of quaint shops and an imposing beige stone church. Right next to the entrance steps is a pub with 'The Black Bull' in gold on its frontage.

The hotel that Klint's booked for us—a low-slung two-storey stone-and-plaster building with an uneven slate roof—is in a valley near the village. Inside, it's old and characterful with dark oak beams criss-crossing the ceiling and a flight of narrow stairs leading up to the rooms. A bar doubles as a reception desk, and an adjacent dining area has a number of empty wooden tables. I spy a couple of faded Brontë biographies displayed in a snug next to the bar, which could come in handy for a post-dinner read—though, as if we've arrived mid-morning, there's a while to wait until dinner.

Before even introducing himself, Klint, ever the historian, asks the burly pleasant-faced guy behind the bar about the history of the place. Gareth Rumsey (as his name badge states) is barely older than we are, but he seems to have a ready supply of facts. Apparently, it was a sixteenth-century rest stop for horses to take a load off while their shoes were being shod. Then it was turned into a wayfarers' hotel. After a few more minutes of chit-chat, Klint asks about the room; and Gareth admits, pleasantly, that check-in isn't until two but we can relax and have a drink at the bar if we like. I look at the array of coloured bottles on the shelves. It's too early to start drinking, though I could murder a G and T.

'That's OK. We'll explore the town and have some lunch,' I tell him. Klint glances over at the empty restaurant. I assume he's about to ask if he can take his laptop in there later on to finish his notes, but then he notices Gareth staring at my forearm.

Damn, it's warm in here, and I pushed up the sleeves of my cardigan without thinking.

'Yes, good idea. I'm starved,' Klint says. 'Do you mind looking after our luggage?' He hands Gareth his shoulder bag containing his laptop, which effectively distracts him. The mark on my arm, a crescent of teeth, looks worse than it is; and it's not painful. But it's not something I particularly want to explain to a stranger. Usually, if anyone asks, I say I had a run-in with a dog. But Gareth looks the discerning type, and I don't think he'll believe me.

We beat a hasty retreat to the village.

'I'm sorry,' says Klint unprompted, his voice thick with guilt as we stroll along the high street.

'Don't worry about it. It'll go away in a few days,' I reply stiffly. He's apologised numerous times, and it's bordering on overkill. Short of wearing metal armguards to bed, I'm not sure what I'm supposed to do.

I peer inside a café with a sage-green frontage. It looks homely, yet tasteful and not too busy. However, it is September, so we've missed the peak tourist season. I bet Haworth is heaving with Brontë fans during July and August.

'Is here OK for lunch?' I ask Klint.

He shrugs. 'Sure.'

We step inside and silently queue behind a tall dark-haired guy who's wearing an old-fashioned black silk coat with long tails and a high collar. From the back, his Victorian vibe is eye-catching enough to make me contemplate him and wonder what the deal is—maybe he's attending a themed wedding? His confident stance and the timbre of his voice suggest he's hot, but it's not confirmed until he turns to extract a bottle of drink from the fridge, and I get a better look. Shortish dark wavy hair, perfect pale skin, classic bone structure, along with a pair of deep brown eyes and sculpted lips. I swallow. Hot indeed. Maybe he's an actor who's in a period film? He's got that air about him. A guy like him could definitely inspire a Brontë book boyfriend.

Thankfully, he pays and breezes past in a cloud of mystique before I get too flustered. Klint hates it when I check out other guys, but it's just *looking*, and he looks at other women all the time. As my eyes have been wandering, I let him off the hook for perving at the café server since she's attractive and for being enticed to order a gigantic slice of carrot cake. Klint loves cake almost as much as he likes steam and studying.

***

After lunch, we explore the main street of the village, which doesn't take long since it consists of pubs, curio shops, and cafés. We walk back to the hotel, the tense atmosphere between us eased thanks to a good lunch.

'The Brontë Parsonage is through there.' Klint nods to a lane leading up to a car park and a leafy enclave. 'You could go now if you wanted.'

I frown and stare at the road ahead, my stomach clenching.

'Mum is calling around three, and it shuts at five,' he presses.

'Doesn't give me much time,' I say, feeling coerced into going before I'm ready.

'Isn't two hours enough?'

'I want to have a good poke around, see if anything jumps out at me.'

'Suit yourself.'

Why is his mother calling again? He spoke to her two days ago. I don't voice that thought out loud, though. Klint and his mother, Lydia, have a special bond that requires regular communication. His dad is often away on business, so she calls Klint 'for a little chat' because she has nothing better to do, which is fine. But he doesn't like me listening in. God knows why as their conversations are hardly scintillating. It's mainly gossiping about people I don't know. Then again, I'm probably just jealous he has a mother to talk to.

'I'll go and read *Wuthering Heights* downstairs so I don't disturb you,' I tell him.

'OK, thanks.'

I sigh quietly as we walk. Maybe I *should* go to the parsonage, though it does look like rain. The sky, which was clear blue before, is now filled with scudding grey clouds. The shadowy moors slope up behind the village, and below the road we're walking on, lush green fields sectioned with stone walls stretch away into the distance.

'It's lovely here,' I comment. 'The air is so fresh and bracing. I can see why the sisters liked going for walks.'

'Bet it's bloody freezing in winter, though.'

'Yeah, probably why they're filming now before it gets too cold.'

'Who's filming?'

'I got the impression there might be a movie being made.'

'What makes you say that? I didn't see a film crew or anything.'

I don't want to mention the guy from the café in case Klint thinks I was checking him out (which I kind of was).

'Oh, I thought I saw something happening up by the church, but it was probably just a bunch of tourists with large cameras.'

Back at the hotel, I ensure the sleeves of my cardigan are firmly pulled down, but Gareth doesn't mention anything as he smoothly checks us in. We lug our bags up the flight of steep stairs and down an even narrower hallway to room 6.

Klint looks around at the blue-walled room, which is dwarfed by a double bed with a flowered bedspread, and purses his lips. He doesn't say anything, but I know what he's thinking: poky! But I like it; it's snug. A high window lets in the cool breeze and displays a view of the darkening sky and a glimpse of the moors. I'm glad I decided not to go to the parsonage today. An hour downstairs with Cathy and Heathcliff is preferable to getting rained on or listening to Klint and his mother gossip.

'I'll just wash my hands,' I say, heading into the en-suite, which contains a shower and a sink. I had a messy panini for lunch, and I don't want to mark the pristine pages of my new book with greasy fingers.

Klint pokes his head in. 'Not enough room to swing a cat,' he comments, eyeing the small shower stall and the even smaller sink that are jostling for space.

'Hah, yeah. Lucky you're not six foot six.' Klint is a respectable five foot eleven, but reed thin. If he turns sideways in a certain light, he sometimes looks invisible.

Finished washing my hands, I carefully soap and rinse the wound as well while he watches. I'm not doing it to make him feel bad. I don't want it to get infected, and a sticking plaster will pull off my arm hairs.

'Do you think I should say something to Mum?' he asks in a concerned tone. 'It's happening quite frequently.'

'If you want to, but she'll blame me and probably book you an appointment with her psychiatrist.'

Turning off the tap, I gingerly pat my forearm with the towel. There's a hint of a purple bruise forming around the teeth marks.

I don't care what Klint tells his mother about his sleep biting habit—I just hope it doesn't happen again tonight.

Chapter 2

All through the night, your glorious eyes
Were gazing down in mine.

(Emily Brontë, 'Stars')

Maybe talking to his mother is good for something as there's no reoccurrence. I leave Klint happily tapping away on his laptop in our room after breakfast and make my way up to the Brontë Parsonage. The sky is overcast with patches of blue, but it's not too chilly. Last night, a high wind whistled disconcertingly round the eaves, making me glance up from my book from time to time. There's something thrilling about reading a novel that was inspired by the landscape outside your window. I hope I can walk on the moors while we're here. I want to be fully immersed in the Brontës' world.

Charlotte, Emily, and Anne's home is fronted by a neat strip of green lawn and faces Haworth Parish Church and its dilapidated graveyard. The two-storey house isn't manor-sized, but its brown brick frontage has an imposing quality.

The fact that it's liberally set with windows strikes me as macabre. For the sisters, there was no escaping that graveyard view or being reminded of their own mortality on a daily basis.

The gabled front door is wide open, but there's no one on the doorstep to check my online ticket, so I head up the flagstone steps and go inside. Despite the cold look of the exterior, the light-blue-painted hallway is surprisingly warm. The home feels well cared for, beloved.

A girl around my age comes out of the room on the left. She's pale with large eyes and shoulder-length brown hair. Apart from her modern clothing, there's something antiquated about her face, like she could almost be a long distant Brontë cousin. 'Hello, have you got a ticket?' she asks.

'Hi, yes.' I show her my phone.

'Great, that's valid for a year in case you want to visit the parsonage again.'

'I might actually, so that's good to know.'

She smiles, revealing wonky front teeth that add to her wistful charm. 'Well, feel free to wander around. It's not too busy this morning, so you'll probably have the house to yourself.'

This is what I want to hear. There's nothing worse than trying to soak up the ambiance of a historical home whilst jostling elbows with other tourists. If something intrigues me, I might need a decent length of time to look at it, and I don't like being forced to hurry. Klint hates going to museums with me because he'll have whipped around in an efficient manner and be ready to leave while I'm still staring at the first exhibit.

'Where should I start?' I ask the girl, whose name badge says 'Bridget'.

'The parlour.' She gestures to the room on the left. 'That's where most people like to go first. It's where the novels were written. Oh, and look out for the *E* carved into the table, courtesy of Emily.'

'Thanks. Will you be around if I have any questions?'

'Dain's our on-site Brontë expert, but I should be able to answer anything as well.'

I note that her eyes widen, and her cheeks glow at the mention of him. Something's going on there. Is he her boyfriend? Do they have illicit trysts up on the moors during lunch breaks? She doesn't look the type.

The girl turns to greet a couple who are approaching the doorway, and I take out my phone to type 'DAIN' into my notes app. If he's the Brontë expert, he'll be a good person to hit up if I come across anything that requires further analysis.

After moseying around the downstairs rooms (the small neat parlour where the sisters wrote, Mr Brontë's austere study, the tiny household kitchen, and the makeshift office for Charlotte's husband, Arthur Nicholls), I make my way upstairs. There are five rooms. The one belonging to their brother, Branwell, is a mess—a jumble of sketches, poems, clothing, and even a (fake) beer spillage. It was part of the set of the film *To Walk Invisible*, so it's been left to showcase him as the slovenly ragtag of the bunch. I have seen the film, and he definitely gets the short shrift in that. But judging by the proximity of the bedrooms, living with such a disruptive force in their midst must've taken its toll on the sisters. I'm guessing they escaped into their writing or headed out onto the moors to get some relief from his drama.

The other four upstairs rooms are labelled as belonging to the maid, Mr Brontë, Charlotte, and the children. I'm leaning against the banister on the landing, wondering which room was Emily's, when I hear someone coming up. I glance over into the stairwell. As a mop of dark hair and clean profile bob into view, I realise with a shivery thrill it's the guy from the café. The adrenaline rush is quickly followed by a strong urge to run away, but that's a dumb move since he's about to see me.

He reaches the top of the stairs, and I can't help gawking at the full spectacle. In the blink of an eye, I'm back in the nineteenth century. He's not wearing the coat but still dressed in formal suit attire: white round-collared shirt with the sleeves rolled up, black pinstriped waistcoat with a gold fob watch chain, and slim black wool trousers. He has the look of a young curate. But back in the day, he probably wouldn't have been coming up here since there are young ladies' bedrooms.

'Hello. You look lost in thought,' he says. My eyes flick to the name badge on his waistcoat: DAIN. OK, so he's the Brontë expert. That kind of explains the Victorian get-up and, since he's stunningly good-looking, the blushing girl downstairs.

My pulse rate increases. I hardly know what to say. 'Oh, I was wondering which bedroom was Emily's. Was it the children's room?' I ask, blushing a little myself as it's a lame question.

But Dain seems eager to supply the answer. 'Yes, it seems so as one of her diary papers has a self-portrait sketch of her in there.' He gestures to the room, and I head over to have another look. For some reason, I *am* drawn to this room.

'Wow, it's really small. Wasn't she tallish?'

'Yes, five foot seven—the tallest of the sisters. That's the stool she used to take out on the moors with her to write,' he says, coming over to stand next to me. 'There's also some graffiti on the walls, which we think were made by the children when they were younger.' He points, and I peer in further and see some scratchings, but they're too faint to make out. I believe if he believes.

'She liked lying in bed at night and looking up at the stars.' His tone turns dreamy. 'Without any light pollution, the sky would've been awash with them. The view from this window inspired her to write the poem "Stars", which was included in *Poems by Currer, Ellis, and Acton Bell*, published in 1846.'

I glance up at him, impressed. He does seem to know his Brontë stuff.

'Are you in Haworth for the day or staying for longer?' he asks conversationally when we've moved back onto the landing.

He's knowledgeable, maybe even an academic, and his obvious enthusiasm for the Brontës is rubbing off on me. So I feel in a safe space to admit, 'For a few days. I'm actually hoping to find a topic for my DPhil.'

Dain's dark-brown eyes lock on mine. 'Oxford?'

I nod, mentally kicking myself for not saying 'doctorate' and hoping he won't pigeonhole me as an intellectual snob because I don't think I am.

'What did you do your master's in?' he enquires.

'Feminism in nineteenth-century American literature.'

He leans against the stair banister and folds his arms like he's settling into debate mode. 'You can't go wrong with the Brontës. They're endlessly fascinating, and there's plenty of background research material.'

'Hmm, I'd have to be *really* interested in the topic to write 100K on it. But they are an intriguing bunch of women.'

Dain frowns as if 'intriguing bunch of women' isn't a phrase he'd use to describe them. 'Have you read the big three: *Wuthering Heights*, *Jane Eyre*, and *The Tenant of Wildfell Hall*?'

I nod, relaxing a little as he's easy to talk to. 'I'm re-reading *Wuthering Heights* at the moment. We did it for high school English, and my take on it now is a bit different, but I'm enjoying it.'

Dain gives a quick pleased smile, and his face glows. I stare at him, a little bewitched. He is quite something. 'That's one of my faves. I'd also suggest reading *Agnes Grey* and *Villette*. Both give excellent insight into Anne's and Charlotte's strong characters and the plight of women at the time. For biographies, there's *The Life of Charlotte Brontë* by Elizabeth Gaskell, though she chose to use artistic license for some of it ...' His dark eyes gleam with amusement. 'And also *The Brontës* by Juliet Barker. It's more based on fact than flights of fancy. *The Brontë Cabinet* by Deborah Lutz is also fascinating. Some of the objects she mentions are in the display room next door. We have a good selection of titles in the bookshop downstairs too if you want to buy any physical copies.'

'OK.' As he's speaking, I'm busily typing the books he suggested in my notes app while sneaking glances and wondering how to keep the conversation going.

'If you want to pick my brains, we could also have a session in the Black Bull. It's where Branwell used to drink,' he says casually. It appears he's thinking along the same lines.

I pause in my typing, my eyes flicking to his. *Did he just ask me out?* I know instantly that (*a*) I want to go and (*b*) it's going to be difficult to get it past Klint.

Luckily, Dain takes my silence for ignorance rather than rejection. 'Do you know anything about their brother?'

I push down my stomach flutters and try to act nonchalant. 'A little. He wasn't a great artist and caused them all a lot of misery with his drunken rants—I've seen the *To Walk Invisible* movie.'

'That was damning. He's often scorned, but in my opinion, he was an important creative catalyst. If it wasn't for Branwell, I doubt we would've had characters like Heathcliff, Rochester or Huntingdon. He was an integral part of their life, physically and emotionally.'

Dain is speaking my language. 'I was just thinking something along those lines.'

He smiles, looking expectant, and I know he's waiting for an answer to his invitation to the pub. To bide my time, I shakily type 'BRANWELL CATALYST' in my notes app while he watches.

I clear my throat. 'OK, well, picking your brains might be a good idea. I'm Lizzy Doyle, by the way.'

'Dain Whitmore.' He doesn't unfold his arms to shake my hand, so I keep mine anchored by my side. I don't think touching him is a good idea by the way my stomach flips when I think of it.

'Whereabouts are you staying?'

I tell him the name of the hotel, and he raises an eyebrow. 'Ah. I hope you're not the nervous type?'

I don't reply as I'm not sure what he means by asking that and because I *am* the nervous type.

The couple who entered after me have come part-way up the stairs. They pause to look at Branwell's portrait of the sisters, and I hear them discussing it in low voices.

Dain extracts a small pad and pencil out of his waistcoat pocket and scribbles on it.

'Here's my number anyway if you want to get in touch while you're here.' He hands me a slip of paper, and I know

I'm smiling a little too brightly as I take it.

'Uh, thanks. Well, I guess I'll check out the bookshop.'

Dain nods. 'Nice chatting, Lizzy! And message me anytime. Like Emily, I'm a bit of a night owl.' OK, that definitely sounded flirty. This could be a bad idea. He saunters off down the stairs to talk to the couple, and I head through to the adjoining display room, which is full of Brontë paraphernalia.

I can't help feeling discombobulated by Dain as I wander around. Not only is he completely my type lookswise; he's also intelligent, interesting, and amenable to meeting up. It's not a wise combination for me, and I know Klint would hate him on sight.

I go down another level to the brightly lit bookshop, which is chock-full of books, mugs, key rings, even stick-on tattoos of Brontë book quotes.

Idly, I pick up a mug and look at the price before heading over to the bookshelf. But I can't discount the fact that Dain appears to be a walking Wikipedia when it comes to the Brontës. If anyone can inspire me to come up with a research topic, I'm putting my bets on him.

Maybe Klint can be persuaded to let go of the reins a little. I just need to manage the situation carefully.

Chapter 3

Keeper flew at his throat forthwith, and held him there.

(Elizabeth Gaskell, *The Life of Charlotte Brontë*)

Upon my return to the hotel, I dive into the last quarter of *Wuthering Heights* for the rest of the afternoon and early evening. I don't feel like reading in the restaurant. Yesterday, Klint spoke to his mother for an excruciating hour and a half, and my butt went numb. So I lie on my side of the bed, trying to tune out the annoying tapping and clicking noises he's making on his laptop. I'm on edge and overly excited after talking to Dain to the point where I keep shifting position restlessly, making the bed bounce, and Klint comments that someone's got 'ants in their pants'.

Around six, Klint and I descend to the dining room for dinner, where we peruse the menus and give the waitress our orders: a burger and fries for Klint, sausage and mash for me. He also orders a pint of local cider to go with his meal, which surprises me. Klint hardly ever drinks alcohol unless it's a special occasion. Either his thesis is coming along swimmingly, or he's feeling tense and needs to relax.

'G and T, Liz?'

'Yes please. A double.' Might as well take advantage of this. I'm not a huge drinker, but I haven't touched alcohol in months.

'So how was the parsonage?' Klint enquires after the waitress has left. 'Sorry I didn't ask before. I was dealing with a tricky section.' *OK, hence the cider. He needs to relax.*

'Oh, good,' I say with a shrug.

He cocks his head and surveys me. 'Nothing you saw that might be worth pursuing?'

Only a tall dark handsome stranger, I think, instantly feeling guilty.

'Ah, not yet. But I did buy some books from the shop. One of the guides recommended reading a few more Brontë novels and a couple of biographies. There's also an artefact study that sounds interesting. So I've got enough to keep me busy.'

This is the point where I should probably mention to Klint that the said guide kindly invited me to the pub so I can pick his brains about the Brontës. But the timing and my demeanour aren't right. Dain is far too sexy to feign nonchalance, and I know if I say anything now, I'm going to sound overly eager. There has to be a delay so I don't care as much.

Our food arrives, and between mouthfuls, Klint tells me about some aspect of his research. But the sound of a raised voice penetrates our conversation. One of the pub's patrons, a middle-aged gentleman, is propping up the bar and wanting another drink. Gareth is refusing to serve him one.

'Aww, come on,' the man slurs. He slaps a note down on the bar, but Gareth doesn't pick it up.

'You've had enough. It's time to go,' he says and comes round the other side of the bar and attempts to grab the man's arm, but his grip is abruptly shaken off. The man staggers backwards, telling Gareth to keep his 'fucking hands' off him. I watch the scene, fascinated, whilst forking peas and mashed potato into my mouth.

'Lizzy.' Klint shakes his head, indicating that I shouldn't stare.

'This is brilliant,' I whisper to him. 'It's like something out of *Wuthering Heights*. The locals definitely have a wild spirit even in this day and age.'

Klint looks amused and glances at the bar, where the man is again demanding a drink. 'Yes, they are a bit rough and ready.'

The scene escalates to the point where the cook comes out of the kitchen, and he and Gareth manhandle the guy into the foyer, where a lively discussion ensues. The man wants to drive home. Gareth wants his keys. There are scuffling noises.

'Jesus,' mutters Klint. 'Drive? In his state?'

Gareth comes back in and is on the phone, asking to be put through to the police. He speaks in a low rumble, saying something I can't hear. He disappears again, I assume, to await their appearance.

'Good job,' says Klint, putting his knife and fork together neatly on his empty plate. 'The police will sort him out.'

The cook, a large man with a bushy beard and a striped apron, comes over with a sheepish expression. 'Sorry about that.'

'Is everything OK?' asks Klint.

The cook sighs. 'He's a regular, a local businessman. We've had him barred before, but it only lasts three months, and he's back again.' He glances at our empty plates. 'Can I get you some dessert?'

'Yes, that would be great, thanks,' I say. If we stick around, there might be some more drama.

While we're waiting for dessert (and the police) to appear, I go for a poke around the dimly lit back of the restaurant as I glimpse some photos on the wall. There's nothing too exciting—only some old black-and-white shots of the hotel. I move around the corner, and my gaze lands on a gold-framed certificate proclaiming, 'THIS PLACE IS HAUNTED!'

It states that the Ghost Research Foundation has undertaken a study and found "conclusive evidence" of ghost phenomena within the building—and to "watch out as there are ghosts about". I groan inwardly. That must be why Dain asked if I was the nervous type. Did Klint know about this when he booked our room? I hotfoot it back to the table, where he's on his second pint of cider, and sit down hurriedly.

'Oh, hey, do you want another G and T?'

'No thanks. Did you know this place was haunted before you booked it?' I say accusingly.

Klint raises his eyebrows at my tone.

'Um, no, I didn't. What makes you think it is?'

'A certificate in the back over there. Some research foundation did a study, and they found *conclusive evidence of ghosts.*' My voice rises an octave, but Klint doesn't look fazed.

'Calm down. It's probably a marketing ploy. They have to say something to get people to stay here since it's out of town.'

I take a deep breath. 'If that's the case, it would've been front and centre on their website when you booked. The fact that it's on a certificate hidden in a back room suggests that it's legit. We can't stay here.'

I *cannot* stay in a haunted hotel. I'm the sort of highly strung person a ghost would appear to, and I *do not* want to see it. Once, I stayed in a spooky hotel with a group of friends on a murder mystery weekend, and it was horrible. Of course, everyone else slept like a baby. I was wide awake all night, and had a panic attack every time a floorboard creaked.

Klint clicks his tongue. 'It's too late to find something else, so we'll have to stay tonight at least. Even if it is haunted, which I highly doubt, a ghost isn't going to hurt you.'

'It said "phenomena", so it's more than just one!'

The cook comes in with our dishes of chocolate cake with caramel sauce and vanilla ice cream. 'Here you go.' He sees my mournful expression and enquires, 'Everything all right?'

Klint answers for me. 'Lizzy is worried there are ghosts floating around.'

The cook smiles at me reassuringly. 'Nothing to worry about. I've been working here for seven years, and I've never seen anything.'

My anxiety eases. 'So the certificate I saw is silly nonsense?'

'Well ... I wouldn't say it's entirely unfounded. But it's only people staying in room 6 on the old side of the hotel that tend to complain about things going bump in the night.'

My anxiety returns doublefold. 'But we're in room 6!' I exclaim, staring at him wide-eyed in horror.

The cook gives me a pitying look and decides this is a good time to slink off back to the kitchen.

'Maybe we can shift rooms,' I say to Klint, who's digging into his pudding with gusto.

'I think you're being overly dramatic,' he replies, licking ice cream off his spoon. 'Nothing's going to happen. I've watched those ghost shows. They set up their cameras and audio equipment in a "supposedly" haunted house for a night. There's always a massive build-up, and it's usually a big let-down because nothing whatsoever happens. So if you do see anything, I'll be mightily surprised. Anyway, I'll be there. Just wake me up if you're scared.'

I reach over to place my hand on his to show my gratitude, which he allows. But after a moment, he moves it away, saying softly with a side glance at the bar, 'Sorry, you know how I feel about PDAs.'

I bite my lip. *There's no one around! Unless he's worried a ghost might see.*

Lying in bed later, I roll towards Klint and spoon against him hopefully, but he doesn't respond. I rub his arm gently, and he tenses. 'I'm not in the mood,' he says.

I sigh and roll onto my back. I was hoping sex would enable me to drop off to sleep afterwards, therefore solving the ghost issue. But it seems Klint isn't going to help me out. 'Do you mind if I read then?'

'Go for it.'

I delve into *The Life of Charlotte Brontë*. I'm half a chapter in when Klint's head swivels. 'Can you turn the light off now?'

'I was hoping to keep it on.'

'All night? No way, I need it dark.'

'I won't be able to sleep if it's dark! We're in room 6, remember?'

'Honestly, Lizzy, you're being ridiculous. Turn the light out please. I'm tired,' he huffs.

Mutely, I put my book on the bedside table and flick off the light, plunging the room into pitch darkness.

There's a rustle as Klint gets comfortable on his pillow. 'Thank you. Now close your eyes and go to sleep. Nothing's going to happen.'

Dutifully, I pull the covers up to my chin and shut my eyes. But a crinkling noise in the corner makes my heart leap in fright. 'What was that?' I switch on the light and sit bolt upright. 'Oh, it was my make-up bag falling over,' I say with a giggle, relieved. I turn the light out again, and Klint heaves a deep sigh.

'Good night, Lizzy.'

It's past midnight. I'm exhausted and desperately wanting to sleep, but my overactive imagination isn't letting me. One minute, my eyes are shut; the next, they're flinging open and peering into the black room because I'm convinced a white ghostly form is going to appear even if Klint said it wouldn't. What does he know? He's fast asleep!

When nothing does actually happen, I manage to calm myself down and drop off into a deep sleep. I dream I'm in the parsonage, in Mr Brontë's bedroom.

Dain is standing over by the window, looking out with his back to me. I know it's him because he's wearing his black long-tailed coat. Wondering what he's staring at, I start to walk over, but the coat he's wearing morphs into a black high-necked Victorian mourning dress with puffy sleeves. He turns, and I see it's definitely Dain. But he's got long dark hair, and it's been fashioned into the style of the period—parted in the middle and looped back on either side.

A big brown dog materialises at his side with its muzzle lifted, and a watchful gleam in its eyes. It takes a step forward, growling, causing Dain to say sharply, '*Stay, Keeper*' and I recognise it as Emily Brontë's bull mastiff. I reach out my hand to pet him, and Dain (or is he now Emily?) shakes his head. 'I wouldn't if I were you.'

Keeper crouches and springs, flying through the air, snarling—his bared teeth dripping with saliva and aimed directly at my neck. I scream, instinctively flinging up an arm to protect myself, but his jaws snap shut around it. I scream again and kick out, my foot connecting with soft bulbous flesh. A howl of pain sounds in my ear, and struggling awake, I realise it's not Keeper who's biting my arm—it's Klint. And I've just booted him in the balls.

Chapter 4

'Ma'am,' she would whisper to Mrs. Bretton,
'perhaps your son would like a little cake?'

(Charlotte Brontë, *Villette*)

Heading down to breakfast the next morning, we're the worse for wear. I'm hardly speaking to Klint and nursing a throbbing arm while he's got a swollen crotch (not in a good way). We're the only people in the room, which suits me fine.

We sit opposite each other at one of the tables and Gareth comes in with a couple of menus. I suppose he's handsome in a rugged kind of way with his thickset build, tousled sandy hair, and stubble. His clothing—an olive-green fisherman's jersey and jeans thrust into mud-flecked hiking boots—suggests a pastime of tramping over the moors.

'Morning,' he says cheerfully, handing over the menus. 'How did you sleep?'

'Like logs,' replies Klint, avoiding my eyes. I get it. He doesn't want Gareth to think we're troublesome guests. I just pray no one will complain about me screaming blue murder at 4 a.m.

'Did you get things sorted with that guy last night? Did the police arrive?' Klint asks him. 'We went up after dessert, so we didn't see the outcome.'

'Ah, thanks, yes, they did. He was arrested, and is facing another period of being barred. But he did ring up this morning to make sure his tab was settled and said that he'd see me in three months' time.' Gareth looks amused.

'Help yourselves to cereal, fruit, and yoghurt from the sideboard. There's coffee, tea, and OJ too. I'll be back presently for your cooked orders.'

I'm not hugely hungry. Cereal and fruit will do for me, but I open the menu anyway to see what's on offer.

The preface page has a few paragraphs about the hotel's history, which I run my eye over. Near the bottom, there's more information about the ghostly phenomena and who exactly these phantoms are purported to be. There's a female pub owner who fed a bunch of cats and now clangs a bell accompanied by hungry invisible feline ghosts. Also a man with a bag over his shoulder who climbs the stairs, looks around, and vanishes. Not to mention disembodied children's voices, random footsteps, mist, and mysterious handprints on mirrors.

'Oh my god, have you read this? The place is full of spooks!' I say to Klint, feeling unnerved even though it's broad daylight. 'There's even been poltergeist activity: glasses shooting across the room, moving paintings, and curtains opening and closing *of their own accord*.'

Klint laughs. 'Now that would be a sight to see.'

I grip the menu tightly. 'I don't want to see it. We're out of here.'

'It's only another couple of nights,' he reasons. 'And nothing happened last night.' I stare at him. 'Well, apart from ... the other ... I mean, nothing paranormal.'

'I guess not, but I'd rather stay at an Airbnb than here.'

'There wasn't anything available, but I'll do another check this morning.'

'Good. Even if it's a hovel, I'd rather stay there,' I say, feeling relieved.

'I'll remind you of that when you can't sleep because the bed is hard as nails and the plumbing is dire. You'll be begging to come back here.'

'I doubt it. Anything is better than sleeping with ghosts.'

Klint studies the menu. 'What are you having? I like the look of the full English.'

Good to see there's nothing wrong with his appetite— even if his balls are bruised.

After breakfast, I decide to go into the village and leave him to his thesis. This time, he's broken the skin, so I need some medical supplies to deal with it even if antiseptic cream and a sticking plaster won't fix the underlying cause.

Klint's apology can't mend physical hurts, but it goes some way towards soothing my emotions. After his 'I'm so sorry, it must be the stress', a brief inspection of my arm, and murmurs of 'Does it hurt?', followed by a conciliatory hug in the bedroom, I head off.

Trudging along the road that leads to Haworth and battling a fresh headwind, I reflect on his admission that he's stressed. Maybe that's all it is. Stress can affect the body and mind in different ways. But his sleep biting has been happening more often lately. Perhaps I should skip the chemist and go to a pet shop—for a muzzle.

I didn't mention my dream about Dain and Keeper to Klint. But the images, and feelings associated with it, are still vivid in my mind. As I pass by the Brontë Parsonage, I hover on the verge of going up there. Dain might be interested in hearing about it, especially as he seems to have an affinity with Emily. *I could tell him about the dream, see what he makes of it, then be on my merry way.* Of course, I know it's an excuse to see him again; and it could quite likely backfire, painting me as a fruitcake. At this point, I think I'm better off ignoring the impulse and finding a chemist.

However, as quaint and lovely as Haworth is, trying to find a practical shop in the main street proves impossible; and I have to walk down the hill and past the train station. Keeping mum about my ailment is another issue as the elderly male chemist starts asking questions when I rock up to the counter with two packets of plasters, a tube of Savlon, and a couple of bandages for good measure.

'Is this for you? Or a loved one?'

'Me.'

'Do you currently have an injury?'

'Yes.'

'Whereabouts?'

'Um, my arm.'

'What happened?'

'It's nothing. A scrape.'

I didn't expect anyone to be that interested. But it's a small town, and perhaps he doesn't get anyone buying more than aspirin and corn pads.

When he suggests having a look at it and I refuse, he throws me suspicious glances as he scans the items. I grab the small bag he hands me and hurriedly leave the shop, feeling like I'm being accused of self-harming or something.

Walking back through the main street, I pass the café

where we had lunch and happen to glance through the window. There, sitting on the counter under a Perspex cover, is a large Victoria sponge—Klint's favourite cake. It's dusted with icing sugar and oozing cream and jam. It's also fresh and virginal—no one's taken a slice out of it yet. Perfect!

I push open the door and go in.

The girl who served us last time is writing something in a notebook but looks up and smiles. She really is pretty—green eyes, long wavy auburn hair, clear pale skin, and a sprinkling of freckles across high cheekbones.

'Hello again. What can I get you?'

Oh, she remembers me from the other day. It feels like a lot's happened since then.

'Hi, a latte and a slice of the Victoria sponge to go, thanks.'

'Sure.'

As she's changing the coffee filter, I see her notebook is still open. There are a couple of verses of what looks like poetry, but the writing is upside down and too small to make out. God, I'm nosey.

'Are you staying in Haworth?' she enquires conversationally as she froths the milk.

'Yes, just out of the village.' I tell her the name of the hotel.

'Nice. Holiday?'

'No, my boyfriend, Klint, is writing his doctoral thesis on nineteenth-century steam engines. So we're here for a few days. We've been visiting museums in various towns up this way so he can see some working ones. Haworth's steam train is also a big draw.' *Not that he appreciated riding on it.*

'Sounds interesting.' She takes the cover off the cake and cuts a generous slice.

I shrug. 'If you're into steam.' That comes out sounding resentful, so I add a brighter 'We live in Oxford, so I'm enjoying seeing some different countryside'.

'Have you visited the parsonage yet?'

'I did, yesterday. You must be over the Brontës, working so closely to the house.'

She shakes her head. 'I love them. Read all their books a million times, and I still can't get enough.'

Her eyes shine, and I blink, surprised. Wow, she isn't putting it on either. Her enthusiasm reminds me of Dain's, and it encourages me to say, 'I'm thinking of doing my own thesis on them. Maybe something about how their books reflect the hardships women faced at that time.'

'Oooh, yes. You could also mention the circumstances in which they wrote. The sanitary conditions up there were terrible. I believe they were constantly getting sick.'

'Yes, I've been reading *The Life of Charlotte Brontë*, and it touches on it. I had a few other titles recommended to me as well.'

The girl smiles benignly, handing over my coffee and cake. 'You met Dain, didn't you?'

'Uh, yes. How did you know?' I say with a smile.

'He's always loading tourists up with books. I think he single-handedly sold all the copies of *Wuthering Heights*, *Jane Eyre*, and *The Tenant of Wildfell Hall* in the parsonage bookshop this summer. They had to order more copies.'

My smile falters. *Oh, so I'm not special.* She seems to know an awful lot about him. *Are they friends?* I wonder. *Or is she his girlfriend?* She's on a par with him lookswise.

'Did you tell him you want to do some research?' she asks.

'Yes, he said I could pick his brains if I needed to.' I take a sip of my latte. It's delicious. It's a pity I got it to go. I'd like to talk to her more, especially if she knows Dain. That's probably why he was in here.

As if she's reading my thoughts, the girl says seriously, 'You totally need to talk to him.'

'Do I?'

She nods emphatically. 'Yes! He's very knowledgeable about the Brontës. You'd be doing yourself a disservice if you didn't. I'm Joelle, by the way, his ex.'

'Lizzy,' I offer. Aha, I knew it! But *ex*-girlfriend? Interesting.

'OK, I will then. I wasn't sure about it as I didn't want to take up his time.'

Joelle laughs. 'Are you kidding? If you want to talk about the Brontës, he'll make time.' She leans forward and lowers her voice, as if telling me a secret. 'If you ask me, I think he's slightly obsessed ...'

My heart thuds. OK, that clinches it—fate in the form of his ex-girlfriend urging me to get in contact. I need to message him. And soon.

Chapter 5

The blood ran down and soaked the bedclothes:
still it wailed, 'Let me in!'

(Emily Brontë, *Wuthering Heights*)

Cake and medical supplies in hand, I walk back to the hotel, ruminating on this latest development: Joelle and Dain. A likely couple. But why did they break up? By my reckoning, they should be deep in domestic bliss, expecting the pitter-patter of little feet or at least have a puppy or two. Except ... they're not. Was Dain too into the Brontës for her liking? But she said she loved them as well, so that can't be the reason, though she did say he was 'obsessed'—it's quite a strong word. Maybe he was into having séances to commune with the sisters, or she caught him dressing up as Emily? Hmm, more likely little Miss Paleface who works at the parsonage has caught his eye, and he's dumped Joelle for her. Stranger things have happened.

Either way, it's conjecture on my part. Dain's love life is

his business. I shouldn't even be wondering. I have to remind myself he's simply a source of information and one that I need to access since we're leaving in a couple of days. If I can sweeten Klint up with this Victoria sponge, I should be able to tread freely and meet with Dain without setting off his paranoia.

The bar area of the hotel is empty when I walk in, and the whole place is deathly quiet. Now that I know about all the spooks living under the roof, the cosy vibe has changed into more of a creepy one. I try not to think about the woman with her clanging bell and ghostly feline friends or, as I'm climbing the stairs, the man with the bag over his shoulder who vanishes at the top. Why oh why did we have to get put in room 6?

The door handle to our room turns halfway but won't budge. Has Klint locked it from the inside? Or gone out for a walk? That would be unfortunate since I'm feeling peckish, and the Victoria sponge looks delectable—he might miss out. I jiggle the handle, then knock. 'Klint?' I call softly. 'Are you in there?'

There's no reply, so I pull out my phone and send him a message, but he doesn't respond. I call, and it goes to voicemail. I knock louder, feeling uneasy all of a sudden, like there's someone in the hallway with me. It's a weird sensation of being watched by unseen eyes. A cool breeze strokes my cheek even though there are no windows. I rattle the door handle in a panic. 'Klint! It's me, Lizzy. Let me in!'

The door flies open, and Klint stands there, looking flustered. I plunge into the room. 'Thank God.' I slam the door and lock it, hoping that whatever's in the hallway respects solid wood.

'What's with you?' Klint eyes me as I take a deep shuddering breath.

'Why the hell didn't you answer the door? Didn't you hear me knocking?'

'Sorry, I was on the loo! It was a critical moment. I couldn't just jump up—'

'I messaged you—'

'I wasn't on my phone.'

With the lack of sleep, my sore arm, and my highly emotional state from the ghost eyes, I feel like I might burst into tears at the slightest provocation. However, Klint doesn't push it. 'It's OK, you're tired. I'll put the kettle on and make us a cup of tea.'

He gently steers me towards the bed. Settling back against the headboard with my knees pulled up, I watch him flick the switch of the in-room kettle and tear open a couple of PG Tips teabags. The familiar motion of tea making calms me down, and I start feeling silly for my outburst. It's not his fault he was on the toilet—it was bad timing all round. Maybe I was conjuring up a presence in the hallway. I do have an overactive imagination.

I proffer the cake container to him. 'Here you go. You can have this with your tea.'

Klint smiles upon seeing the cake, and for a moment, I'm reminded of why I fell in love with him. He's not classically good-looking like Dain by any stretch of the imagination; his nose is long and narrow, his lips thin, and his chin pointed. With his owlish glasses resting on angular cheekbones, unshaven jaw, and dishevelled light-brown hair in need of a decent cut, he's the epitome of an intellectual Oxford student. His resting expression is typically stern, but when he smiles, his face lights up with a childlike air that I find endearing and quite sexy.

Suffice to say, he swoops on the cake, takes a large bite, and groans like he's in ecstasy. Icing sugar falls on the bedspread, but I don't mind. It's nice to see him happy for once. After a couple more blissful bites, he asks, 'Did you get this from the café?'

'Uh-huh.'

Finishing the cake, he wipes icing sugar from his lips. 'Mmm, I could eat another three of those.'

'Good?' I notice there wasn't any offer of a bite for me. Klint doesn't share cake unless he's forced to.

'Really good. Thanks.' Klint hands over a cup of tea and

sits cross-legged facing me on the bed, taking a sip of his own.

'So I got talking to Joelle, the server at the café.' I blow on my tea to cool it down.

'Oh, been making friends with the locals?'

I nod, shifting my arm, and he spies the paper bag on which it's been resting.

'Did you get some stuff at the chemist?' he asks.

'Yes, some plasters and cream.' I brush over that to keep him on track. 'Anyway, I found out Joelle is the ex-girlfriend of the guide at the Brontë Parsonage. You know, the guy who recommended the books to me.'

'Is it a he? I assumed it was a woman.'

'I didn't say it was.'

'No, you said "one of the guides".'

Klint can be pernickety about details, and he has an excellent memory. It's all the footnotes he writes.

I take a breath. 'Anyway, she said *he* loves discussing the Brontës. He seems to be a wealth of information about them, so I thought it might be a good idea to follow up. I got his number.'

OK, that's a teensy, tiny tweak of the truth; the number was given to me yesterday by Dain himself.

Klint presses a finger into a dusting of icing sugar on the bedspread and licks it. 'I guess you should meet with him then and see if he can spark any interest. Saves time as well since we're only here for a couple more days.'

I nod. 'Yes, that's what I thought. I'll suggest lunch tomorrow at the Black Bull, if he's free.'

For a moment, I think Klint's going to invite himself along, but he drains the rest of his tea and says, 'That works. I've got an appointment with the station manager tomorrow at noon, so you might as well meet with your Brontë expert then.'

'Great. I'll message him.'

Cake—it works every time.

***

Before bed, I sort out my arm in the minuscule bathroom, applying cream, pressing on a couple of sticking plasters, and winding the bandage around it for good measure. I probably should see a doctor, but I don't want to get Klint in trouble. It's not domestic abuse; it's a nervous habit from his childhood that has flared up because of something that happened a few months ago at a party we went to. There was alcohol involved, and it was messy all round. I had to tell him because he would've found out anyway as there were multiple eyewitnesses. Though I wasn't completely to blame, now Klint doesn't trust me, even to go out with the few friends I do have. But as I've been making excuses and saying I want to stay in, they've started not inviting me to things anyway. And on top of that, he's sleep biting again. I guess it's his subconscious dealing with it. But how can I say all that to a doctor?

I hook the metal bandage fastener into place and look at my mummified arm. At least if it happens again, he won't be able to get at the skin—unless he manages to get my neck this time. I start brushing my teeth, and there's a light rap on the door.

'Are you nearly finished, Liz?'

'Yes, just a sec,' I mumble with a mouth full of toothpaste foam.

I rinse and spit, avoiding the mirror in case a ghostly handprint appears. I'm not looking forward to another sleepless fear-fuelled night keeping one eye open for ghosts. While Klint uses the bathroom, I read some more of *Villette* to distract myself. The wind has picked up again, strong and insistent, rattling the windowpanes. Small gaps in the frame let in air, so the curtains billow at intervals. But thankfully, they don't open and close of their own accord.

My phone is silent as the grave on the nightstand. I sent Dain a carefully worded message before dinner, asking if he wanted to meet for lunch at the Black Bull tomorrow. But there hasn't been a reply. I glance at it again for the millionth time, my stomach twisting into a figure eight knot. After the effort I've made to arrange this, it would be a shame if he didn't want to meet me after all.

I resume reading. A short while later, my phone buzzes, and I know it's him. Dreading that it's going be a 'No, I'm busy', I check the message.

Hi Lizzy, of course I can meet you for lunch. I can do 12 at the Black Bull? Looking forward to our discussion. Dain.

A grin spreads across my face as nervous anticipation leaves my body, and a Zen-like calm takes over. It's the perfect response—friendly, yet professional. I send a quick message back confirming the time and put my phone in sleep mode just as Klint comes out of the bathroom. I switch out my light and scooch down under the covers.

'You OK?' he asks, getting into bed.

'Yes, why wouldn't I be?'

'Last night, you were a nervous wreck and wanted to keep the light on.'

'Oh. Well, nothing happened, did it? Maybe it's all a bunch of bullshit,' I reply, trying not to think about what's out in the hallway.

'Exactly. I'm glad you've come round to my way of thinking.' Klint hooks a finger under the strap of my mauve satin camisole. 'Is this new?'

'No, just haven't worn it before.'

'Pretty colour.'

'Doesn't go with the bandage,' I joke.

'We can keep the light on if you like,' he says, pulling the strap down and kissing my shoulder. 'You know, for a bit longer ...'

I nod, feeling surprised. *Reader, it's the first time he's wanted to have sex in quite a while.*

Chapter 6

His presence in a room was more cheering
than the brightest fire.

(Charlotte Brontë, *Jane Eyre*)

As I shower and dry my hair the next morning, I'm in a jubilant mood. Thanks to Klint's amorous attention last night, we both had a decent night's sleep; and no biting occurred, in dreams or otherwise. It feels like we've turned a corner, and we're on the mend.

Dain will be the true test, though.

I step outside the hotel, expecting a patchy blue sky like we've had for the past few days. Instead, a dense grey fog greets me—it's a real pea-souper, wrapping itself around my body like a shroud. I can hardly see ten feet in front of me. Shivering, I zip my windbreaker right up to the chin, wishing I had my beanie. At this rate, the damp will play havoc with my freshly diffused curls. I speed up with the intention of arriving at the Black Bull five minutes early so I can defrizz and check for stray mascara streaks in the ladies'.

I'm not usually this concerned about my appearance, and really, my hair and make-up are the least of my worries. But I need to feel confident that I'm putting my best face forward since I'm throwing myself into the den of temptation. If I walk out unscathed, I'll know that all the shit that Klint and I have gone through in the last few months has been worth it. It will prove that we're meant to be together.

The square clock tower of Haworth Church comes into view through the fog as I approach the town. Shortly after, the soot-stone frontage of the Black Bull appears swathed in a moody swirling mist. I feel like I've stepped into the pages of one of the sisters' Gothic novels and half expect Mr Rochester to come clip-clopping up the street on his horse. But there's only an indistinguishable figure walking ahead of me with muffled footsteps in the eerie quiet.

The Black Bull is cosy and inviting after the wet chill of the fog. A quick glance around the pub's dining area reveals a crackling fire and a few patrons enjoying the warmth and a meal, but no sign of Dain. I make a beeline for the ladies'.

I scrunch some life back into my limp curls with shaking hands. *Calm down, Lizzy. It's just lunch, not a date!* Wiping a finger underneath my left eye, I attempt some deep calming breaths, but they come out more like shallow hacks. *Breathe! You've grown as a person. You are now stronger, wiser, and more mature than three months ago. You will not succumb to the charms of Dain Whitmore!*

After my freak-out in the loo, I pull myself together, order a sandwich at the bar, and sit composedly in the corner by the window, sipping a glass of apple juice.

Noon comes and goes, and my palms are a sweaty mess. But at 12.05 p.m., the door to the pub opens, and Dain comes strolling into the bar area. He greets the bartender. There's a friendly exchange I can't quite hear, but I catch the stray end of it: 'I'm meeting with someone ...' He looks round and catches sight of me, and a small smile plays around his lips. I force myself to sit up straight and smile in return as he comes over.

'Hi, sorry I'm late,' he says.

'You're not,' I reply, pleased that my voice shows no sign of the previous inner turmoil.

He's as gorgeous as ever and wearing a long black overcoat and a deep-green scarf, which he unwinds from around his neck and hangs on the back of the chair opposite me. He unbuttons his coat, and underneath, I glimpse his white shirt and waistcoat attire. He stretches his fingers to the fire for a moment and breathes a sigh of relief. 'That's better. The fog is freezing.'

'Do you have central heating up there at the parsonage?'

He laughs. 'Unfortunately, we're reliant on the same rudimentary heating system as the Brontë family, namely fires in all the grates. But I have been running up and down the stairs all morning, so it wasn't too bad—we had a bus tour,' he explains, seeing my blank expression.

'Ah.'

He shrugs off his coat and hangs it on the chair, covering his scarf. 'Anyway, have you ordered? Are you OK for a drink?'

I indicate my apple juice. 'Yes, thanks. And I ordered the torched goat's cheese sandwich.'

Dain's soulful eyes light with merriment. 'That's my fave. I call it "the tortured goat". I'll get that too.' He smiles at me, and the effect is quite devastating on my attention-starved libido. Shit.

He goes off to order, and I slump back against the wall cushion, feeling blood rush to my cheeks and tingles in places I shouldn't be tingling. Jesus, what was I thinking? If he can floor me with a smile, there's no hope for keeping this professional in my head.

I take a shaky sip of cold apple juice and quell the urge to run. *Tortured goat indeed.*

He comes back carrying a tall glass of fizzing Coke, and I

steel myself. If I can ignore his attractiveness, I should be fine. I'll mention Klint as soon as I can; that should stop any potential flirting dead in its tracks—on my side anyway.

'So how are you finding the hotel?' he asks, placing his drink on the table and settling into his chair.

'It was fine until I found out it was haunted.'

'Mmm, yes, I didn't think I should tell you that,' Dain says. 'Especially if you're staying there by yourself?' He phrases it like a rhetorical question, but it's one that needs answering.

'I'm with my partner, Klint. He's doing some research in Haworth for his doctorate.'

Dain doesn't react outwardly to this information. He takes a sip of Coke and says, 'That's good you're not alone, especially at night.' I breathe easier. Now he knows I'm not single. But I happen to see him glance covertly at my ringless left hand resting on the table.

Right. MORE KLINT.

By the time our sandwiches arrive, I've filled him in on Klint's teenage obsession with trainspotting (*not* the Scottish book, I add); his undergraduate degree in nineteenth-century history at Oxford, followed by a master's with distinction on the Industrial Revolution; and his current DPhil on steam engines. Feeling like we're running out of time to discuss the Brontës, I steer the conversation back to Dain, who's tucking into his sandwich.

'So how did you end up volunteering at the parsonage?'

'It's a story in two volumes featuring a hastily shelved acting career and an aunt.'

I take a bite of sandwich and smile to myself. Cute that he's referencing his life like the way books used to be printed.

'Sounds intriguing.'

Dain leans back in his chair and folds his arms, which I'm starting to recognise is his go-to pose for having an in-depth conversation. 'In high school, I was consumed by the idea of being the next great British theatre actor. You know, following in the footsteps of Laurence Olivier and the like. My parents encouraged me by paying for acting lessons and taking me to see local plays, and occasionally, we did the odd trip to London to the West End—we lived in Leeds, so it was a big adventure,' he explains.

'Gotcha.'

'When my school put on a production of *Jane Eyre*, I auditioned and got a leading role.'

'Great! Mr Rochester, I presume?'

'No,' replies Dain dryly. 'His wife in the attic. I was at an all-boys school. I had to wear a dress and a wig.'

'Oh dear.' I suppress a smile, but not very well.

'Yes, you may well laugh. Anyway, I got to know *Jane Eyre* inside out, back to front, and sideways. And I came to appreciate the storytelling and writing skills of Charlotte Brontë. I started reading another of her books, moved on to Emily, then Anne. By the time the play opened, I was a fan of all of them.'

'How did the play go, though?'

He rolls his eyes. 'It was a disaster. I got stage fright in front of 200 people.'

'Oh no! What did you do?'

'I managed to shuffle, moan and wring my hands. Luckily I didn't have any speaking lines. I gave up acting after that.'

The woebegone look on his face makes me want to giggle and hug him simultaneously. I clear my throat, trying not to laugh. 'OK, so the acting was a no go. What about the aunt?'

'My mother's sister, Abigail, lived here in Haworth. We used to come and stay with her when Dad went away on business trips. Since I was a fanboy of the Brontës by that stage, I used to spend a lot of time hanging around the parsonage and exploring the moors. At the time, I quite fancied myself as Heathcliff.'

'I can imagine,' I say, caught up in a romantic imagining of Dain striding over the moors, looking angsty and windswept.

'Fast-forward ten years, and the lot at the parsonage got sick of me showing up and answering tourist questions ad hoc and suggested I become an official volunteer instead. I was studying the classics at Leeds Uni at the time, but I volunteered during the holidays. Then when my aunt died, I moved here permanently. My great-grandmother was friends with the Brontës' maid, Martha, by the way,' he adds casually.

I've been chewing on a bite of sandwich, and I gulp it down. 'Seriously?' Martha Brown was mentioned a lot in Charlotte's biography, so I know exactly who he means.

Dain nods. 'Yeah. Crazy, eh? It still blows my mind. Martha knew them when they were alive, and she was there nursing them during their final days. Well, Charlotte and Emily, not Anne.'

I lean forward with interest. 'Did your aunt tell you any stories that had been handed down to her?'

'Plenty when I was younger. It felt like having a privileged window into their lives. A lot has been kept out of the history books, especially certain things,' he says, his tone lowering an octave.

My ears prick up at that. *Certain things.* 'So you're saying you know stuff about the Brontës that no one else does?'

He downs the last of his Coke and taps his nose. 'Possibly. But if I do, I'll be taking them to my grave. I was sworn to secrecy by my aunt, God rest her soul.' He winks at me, and I'm not sure if he's joking or trying to arouse my interest by being mysterious.

Even though I'm burning with curiosity, I decide not to bite on the dangling carrot. 'So do you live in the village?'

'Yes, my aunt left her house to me since she didn't have any children.'

'Wow, lucky you.' *Does he live alone?* I wonder.

Dain supplies the answer without me having to ask. 'It's just me and Tabby, her cat. She's named after the Brontës' other maid, Tabitha, who lived to ninety. I'm not so sure her namesake will even make it to next year. She's always getting into fights with the tom next door. But I think he secretly adores her.'

I giggle at that, and Dain grins widely. I'm definitely getting the sense he likes a captive audience. It's a pity his acting career never took off. How does he earn money if he's volunteering? He probably doesn't have a mortgage if he owns his aunt's house, but there must still be bills. I can't ask about that, though. It's too nosey. He's not living with little Miss Paleface anyway. Perhaps they're just friends since they work together?

'Anyway, enough about me. I've been prattling on. You're too good a listener,' he says, picking up the other half of his sandwich and taking a bite.

'Probably all the lectures I've been to over the years,' I comment, twisting a bar mat between my fingers. *Not that I'd put him in the same league as a dry, dusty lecturer. He's far more interesting.*

'How's your reading going?' he asks.

'Good. I've finished *The Life of Charlotte Brontë*, and I'm almost at the end of *Villette*.'

'Enjoying it?'

'Very much so. It's different from *Jane Eyre*.'

'In what way?'

'In *Jane Eyre*, we know we're rooting for Jane and Rochester. In *Villette*, Charlotte's done a bait-and-switch. Dr Bretton isn't the love interest for Lucy Snowe after all. Well ... he is,' I correct myself after a pause. 'But Lucy can't have him even though he's totally gorgeous.'

Dain cocks an eyebrow, and I flush a little at my effusing about the good doctor. 'Indeed. Did that disappoint you?'

'Initially. But it's often the way in life, isn't it? The person you want isn't the person you end up with. And I know Charlotte was writing from personal experience. You can sense a certain sadness in the prose.'

Dain nods. 'The novel is a homage to Monsieur Heger, the Belgian professor she was in love with.'

'I haven't taken to him personally as a character, but the writing itself depicting the passion and yearning Lucy feels for him under her cold exterior is wonderful, especially after learning about Charlotte's shitty real-life circumstances in the biography. She was alone and horribly depressed after her sisters died.' Agitated, I tear off a piece of the bar mat. Dain doesn't say anything, and I look up to find him watching me intently.

'Poor Charlotte,' he says softly. 'It's agony to read, isn't it? Knowing she's writing in the house at night without Emily and Anne. Knowing that the man she's writing about and desperately loved belonged to someone else. It's tragic.'

I swallow, feeling uncomfortable; he's spot on with his observation. Somehow, he's tapped into exactly what I was thinking and feeling when I was reading it.

I change the subject.

'At the house, you mentioned that you think Branwell was the catalyst for the heroes of the other novels. What makes you think that?'

Dain shrugs. 'How could he not be? You saw how close the living quarters were. Apart from their father, he was a male role model. They were all impressionable. He was heartbroken from his affair with Lady Scott. His pain must've influenced them deeply, Emily especially.'

I nod animatedly. 'Yes! I was thinking she may have used him as inspiration for that bit in *Wuthering Heights* when Cathy dashes her head on the sofa and grinds—'

'"Her teeth, so that you might fancy she would crash them to splinters."' Dain finishes my sentence.

I'm impressed. 'Wow, you know the exact words.'

'I've read *Wuthering Heights* numerous times, and I love that scene,' he says simply. 'But, and here's the ironic thing ...' He leans forward to emphasise his point. 'Branwell wasn't as despised as Mrs Gaskell made out. He was well liked by the village and respected for his intelligence. He fell in love, he was spurned, and he got his heart broken. I don't blame him for being upset about it. Maybe he's watching us right now and feeling glad that someone's sympathetic.'

I peer around the room cautiously, as if I might see a ghostly Branwell lurking and sobbing into his beer tankard.

Dain sees me and chuckles, then abruptly pulls his fob watch out of his waistcoat pocket to check the time. 'Sorry, I have to get back. I didn't realise it was getting so late.'

I'm startled back to the present. Our sandwiches are gone, and our glasses are empty. But my brain is on fire.

Dain smiles at me. 'We only just got started on the Brontës, didn't we?'

'Yes, but what we did talk about was interesting. Thank you for meeting with me.'

He gets up and starts putting on his coat. 'Tell you what. Text me your email, and I'll send you a link to the online Brontë Museum and Library. There are documents, letters, and all sorts of personal artefacts—things that aren't on display in the house.'

'OK, great, thanks.' I quickly text him my email as he buttons his coat with nimble fingers.

'Oh, by the way, is there anywhere I should check out on the moors?'

'Yes, there's the Brontë Waterfall and Brontë Chair. Farther afield, there are Top Withens and Ponden Hall, both said to be inspiration for *Wuthering Heights*. But you shouldn't go alone. It's easy to get lost if you wander off the trail. If you do, at least take a fully charged phone. You should get Google Maps out there. There's coverage.'

I watch him winding his green scarf around his neck. 'You sound like you know a lot about it.'

'I'm a keen hiker,' he says. 'Well, I used to be. Not so much lately.'

You're full of surprises, I think but don't say it aloud.

'Do you want me to come with you?' he offers. 'It should be fine tomorrow or the day after.'

I pick at the ragged edge of the bar mat, incredibly

tempted by the thought of spending more time with him. But it isn't a good idea.

'Thanks, but I should be fine,' I say, thinking that it's better to be safe than sorry. 'I'll probably go with Klint.'

But I know with utmost certainty that he won't want to set foot on the moors.

Chapter 7

Wander as I may through the house this night,
I cannot lull the blast.

(Charlotte Brontë, *Villette*)

'How did it go?'

Klint is sprawled on the bed with his laptop propped on his chest. From what I can see, he's playing a computer game rather than working on his thesis.

I shuck off my damp windbreaker and hang it on the back of the door before answering, 'Good, I think. We didn't talk too much about the Brontës, though.'

Klint scooches into a sitting position, putting his laptop on the bed, and frowns. 'I thought that was the whole point. What did you talk about for an hour?'

'Uh, his childhood. His aunt. His cat.'

He rolls his eyes. 'Sounds fascinating.' His attention returns to his game, and I lie down on my side of the bed, facing him.

'He's sending me a link to the online Brontë Museum

and Library.'

Klint is busy moving soldiers around in his virtual army and doesn't reply, so I close my eyes. 'How was your meeting?'

'It was cancelled. The station manager lives in Keighley and didn't want to drive over in the fog on his day off. We've rescheduled for next week.'

My eyes fly open. *If we're staying in Haworth for another week, I could meet with Dain again.* The thought thrills and dismays me. I can't. I shouldn't. As if it's a warning, my arm, which has been fine all day, starts throbbing.

'Oh. Should we extend our stay at the hotel then?' I ask nonchalantly.

'Could do. I'm expecting another funding payment to come through tonight. Unless you want to shift to an Airbnb? I found one that looked OK.'

I take a deep breath. 'We can stay here. I'm getting used to it now, and there haven't been any paranormal happenings so far.' *It was only my overactive imagination.*

Klint nods in agreement. 'Great, I was hoping you'd say that as I can't be arsed moving.'

After dinner, Klint is in the restaurant, working on his thesis; and I'm lounging on the bed, flipping through the movie channels, having finished *Villette*. The book has put me in a strange restless mood. The hastily wrapped-up ending has me longing for something more satisfying. It doesn't help that the wind has chased the fog away and is moaning at the windows once more. I flick off the TV with the remote and flop back on my pillow. My traitorous mind fills with questions.

Whereabouts in the village does Dain live? What does he do at night? Does he like reading contemporary novels or only classics? Does he wear pyjamas?

I send out my random questions into the universe as I lie there, looking up at the plaster ceiling, feeling silly. Why does it matter if he wears pyjamas or not? But my wonderings have obviously sent out a psychic vibe his way because, when I look at it, my phone shows an email notification from him. The back of my neck prickles. Spooky.

I grab my laptop from my tote and fire it up. Might as well see what he's written properly.

Hi Lizzy,

Great chatting with you today, even if I did hog the conversation. You wanted to discuss the Brontës, not hear my life story! Anyway, as promised, here's the link to the museum and library collection, where you can browse as much as you like. If you want to talk about anything, I'm around the parsonage most days. Just follow the sound of someone lecturing.

Best,
Dain

A link has been added below his email. Clicking on it opens up a page to a catalogue of items relating to the Brontë family: original letters, diary papers, documents, poems, artwork, items of clothing, and household artefacts. Wowser, it's like being given the key to a treasure trove.

Before I can overthink it, I send him a reply.

Hi Dain,

I checked out the link you sent. Oh my god, it more than makes up for you hogging the conversation. Not that you did. I enjoyed chatting with you too. Thanks so much for this. I see I'm going to be up to my eyeballs in Brontëana tomorrow.

Looking forward to it :-)
Lizzy

Overly friendly? Possibly. Maybe I should've slept on it and sent a more formal reply in the morning. But it's too late now.

I put my laptop away, mentally kicking myself, but my phone lights up again. An illicit thrill goes through me: Dain's sent a WhatsApp message. This is getting more personal.

Swallowing hard and listening for Klint's footsteps in the hallway, I check it.

Hi, me again. Hope you don't mind me messaging here. Easier to chat. Enjoy your Brontëana browsing!

Hmm, that doesn't necessitate a reply, but I should probably say something. Otherwise, it will look rude.

Hi, no, it's fine. Yes, I will. Thanks again!

I wait as I see he's typing a reply. Yikes, if Klint were here, this could get awkward; he'd be asking who I was messaging.

Dain: *Which bit are you up to in Villette?*

Me: *I just finished it.*

Dain: *The ending is depressing, isn't it?*

Me: *Lol, yes, a little.*

Dain: *The bit with the wind shrieking like a banshee and Lucy wandering through the house always gets me. It's Charlotte herself of course. I know what she means. I've been there at night, and it does sound like someone screaming.*

Me: *What? Please tell me you didn't stay at the parsonage overnight!*

Dain: *OK, I won't.*

Me: *But you did?*

Dain: *I did.*

Me: *Wow, you're brave! How come?*

Dain: *It was a dare. I wouldn't do it again. I didn't sleep very well.*

Me: *I'm not surprised. Which room were you in?*

Dain: *Mr Brontë's. The bed is flipping uncomfortable.*

Me: *Lol. Was it spooky?*

Dain: *Sooo spooky. You should've seen me cowering under the bedcovers with two lit candles on either side. Then they blew out, and I screamed. Loudly.*

I can't help laughing at this. I wish I could hear the story in person.

Me: *LOLOLOL*

Dain: *I'm surprised I made it through the night!*

OK, this is pertinent. I'm going to tell him about my dream.

Me: *Weirdly, I dreamt about you in Mr Brontë's bedroom. The night after I met you at the house. It was quite vivid.*

I cringe, blushing, wondering if he'll think it was a sexy dream.

Dain: *What was I doing?*

Me: *Standing by the window, looking out. But when you turned around, you were wearing a black dress and had a Victorian woman's hairstyle. Kind of odd since you told me about dressing up as Mr Rochester's wife. Though I think in the dream you were Emily.*

Dain: *What made you think that?*

Me: *Emily's dog Keeper was there, and you told him to stay. I reached out to pet him, and he flew at me and bit me on the arm. Then I woke up.*

Dain: *Wow, intense! Dogs usually mean friendship, but dreaming specifically of Emily and Keeper is interesting. The house does have a strong energy. I have strange dreams sometimes too.*

Me: *Let me know if you have any of me dressed as Heathcliff.*

Dain: *Hahaha, I will!*

Me: *Speaking of sleeping, I should go.*

Dain: *Me too. Tabby needs her nightly saucer of milk, or she gets cranky.*

Me: *Goodnight, and goodnight, Tabby.*

Dain: *Sweet (non dog biting) dreams.*

I flip over my phone on the bed and flick on the TV to a random news channel in case Klint comes in unexpectedly. My hand is shaking. Fuck fuck fuck! Dain knows I have a boyfriend. Why did he message me? Even more concerning was my eagerness to engage. I should've just left it alone.

I bury my face in the pillow. My arm is throbbing madly, and the fire in my brain is back. Dain is too good-looking, funny, and interesting—he's too dangerous all round. And I'm too weak.

In the bathroom, I splash water on my hot face over and over in an attempt to cool the furnace. Patting it dry with a hand towel, I feel better. I'm completely overreacting. It was a casual chat—not that flirty, more friendly than anything. I have to dial it back in future so I don't get sucked in. Mute my WhatsApp notifications so I'm not as accessible if he messages. Yes, I'll do that. Phew, problem solved.

Having sorted out my WhatsApp, I'm lying on the bed serenely and flicking through the channels on the TV when Klint comes into the room with a face as black as thunder. My stomach drops.

'What's wrong?'

'There's a delay in the funding payment, an admin screw-up at the university's end.'

He deposits his laptop on the bed and paces around, pouting petulantly.

'We'll be OK,' I say reassuringly. 'Haven't you still got some money in your account?'

'No, I spent 200 on a conference ticket, and it hasn't been reimbursed yet.'

I raise an eyebrow at this but can't say anything; it's his funding—he can do with it what he likes.

He continues striding in the space next to the bed. 'Do they expect me to exist on vegetable soup and toast?'

'Add a few kidney beans and a sprinkle of cheese, and you've got a balanced meal,' I say, trying to be helpful, but it comes out sounding flippant.

Klint scowls at me. 'Very funny. I need to pay for another week's stay here tomorrow. Gareth's a nice guy, but he's not going to accept my TAG Heuer to hold the room.

And my credit card is maxed out.'

I sigh inwardly. I loathe it when he rants about money. It's not like his parents don't have a healthy joint bank account. 'Can't you ask your mum for a loan until you get paid?'

He screws up his nose as if he's stepped on dog shit. 'That's not an option. I'd rather sell my body on the street.'

'Well, I'm sure that it won't come to that,' I say soothingly. 'We can use some of my savings. I don't mind.'

'Is that OK?'

'It's fine.' I'm tired and not in the mood for Klint's haranguing. 'Let's go to bed and sort it out in the morning.'

He stops pacing and places a kiss on my forehead.

'Thanks, Lizzy. You're a brick. I'll use the bathroom.'

I nod, glad I've assuaged his stress. He pauses by the bathroom door. 'Did you end up watching a movie?'

'No, I couldn't find one I liked, so I read.'

'Did that guy send through the link?'

'His name's Dain, and yes, he did.'

'Great! Let's hope you find something that sparks your interest.' He disappears inside the bathroom and closes the door behind him.

Little does he know, something has sparked my interest, but it's not in the museum.

Chapter 8

I felt such a craving for support and companionship
as I cannot express.

(Charlotte Brontë, letter to a Brussels schoolfellow)

I lie awake for ages after Klint has dropped off to sleep. All my good intentions about resisting Dain's charms have evaporated like the Haworth fog. Now all I want is to see him again—and as soon as humanly possible.

I, Elizabeth Doyle, am not a sweet angel, though I've tried to be. Klint even dragged me along to his church, insisting I confess my indiscretion to an unempathetic priest. But it hasn't cured me of my 'fall from grace'. If he thought repenting and forty Hail Marys would do the trick, he was wrong.

It feels like I'm deliberately trying to sabotage my relationship. Am I that bored that I'm seeking Dain out for mental stimulation? Or is there something else going on?

I must drop off to sleep because I'm jolted awake in the

middle of the night by a sharp pain in my right shin. Then another in my ankle. Groggily, I open my eyes to find Klint sitting up and kicking out at me. Hastily, I draw my feet out of range, but not before he delivers another swift strike to my shin with the accuracy of a FIFA footballer.

'Ow, stop it!' I cry, now fully coherent. 'What the fuck are you doing?'

'You stop it. You know I hate my feet being tickled,' he mumbles sleepily, lying back down and yanking the covers up.

Huh? I lean over his shoulder to assess if he's sleep talking or not. Klint has a number of odd night-time habits, so I wouldn't be surprised if he was. It's amazing I've actually managed to get any sleep in the last four years of being with him.

I prod his shoulder tentatively. 'Are you awake or asleep?'

'Awake, thanks to you.'

'I didn't *do* anything. I was asleep!'

'Whatever.'

He sounds in a right sulk, so I don't push it. Great. Now not only do I have a sore arm, but I'm also going to have plum-coloured bruises all over my leg. I curl into a tight ball and hug myself.

Black clouds are gathering. Maybe I should go back to

Oxford and leave him to it before they engulf me.

***

The next morning, Klint and I are in the breakfast room, quietly bickering about what happened. He still believes I was playing a joke on him, to which I'm incredulous.

'Have you *seen* my leg?' I hiss. 'I know you're a sensitive sleeper and liable to react to anything untoward. So why would I inflict that on myself?'

My shin is developing a couple of lovely large violet bruises as I predicted.

Klint shrugs. 'Masochist tendencies?'

We draw apart as Gareth comes bustling in with the breakfast menus. 'Good morning. How are we today?' he chirps breezily, then sees our hangdog expressions.

'Everything all right?'

'Not really,' says Klint.

'What's wrong?'

'A problem with the bed.'

'Which room did I put you in?' Gareth enquires.

'Six,' I say.

He hands over the menus and leans against a nearby sideboard. 'Ah, yes, room 6. That can be tricky. Things do tend to happen in there.'

'What things?' asks Klint suspiciously.

'Some guests have complained about the bedcovers being pulled off.'

'Anything else?' I ask.

Gareth looks sheepish. 'Ah, foot tickling, but nothing more serious than that.'

I shoot a triumphant glare at Klint. 'See! It wasn't me.'

Klint has gone pale and, to my surprise, looks freaked out.

'Um, I need to extend our stay for a few more days. But can we have a different room please?' he says to Gareth. 'One that doesn't have errant foot-tickling ghosts?'

Gareth sorts us out after breakfast. He doesn't seem to mind changing our room, but I feel sorry for him. I bet he wishes he works at a hotel that wasn't haunted.

'Right. I've put you in room 9. That's on the newer side of the hotel. We haven't had any reports of things happening in there.' He hands over the key to Klint, and I feel relieved. I wish he'd put us in that room in the first place.

Klint heads off upstairs, but I linger by the bar to talk to Gareth. 'Um, I don't suppose you have a map of the walking trail on the moors?'

'Yes, I do actually.' He reaches beneath the bar and brings out a white piece of paper with black markings that looks home-made.

'This is us.' He points to a spot. 'You can start from here and join up with this path.' He points to another spot. 'Which takes you past the reservoir and Ponden Hall. It curves around and takes you up to Top Withens, here.' He jabs at the map. 'Then past the Brontë Waterfall and back to Haworth. It's about a five-mile round trip.'

'Thanks. A guide at the parsonage mentioned those sites, so I was keen to check them out.'

'It wasn't Dain Whitmore, by any chance?' Gareth asks casually.

My heart flutters. 'Uh, yes, it was. Do you know him?' I ask, feeling a blush forming for no reason other than his name being mentioned.

Gareth nods. 'Yeah, it's a small town,' he replies somewhat gruffly and turns away to tend to something behind the bar.

Our conversation appears to be over. 'Well, thanks for the map,' I say awkwardly.

He hitches a shoulder in my direction. 'No problem. Let me know how you get on in room 9.'

We pack our bags, jamming in clothes and toiletries, and swiftly leave room 6. Klint is doubly keen to vacate it since it appears he now does believe in ghosts. Him freaking out would be amusing—if my bruised leg wasn't aching.

Room 9 has a similar homely decor but is larger because it has twin beds, which Klint suggests we push together.

'Fine, but can we do it later? I want to make a start on the Brontë catalogue,' I tell him, feeling irritable. To be honest, I'm not fussed about making it into a double. I need a good night's sleep without him thrashing around next to me.

I collect my laptop and head back down to the restaurant, giving him the room to work in. After setting up on one of the tables, I risk a look at my WhatsApp. Nothing from Dain. That's good. If he'd sent a message, I'd be in a quandary about whether to reply or not.

Half an hour later, my eyes are blurry from peering at Charlotte's tiny book manuscripts and poring over Emily's illustrated diary papers, trying to decipher her writing. It's all fascinating stuff, but it's making me think about Dain more than ever. I check WhatsApp again. I can see the last time he was on there: thirty minutes ago. Pretty much when I was.

Was he chatting with someone else? Or revisiting our conversation and thinking about me?

Through the lattice window, the sky is clear, though the trees are swaying. The wind never seems to stop blowing here. But maybe a strong blustery breeze plus a visit to the parsonage are what I need to clear my head. I shouldn't go there, but I'm feeling disinclined towards Klint, and I'm craving some kind of interaction with Dain. Anything will do, even if it's two minutes before he gets whisked away by Brontë fans.

Pushing my laptop into my tote bag, I slip out through the side entrance, deciding not to message Klint. He's busy, and I need some space. If he wants to know where I am, he can message me for once.

***

I've been wandering around on the upper floor of the house for twenty minutes with no sign of Dain. But when I venture down the stairs, I hear his voice coming from the kitchen. I linger on the bottom step, eavesdropping.

'The sisters often read and studied while doing household chores. Take Emily, for instance. She used to knead bread dough while learning German ...'

I smile to myself. He does have a bit of a lecturer tone.

A woman asks, 'Would she have written *Wuthering*

Heights in here?'

'She definitely would've been thinking about it and jotting down notes, but chores took priority during the day. She did most of her writing at night around the parlour table with Charlotte and Anne. *Wuthering Heights* is approximately 110,000 words, and it was written in nine months, which is between 400 to 450 words a day—an amount that she feasibly could've written with her quill once Mr Brontë went to bed. Don't forget they were also keeping their publishing efforts a secret from him—'

Another woman's voice interrupts. 'Are *you* a writer?'

Dain pauses. 'I dabble,' he says, sounding self-conscious.

I prick up my ears at that. *I bet he writes poetry. He looks the type.*

A small group of middle-aged women file out of the kitchen, chattering, and turn left towards the parlour. I freeze; I shouldn't be here. If Dain follows them into the parlour, I can sneak out the front door. I'm about to take a step. However, he comes out of the kitchen, turns right to go upstairs, and we almost collide.

'Lizzy!' he exclaims, looking surprised.

My retinas burn at the sight of him. This handsome dark-haired version with his eyebrows raised and lips parted is definitely better than the inanimate one in my imagination. I chew my lip, feeling a blush starting. 'Hi, um,

I was just ...'

'Getting mileage out of your yearly ticket?'

He grins at me lazily, probably guessing I've sought him out after our messaging flurry last night, and my cheeks flush even redder. I shouldn't have come. I'm making it pretty obvious I fancy him despite the fact I have a boyfriend. I grip the banister tightly, feeling awkward as hell. 'I should ...'

'Have you had lunch?' he says at the same time, our sentences tangling.

I shake my head.

'Want to join me? I'm happy to share my sandwiches. I usually make too many,' he says lightly.

I relax at his casual tone, and my awkwardness fades away. 'OK, thanks, if you don't mind. I was getting peckish hearing you talk about Emily's bread.'

Dain chuckles. 'Oh, you heard that?'

'I did. Not that I was eavesdropping or anything.'

He raises an eyebrow, and I laugh. 'Well, maybe a little. You did say to follow the sound of someone lecturing ...'

'So you were looking for me?' He sounds like he needs affirmation, but I'm reluctant to give it to him because of what that will mean.

I shift my eyes from his and shrug. 'I just happened to be

coming down the stairs.'

'Hmm,' he says softly under his breath, his forehead creasing, as if he's trying to figure me out.

'You mentioned something about sandwiches?' I say meekly.

Chapter 9

I was not only going to hide a treasure—
I meant also to bury a grief.

(Charlotte Brontë, *Villette*)

Dain takes me around the back of the house, where there's a stretch of roughly mowed lawn with a couple of wooden benches set off to the side under some trees.

'It's quite sheltered here. There aren't any gravestones, and there's a smidgeon of sun,' he remarks as if he's been weighing up all the different locations we could have lunch.

'Sun is definitely a bonus,' I say, sitting down on the nearest bench and tilting my face to the warmish September rays.

He sits beside me and unwraps the large foil packet of sandwiches he's been carrying. 'Here you go. Get that down you.'

I can't help giggling at the giant doorstep filled with ham and cheese that he hands over. 'Wow, that's certainly a man-sized sandwich! Luckily, I'm hungry.'

'I don't do things by halves.' The way he says it makes me wonder if he's full-on in other ways too, and I chew on my sandwich to distract myself. After we've munched steadily in silence for a while, Dain unscrews the lid of a silver thermos.

'What's in there?'

'Hot chocolate, Cadbury's finest.'

'Gosh, fancy.'

'Usually, it's tea. You've caught me on a decadent day.'

He grins at me, and I can't help but smile back, feeling glad I decided to have lunch with him after all; he's so convivial and easy to talk to. I guess, being a guide, he's used to making small talk with people, though he's less formal with me now he's outside the house.

'Sorry, there's only one cup, so we'll have to share. But we can take turns sipping from opposite sides,' he says airily, pouring out the hot chocolate and handing the steaming cup to me. Hmm, he's also got a borderline flirtatious manner, which makes him doubly attractive.

'So did you have a look at the catalogue?' Dain finishes his sandwich, brushes crumbs off his trousers, and leans back on the seat, folding his arms and stretching out his long legs. I run my eyes over them. I'm a sucker for tall guys, and he's got a great set of pins.

I try to focus. 'Ah, I did, thanks. There's a lot in there.

I'm working my way through it. And I made some notes about *Villette* too.'

'Anything stand out?'

'Lucy's depressive episode is interesting for the era. A literary analysis of how the taboo subject of depression manifests itself in the Brontës' writing could be absorbing.'

'You could include Cathy gnashing her teeth,' Dain quips.

I smile. 'Exactly. Oh, and when Lucy buried Dr John's letters away from Madame Beck's prying eyes, that was intriguing.'

Dain inclines his head towards me. 'I'm not sure I remember that bit.'

I check the notes app on my phone.

'Lucy goes into the town to find a glass jar, rolls up the letters in oiled silk, binds them with twine, and gets the shopkeeper to stopper and seal it so it's airtight. Then she buries the jar in a hollow beneath a pear tree, covers it with some leftover mortar she finds in a shed, and replaces earth and greenery over the top.'

'Ah, yes, I remember it now,' he says, looking away.

'The process was so detailed, like Charlotte was recounting it rather than making it up. It makes me wonder if she did actually hide something.'

Dain holds out his hand for the empty hot chocolate cup,

which I've inadvertently finished. He fills it, takes a sip, and leans back against the bench again before answering. 'What would she be hiding?'

'I don't know. Her own letters she didn't want anyone to see?'

'It's not unfeasible. Charlotte did draw on real life a lot for her books. *Shirley*, for instance, had the locals chortling because they recognised themselves in it.'

'I'll have to read that one.'

'The main character is also meant to be a study of Emily.'

'The mysterious Emily. There's so much hearsay about her floating around. Do you think she had an affair with William Weightman?'

Dain screws up his nose. 'I suppose you're referring to the *Emily* movie. There was an opportunity according to the dates for something like that to occur, but there isn't a shred of proof.'

'None that we know of,' I say.

'To be honest, I think he was too namby-pamby for her. She had quite a strong character. Anyway, how are things at the hotel?'

'Oh, fine,' I say, a little surprised at the swift change of subject. *Did he get bored talking about Emily's non-affair?*

'But we had to change rooms because things got a little

spooky last night. I've got the bruises to prove it.' I hike up my jeans leg to show him the rather nasty-looking bruises on my shin.

'Ouch,' he says, inspecting my leg closely. 'What happened?'

'A foot-tickling ghost.'

Dain raises an eyebrow. 'Do I want to know about this?'

'It's a long story ...' I'm about to give him the shortened version, but I notice he's still staring at my shin—and not in a concerned brotherly fashion. I pull my jeans leg down hurriedly. 'But I'll live.'

'No more dreams about me?' he says teasingly.

'Hah, no.' *But I'm kind of hoping there will be.*

He starts gathering up the lunch detritus. 'I need to get back, but we could meet up again for another chat before you go.'

I hesitate.

'Only if you want to.'

I take a breath. 'We're here for another week due to Klint's schedule, so yes, I'd like that. Thanks for the sandwich and hot chocolate.'

Dain rests his hand on mine briefly, and a warm feeling floods my chest. 'Stay and enjoy the sun. Talk soon,' he says.

I watch him lope off down the hill back to the parsonage,

swinging his thermos.

Pleasantly full and wired from the sugary hot chocolate, I sit there in the sunshine, mulling over what we talked about. It was another good conversation. Apart from him staring at my leg for an overly long moment and the tingles radiating from my fingertips, I could almost say we're becoming friends.

***

Of course, my inner cosiness doesn't last. It can't. Walking back to the hotel, I check my phone and am alarmed to see several missed calls from Klint and a message: *Where the hell are you?*

Hastily, I ping him: *I went for a walk. I'm on my way back.*

He replies straightaway: OK. *I was worried.*

Sorry, I was longer than I thought I'd be. I should've messaged. See you in five.

Klint looks up from his computer as I come panting into the room, red-faced and sweaty. I jogged the rest of the way with my laptop banging against my hip. I'm expecting him to be in a foul mood. So when he smiles, I'm relieved, but wary.

'There you are. I want to show you something.'

'What?' I say, sitting on the nearest twin bed to remove my trainers.

He swivels his laptop towards me and points at the screen. 'Look at this.'

I crane my neck to see. It's information about a student research prize for which the winner receives a not-insubstantial amount of money.

'Susan sent it to me. She thinks I should apply.'

'But you haven't finished your thesis yet?'

'The application deadline is early next year. So if I can get my thesis in by the end of November, I should make the cut-off date.'

He pulls the screen back. 'This would look great on my CV when I apply for the lectureship.'

For a second, I'm confused. 'What lectureship?'

'There are rumours of Percy handing in his notice at the end of April, so his position would be up for grabs.'

'Oh,' I say. 'That would be great if you got it.'

'Susan thinks I'll be a shoo-in.' Klint's cheekbones are flushed, and I suspect his supervisor has been singing his praises and overinflating his ego yet again. She thinks the sun shines out of Klint's butt, and if she wasn't at least 60 and happily married with four children, I'd worry she was after him. But I think her sole focus is on Klint bringing prestige to the faculty. I get up to flick the kettle on.

'How was your walk?' asks Klint.

'Oh, um, good. I went up to the parsonage.'

'What for?'

'Just another look around.'

'Did you have lunch?'

'Yes.'

'No cake for me, though ...' he says, assuming I went to the café in town.

'Hah, no, sorry.'

'Never mind. We can go there tomorrow for lunch. I need to get out of this hotel, or else I'm going to go stir-crazy.'

Later on that evening, we're side by side on the twin beds with laptops propped on our knees. Klint is playing his medieval game, and I've been re-reading some of the Brontë correspondence. I pull up one of Emily's diary papers and peer again at her cramped handwriting that covers every inch of the page. Thank God for the zoom function. Otherwise, I'd be ruining my eyesight.

I flick to another document, a letter from her publisher. Thomas Newby:

I am much obliged by your kind note and shall have great pleasure in making arrangements for your second novel.

I would not hurry its completion, for I think you are quite right not to let it go before the world until well satisfied with it, for much depends on your new work if it be an improvement on your first.

Basically, he's saying, 'You've written an amazing debut novel. "No pressure" for the second one.' It's dated February 15, 1848—ten months before she died. I've seen this before and passed over it without giving it much thought.

But now, after reading *Villette*, I'm seeing it with fresh eyes. I start getting an inkling of an idea.

I check the date when Anne started writing her second novel, *The Tenant of Wildfell Hall*: spring 1847; then when Charlotte was writing *Jane Eyre*: August 1846 through to August 1847.

Was Emily writing her second novel during this time? She'd finished *Wuthering Heights* in June 1846, so it's hard to believe that both of her sisters were feverishly writing their bestselling novels in 1847, and she was sitting idly by. No fear. Emily would've been out on the moors, thinking up scenes and reading out excerpts to her sisters at their weekly writers' group sessions in the parlour.

She definitely had time to write another book before she died, whether it was partially or fully completed. But what happened to it? Did Charlotte kneel by a blazing fire in the parsonage after Emily's death, her eyes full of tears as she fed in page after page because it was too shocking for publication? It's possible. Right until the end, she was iron-fisted in her duty to uphold her sister's reputation. Even if Emily didn't seem to care what people thought, Charlotte most certainly did. Thanks to Anne's loosely disguised depiction of Branwell as the debauched Huntingdon in *The Tenant of Wildfell Hall*, which I'm now re-reading, there was enough dirty family laundry being aired.

But what if she didn't toss the pages in the fire? What if she hid them where no one would look?

I re-read the passage I've marked in *Villette*, where Lucy buries the letters under the tree, and the one further on where she's still dwelling on it in a morbid fashion. Perhaps this was Charlotte's guilt in plain sight? Maybe she was atoning in some way for not publishing her sister's book? One sentence really speaks to me:

Sometimes I thought the tomb unquiet, and dreamed strangely of disturbed earth, and of hair, still golden, and living, obtruded through coffin-chinks.

The death imagery is striking, and Emily's hair was entwined with Anne's and made into a hair bracelet—one of the more macabre ways the Victorians used to deal with grief. However, her hair was brown, not golden. I don't know. It's only a theory, and I could probably nip it in the bud right now by asking Dain what he thinks of it. However, I know he'll shoot it down in flames and say, 'There's not a shred of proof.' And he's right—it's pure conjecture based on a *feeling* on my part. But if I find something to back it up, he might take it seriously. But what that something is, I have no idea!

Surely, there's no harm in messaging Dain in general, though, since we're now on friendly terms; and he said he does want to meet up again. I peek over at Klint, and he's absorbed in his make-believe battle. Surreptitiously taking my phone from the nightstand, I type, *Thanks again for the giant sandwich. When's good for you to meet up?*

I don't have to wait too long for a reply, and his name appearing on the screen gives me an instant dopamine hit.

Dain: *You're most welcome. What about lunch tomorrow?*

Me: *Can't do tomorrow, sorry. The day after?*

Dain: *Sounds good.*

There's a pause, and I think that's the end of the

conversation, but he sends another message.

Dain: *What are you up to?*

Me: *Now?*

Dain: *Yes.*

I hesitate, my fingers hovering over my phone, reluctant to bring up my theory in case I'm drawn into an online discussion; and it's way too premature for that. I'm still thinking about it. Besides, if I type too much, Klint will want to know who I'm messaging.

Me: *Re-reading The Tenant of Wildfell Hall.*

Dain: *One of my faves.*

Me: *Aren't they all your faves?*

Dain: *You got me (laughing face emoji) How far are you through?*

Me: *Two thirds.*

Dain: *I'll read it again too and take notes. We can discuss it when we meet up.*

Me: *You're going to read the whole thing in a day and a half?*

Dain: *Fast reading is one of my few talents.*

Me: *Well, OK, Mr Speedy Reader.*

Dain: *But just to warn you, I'm also opinionated.*

Me: *Lol. I can handle a good book debate. Look forward to it.*

Dain: *Great, I'd better get started!*

I imagine him running to his bookshelf and rifling through his box set of Brontë books and giggle to myself. He's so funny and spontaneous, and I love that he wants to discuss the book with me. It makes me feel special, like he values my opinion. Yes, he is slightly obsessed with the Brontës, but is that a crime? To be honest, I find it endearing.

Chapter 10

Pride refuses to aid me. It has brought me into the scrape,
and will not help me out of it.

(Anne Brontë, *The Tenant of Wildfell Hall*)

Klint still wants to go to the café the next day. I was hoping he'd change his mind once he saw it was inclement weather, but no such luck. The lure of cake sees him donning his waterproof jacket just before noon.

'Are you ready?' he asks.

'It's terrible out there. Can't we go another day?'

'We'll take an umbrella.'

So, much against my will and battling a howling gale that no umbrella could possibly withstand, I drag my heels into the village, knowing there's a good chance that we'll bump into Dain. I'd rather he and Klint didn't meet if at all possible, but it appears circumstances in that regard are beyond my control.

However, he's not there when we arrive nor when we've finished ordering, so I breathe a sigh of relief. Klint heads to the back of the café to snag a table as it's quite busy. The cold and the rain are driving people inside to order warm soup and hot drinks.

Joelle is her usual bright, breezy self as she bustles around, making our coffee and getting food out of the cabinet. I haven't consciously thought of her being with Dain. But seeing her luscious long red hair swishing around and her pert bottom encased in skintight jeans sets off an unwelcome stab of pure jealousy. Lucky cow. Well, maybe not so lucky since they've broken up. But still ... she's the standard he goes for.

Pushing down my feelings of inferiority, I attempt a smile when she makes conversation.

'How's the thesis topic going?'

'Still thinking about it,' I say.

'Did you manage to talk to Dain?'

'I did, thanks. It went well.' A blush flares at the base of my throat, which I hope she doesn't observe. The last thing I want is her thinking I've developed a crush.

I pay and take the tray with our lunch, disappearing before she can ask too many questions.

As Klint drones on opposite me, I tune out and eat my quiche and salad, feeling melancholic. I wish I were here chatting with Dain about *The Tenant of Wildfell Hall*, not listening to him go on about steam engines.

My silent wish is answered. The door opens. There's a swoosh of an umbrella closing, and Dain appears in the café. He's wearing his Victorian coat and looking good enough to eat twice over.

Stomach clenching, I duck my head down, glad that Klint has chosen a seat off to the side. He's also facing me, so he can't see Dain nonchalantly leaning on the counter, chatting with Joelle. Half listening to Klint, I watch Dain out of the corner of my eye. *Is he perving at his ex-girlfriend's firm bottom and wishing they were back together?* The thought depresses me further, and I close my eyes briefly. I open them to find Dain walking towards the table, clutching a couple of paper bags and gazing straight at me. My heart grows legs and tries to run, but I'm caught.

'Hi! Joelle said you were here. I'm on the Scotch egg and apple tart today,' he says, indicating the paper bags with a tilt of his head and a smile.

I wish I could smile back and talk about his food selection. But damn, if he goes on about it being different from the norm, Klint will suspect we've eaten lunch together more than once.

I shake my head softly, and he gives me a strange look. 'Uh, hi,' I say. 'Klint, this is Dain, the guide at the Brontë Parsonage that I told you about?'

Klint pauses with a forkful of quiche midway to his

mouth, then puts it down, silently scrutinising Dain. He's sizing him up as competition—I just know it.

'Hello, Dain. Nice to meet you,' he says in his 'I know my intellect is superior than yours' tone. 'Lizzy has had her nose in her laptop ever since your meeting. You've sparked an interest in something, though in what, she hasn't yet divulged.'

Dain seems unsure how to respond since Klint's comment sounds vaguely accusatory. 'Glad to hear it. Anyway, I should go. I've got a busy afternoon. See you, Lizzy. And nice to meet you, Klint,' he replies and leaves hastily, the café door clanging shut behind him.

I groan inwardly. That was awkward as fuck, and Klint was rude. I don't blame Dain at all for scarpering.

Klint continues eating and doesn't say anything about Dain, which intrigues me. Usually, there's an interrogation.

Eventually, he puts his knife and fork together on his clean plate. 'So that was the Brontë expert.'

I nod.

'He looks like your typical nerdy bookworm. What's with the steampunk get-up?'

'I'm not sure. I didn't think it was polite to ask,' I say, feeling annoyed and not wanting to discuss it.

'Oh well, I guess it's a mystery that shall remain unsolved. Shall we have some cake now?'

***

I'm worried Dain might cancel tomorrow because of Klint's irascible behaviour. So as soon as we're back at the hotel, I message him—from the bathroom.

Me: *Hi, hope you enjoyed your scotch egg and apple tart. Looks like it might be the pub tomorrow if this rain keeps up! (smiley face emoji)*

A few minutes later, I get his reply.

Dain: *Hi. I'm not sure if lunch is a good idea. Your boyfriend didn't seem too keen on me.*

Me (with mounting panic): *He's fine. That's just his personality. He's like that with everyone.*

Dain: *He does know we're meeting up tomorrow?*

Me: *Not yet, but I'll tell him. Honestly, it's all good.*

Dain: OK, *but I don't want to get you into trouble.*

Me: *It's a book discussion in a pub. Hardly illicit.*

Dain takes a while to reply, and I kick myself. Did I overstep the mark by insinuating it's more than that?

After five nail-biting minutes and tearing a square of toilet paper to shreds, I get this:

Dain: *True (laughing face emoji). See you tomorrow!*

He seems OK, thank God. But now I have to tell Klint I'm meeting up with him when I was hoping to 'go for a walk'. Dain might ask if Klint was all right about it, and I don't want to lie to him. But Klint could overreact if I don't step carefully through the minefield.

Frustrated, I flush the toilet and wash my hands. Why am I so fixated on this meeting anyway? We'll be gone from Haworth in a few days, and I'll never see him again. I stare at my flushed face in the mirror. The reason is plain and simple.

The pleasure of Dain's company—even if it's for an hour—is worth risking the inevitable friction with Klint. And the memory of our conversation will be a salve in the months to come. I'm not going to deny myself that.

I'm starting to feel like Helen Graham, Anne Brontë's

soul-tortured tenant. But I haven't kept a diary that I can give to Dain to read about my innocent past. That might be a good thing as he might not find my past as squeaky clean as hers.

I come out of the bathroom to find Klint has pushed the beds together, and he's stretched out on the counterpane, with his shoes kicked off. He smiles encouragingly.

Surely, he doesn't want sex?

'What?' I say suspiciously.

'Come and lie down. I want to talk to you.'

Is this how a relationship should be? Questioning every action, every sentence?

I lie down next to him warily, and he nestles his sharp chin into my shoulder.

'You know I love you, don't you?'

'Sometimes it doesn't feel like it.'

'Sorry if staying here has been a pain ... if I've been a pain. Once this meeting with the station manager is out of the way, we can leave.'

'Have you found out anything more about the documents?'

'Yes, it's a bunch of letters from his great-grandfather written to one of his friends in London. He said there's a lot of factual information about working on the railway here, and I can look through them and take photos.'

'That's great.'

'What about you? How's the Brontë research going?'

'Good. I might have come up with a topic for my thesis.'

'Excellent! I thought I detected the old wheels turning in there.' He taps my temple lightly, and I try not to feel irritated. 'Can you say what it is?'

'Not yet. I still have to do some more research before I lock it in. I also have to find a supervisor who's willing to take me on.'

I've been thinking I might apply to Leeds University rather than Oxford because it's closer to Haworth. But Klint will balk at that. To his way of thinking, it's Oxford or nothing, so I keep my mouth shut.

'Let's have dinner and celebrate with a bottle of wine. Me about to finish my thesis and you starting one.'

'Perfect.'

This is good. It could be my opening to bring up the meeting with Dain.

Klint is two glasses of red wine in, thanks to Gareth recommending a vintage to go with his rump steak. I've ordered a more parsimonious vegetarian chilli and managed half a glass since I'm not a big red wine fan.

There's no easy way to bring it up, so I plunge in. 'I thought I might meet up with Dain tomorrow.'

Klint doesn't look pleased. 'Is that necessary?'

'I've got a few different theories about certain aspects of Charlotte's writing. I want to run them past him.'

'Why not run them past me?'

I look at him. 'Because you're not the slightest bit interested in the Brontës, and Dain lives and breathes them.'

Klint raises his eyebrows. 'That's not fair. I am interested, though I'm not a Brontësaurus like him.' He smirks at his own joke.

I press a stray crumb into the tablecloth. 'It's only a pub lunch, and I'll use my own money.'

Klint winces. His funding still hasn't come through, and he's been firing off emails to check up on it.

'No need to rub it in.'

'I'm not. I was just saying ... in case you're worried about money.'

Klint eyes his rare rump steak, which he's halfway through. 'I wasn't, but since you've brought it up, hopefully your savings will stretch to a steak dinner.'

'It's fine.'

But since I'm in control of the purse strings, he's not exactly in a position to say what I can and can't do.

Gareth swings by with the bottle of wine and asks Klint if he wants a top-up.

'Why not? Since the lady's paying.'

I sigh. Great. Now he's being a martyr.

Klint leans back in his chair and watches as Gareth fills his glass with ruby liquid.

'Do you know a local guy called Dain? He's a guide at the parsonage,' he asks him.

Gareth's hand jerks a little as he's pouring the wine, but his voice is steady. 'Yes, I do.'

'He's not going to run off with my woman if she meets him for lunch, is he?'

I kick Klint's ankle under the table.

Gareth corks the bottle and gives him a small smile. 'I wouldn't worry. Dain's much too busy with the Brontës to run off with anyone.'

He walks off before we can say anything.

'As I suspected,' says Klint cheerfully, attacking his steak once more. 'Go and meet your Brontësaurus with my blessing. And say hi from me.'

I look over at Gareth where he's pouring a pint for a local with a grim expression. What's his problem?

Chapter 11

Oh, how different from the love I could have given,
and once had hoped to receive!

(Anne Brontë, *The Tenant of Wildfell Hall*)

The next day finds me walking into the village, my annotated copy of *The Tenant of Wildfell Hall* tucked into my tote.

The weather has cleared up, but there's a chill wind. Dain messaged earlier, saying he'd meet me in the Black Bull so we didn't freeze to death. That suits me. There's less chance of our fingers colliding over the thermos cup if we're seated opposite each other with a sturdy table in between.

Not that I'm entertaining thoughts of physical contact with him at this current moment. Klint was a little amorous after three glasses of red wine last night, and as the beds were pushed together, we ended up having sex. This morning, we were both a lot more relaxed and connected.

It's strange that Klint is always interested in sex before I meet up with Dain. It's like he has a sixth sense that I'm straying mentally, so he's marking his territory. Maybe it's an inbuilt male thing. But he has nothing to worry about. Like he reminded me again as I was getting ready, a few more days, and we're gone. How can I forget when he's etching it onto my brain?

I spent the morning doing some online digging into the schools of thought around Emily's second manuscript. However, I couldn't find anything of solid merit to back up my theory that it wasn't destroyed. There's so little evidence that it's difficult to piece together what really happened. Trying to write a thesis on it could be like attempting to weave gossamer threads into a substantial woollen blanket. I may have to ditch the idea entirely, unless I can find evidence that points to Charlotte hiding the novel. Maybe Dain's aunt knew something? Her grandmother was friends with the Brontës' maid after all.

Adjacent to the pub, there's a wedding party having their photos taken on the church steps. The bride and her bridesmaids are shivering in thin silk and smiling brightly for the camera despite their arms being covered in goose pimples.

In contrast, the pub is toasty warm, and there's an aroma of steak pie wafting around. Breakfast was a while ago, so I'm starving. Should I order at the bar or wait for Dain? I poke my head into the dining area; and to my surprise, he's sitting at the same table and looking through a notepad, which, I can see from here, is filled with writing. I gulp. He wasn't joking when he said he was going to take notes! I hope I can hold my own in this discussion.

He's watching the bride and groom out the window as they get into a classic car festooned with white ribbons.

'If I ever get married, the ceremony is going to be somewhere warm, not on the verge of winter in a remote English village,' I say by way of greeting. I sit down and rub my arms briskly, looking at the scene. 'Brrr, someone fetch the bride a fur coat!'

Dain grins at me. 'Haworth isn't known for its balmy temperatures this time of year. If you want pneumonia on your honeymoon, this is the place to come.'

We watch as the car moves off down the street, followed by the rest of the wedding party snapping photos.

Dain shifts his gaze to mine, and our eyes lock for a second, making my heart convulse. 'How are you?' he enquires without breaking eye contact.

'Hungry.' I stare down at the menu intently, but I sense him still looking at me. 'I think I might have the fish and chips.'

'Sounds good. Me too. Brain fuel.' He taps his notepad with the tip of his pen. It's jade and has gold edging.

'That's cool,' I say, staring at it. 'Is it vintage?'

He nods. 'Yes. I usually write with a quill, but I ran out of ink.'

'Haha,' I say, but from his expression, I get the feeling he's being serious. *A quill!* Is he into calligraphy or something? 'Um, I'll go and order for us.'

Upon my return to the table, Dain remarks, 'So I've got a couple of questions for you to get the ball rolling.'

I take my copy of *The Tenant of Wildfell Hall* from my tote and place it on the table.

'Fire away,' I say, feeling like I'm on *Mastermind*: '*Elizabeth Doyle, your specialist subject is the Brontës. Your time starts now.*'

'What do you think of the structure of the story? Does it work as a narrative device?'

'Yes, definitely,' I say. 'In the first part of the novel, Gilbert relays the story through letters to his brother-in-law. Then in the second part, it's relayed through Gilbert reading Helen's diary, but it's told from her point of view. The first person tense used for both characters gives the reader full immersion. It's cleverly done.'

'I think so too,' says Dain simply, and I breathe easier. If this is as curly as it gets, I should be OK.

'Do you think Anne Brontë is asking us to have sympathy for Huntingdon?'

'Not really. She portrays him as a man that no one should aspire to be like.'

'Did you personally have sympathy for him?'

'A little, he's a weak-willed man who can't resist vice, and he pays the price for it by dying young. Shades of Branwell indeed.'

'Did you like Helen as a character?'

'She was all right. The switch from innocent virgin to moralistic widow was handled well. But her situation is hard to relate to in this day and age. Women have more freedoms now and are less likely to get stuck in a loveless marriage.' *Though the way I'm headed ...*

'Interesting.' Dain uncaps his pen and makes a note on his pad, but his writing is all swirly, so I can't see what he's written.

'Did you have sympathy for Huntingdon?' I ask.

'No,' he says. 'He deserved everything he got and more. He was a cheating alcoholic, and he abused her.'

I raise my eyebrows and play devil's advocate. 'Wow, speaking of moralistic, I thought you were a Huntingdon slash Branwell supporter?'

Dain's nose wrinkles. 'I never said I condoned Branwell's drunken rants, only that I sympathised with him over having his heart broken and that he served as a catalyst for the male heroes in the sisters' novels.'

'You could apply that to Gilbert as well,' I remark. 'What about the bit where he attacks Lawrence with his whip?' I flick to the section I've marked and read aloud, '"It was not without a feeling of savage satisfaction that I beheld the instant, deadly pallor that overspread his face, and the few red drops that trickled down his forehead." There you go. He's just as ruthless!'

'Hmmm, true,' says Dain, thoughtfully. 'Women always seem to go for the bad boys, even back then ... Why do you think that is?' He's looking at me with a certain glint in his eye, which makes me uncomfortable.

I shift in my seat. 'I don't know. I didn't major in psych. But I'd say it's to do with not having a good male role model growing up.'

Dain's lips twist with the hint of a grin, but his tone is serious. 'Would you class me as a bad boy?'

I stare at him, taken aback. OK, this is getting a bit personal. I don't particularly want to reveal what I think of him. 'Er, I don't know you that well. But based on what I've seen, no, I wouldn't class you as a bad boy.'

'Interesting.' He smirks and jots down another little note, which annoys me. What the hell is he writing? And even more, what is he insinuating?

Our food arrives, hot from the oven, and squirting ketchup on my chips serves as a natural distraction from the way the conversation is headed. I feel exposed—like Dain's picked up on something about my relationship with Klint being off, but he's not coming outright and saying it. He's met him once; he doesn't get to make that call. What about his own mysterious break-up with Joelle? I'm sorely tempted to ask him some awkward questions about that. However, I manage to keep myself in check with difficulty.

We eat in silence, but the atmosphere between us has changed from amiable to suspicious, on my part anyway. It's high time I asked him some pointed questions of my own.

Placing my knife and fork to the side of the plate, I check my notes. 'So Anne was writing *The Tenant of Wildfell Hall* in the spring of 1847, and Charlotte was writing *Jane Eyre*—is that right?'

'Yes.' Dain picks up a chip with his long fingers and dips it in the puddle of ketchup on his plate.

'What was Emily writing during that time? I wonder.'

Dain bites off the end of the chip, chews slowly, and swallows. 'Poetry,' he says eventually.

'Are you sure about that? According to my research, there were no poems produced during that period, which is odd since she was so prolific in the previous years.'

He shrugs. 'Charlotte most likely destroyed them.'

'That doesn't make sense. Why keep her earlier poems

and destroy her later ones? I think the reason there weren't any poems is that Emily was diverting her creativity into writing her second novel.'

'Perhaps.' He swirls another chip.

'So you think it did exist?'

He shrugs. 'We'll never know.' Dain's left eye twitches, and call it female intuition, but I suspect he's hiding something.

I press on into the void. 'Did your aunt know anything about it?'

Dain's reply is to take out his fob watch and check it furtively. 'Sorry. This is an interesting tangent, and I hate to cut it short, but I should be getting back.' He smiles at me, yet it doesn't quite reach his eyes.

'But what about your other notes? You wrote so much.' I gesture at his pad, which he's tucking inside an inner coat pocket.

'That's some writing I'm doing,' he says, not sounding overly keen to talk about it.

'Is it poetry?' I persist, remembering that he "dabbles".

'It's nothing,' he replies abruptly.

'Why are you always so mysterious?' I can't help saying.

Dain's eyes narrow. '*Me*? You're the most mysterious person I've ever met!'

I stare at him, unsure why he's getting so riled up.

'I sat in this very seat and told you stuff about my life, and you didn't offer anything in return. I know *nothing* about you. It's like you've dropped in from outer space, and I can't ...' He stops, breathing heavily.

'Can't what?'

'Never mind. I should go.' Dain gives me a tight smile and holds out his hand, and I shake it mutely.

'Bye, Lizzy. Sorry if I wasn't much help with inspiring a research topic, but maybe the Brontës aren't where your interests lie.'

I take a deep shaky breath when he's gone, feeling like my insides have been dug out with a spoon. I thought we were on friendly terms. It appears we're not.

Call me sentimental, but after I leave the pub, I'm on the verge of tears. That's not how I wanted our last meeting to go. But I wasn't expecting him to lay into me like that. What was he expecting? My life story on a platter? Believe me, he wouldn't want to hear it.

I need to compose myself before I go back to the hotel, so I sneak into the church and hang out there for a while. An exploratory walk leads me to a gold plaque on the floor at the back of the nave. It declares that, interred beneath my feet, are several members of the Brontë family, including Charlotte and Emily. Anne was buried in Scarborough. I send a silent plea to Charlotte to give up her secrets (if she has any).

Afterwards, I wander forlornly around the graveyard that fronts the parsonage, pretending to study the cracked leaning headstones. I'm hoping I might catch a glimpse of Dain—perhaps standing by the door, welcoming a visitor, or leaving from a shift. I can't quite let him go, yet I'm not brave enough to enter the house and go searching for him after his strop.

Should I have opened up more? Why did he want me to? What would that have achieved?

Eventually, the seeping cold, the damp leaf mulch underfoot, and the dreary grey headstones get to me; and I slink away without having seen him.

It's after 4 p.m. when I trudge up the hotel stairs and plod down the hallway to room 9.

'Where've you been?' I can tell by the tone of his voice and the scowl marring his forehead that Klint is deeply pissed off.

'You know I've been at lunch. Hello to you too, by the way,' I say snippily, taking off my jacket.

'A mighty long lunch!'

'I had a look around the village since I might not get another chance.'

Klint gets up off the bed and comes over to me. He

grasps my chin in his hand and tilts my head so I'm forced to look up at him.

'You're lying. I can see it in your eyes. You went back to his place, didn't you?'

Fuck, not this again. Klint's obviously been sitting here, stewing; and now I'm getting it in the neck. I twist away from him and feign calm as I sit on the bed to take off my trainers, but my hands are shaking.

'I didn't go anywhere with Dain. We talked about *The Tenant of Wildfell Hall* in the pub. He left, and I checked out some shops.'

'I don't believe you,' he says, his pointy chin jutting out stubbornly.

'Stop it, Klint.' I get up and fold some clothes in my suitcase that don't need folding to give my hands something to do.

'He likes you. I could tell by the way he was staring at you in the café.'

'He doesn't. That's your paranoia talking.' Well, he doesn't like me *now*, not after our little spat, I think. But I don't say that. Klint requires careful management when he gets into one of his jealous moods. I need to be firm and talk him out of it. 'Even if he did, it's OK for a guy to like me. It doesn't mean anything will happen. You know that. Remember what Dr Millward said? You can control your thoughts and stop them from spiralling.'

But Klint refuses to move on from his conclusion that I've been up to no good this afternoon. He barely speaks to me at dinner and gives me the cold shoulder in the room for the rest of the evening. To make his point even further, he yanks the twin beds apart. The noise of the legs of his bed scraping along the wooden floor sets my teeth on edge. So much for me meeting Dain with his blessing. I've really set him off this time.

Chapter 12

I never liked long walks, especially on chilly afternoons.

(Charlotte Brontë, *Jane Eyre*)

Klint is still in a surly mood throughout the next morning, and by lunchtime, I'm on my last reserves of patience. Silently, I chew on a cheese sandwich and read my book while he slurps his tomato soup. Not that the reading itself is a chore. *The Brontës*, a biography by Juliet Barker, is absorbing. I'm so deeply engrossed I don't realise that Klint's left to go back up to the room until Gareth starts clearing the table.

'Everything all right?' he asks. I'm sure he's noticed Klint's frigid demeanour; it would be difficult not to. His bottom lip was sticking out more than a fresh dermal filler.

'Yes,' I say.

'No more foot tickling, I hope?'

I wish. It might cheer him up. 'No, all good on our side of the hotel.'

However, I did have another weird vision. Last night, I dreamt I was seated with three women at the parlour table in the parsonage. All of us were wearing Victorian dresses, and they were scratching furiously with inked quills on paper. They didn't take any notice of me, but I was included all the same—a warm feeling of trust and camaraderie flowing between us. But I was still very much an observer until the woman opposite, who had the same old-fashioned looped hairstyle as in the previous dream, looked at me with intense grey eyes and said in a low urgent voice, 'Find it, Lizzy', which made me wake up with a start in the darkness. I lay there in a cold sweat, breathing heavily and trying not to disturb Klint. Did I dream about the Brontës? Was Emily speaking to me? It was so vivid that I've been dragging around a mournful nostalgia all day, like part of me wishes I was still there with them rather than here.

'What are you up to today?' asks Gareth, loading our empty bowls and sandwich plates onto a tray. I can't stay at the hotel with Klint acting like this. Maybe if I give him some space, he'll come round.

Closing my book, I make a bold decision. 'I think I might go for a walk on the moors, try out that map you lent me.'

'Wrap up warm if you do,' Gareth tells me with a concerned frown. 'And don't stay out too long. The weather forecast isn't looking too good for later on.'

'I won't. Thanks, Dad,' I say with a grin, and he huffs.

'I don't want any guests getting lost up there. We've got enough ghosts in this hotel as it is.'

'I'll stick to the marked trail.'

'Good. And please take a fully charged phone.'

Huh, that's exactly what Dain said—Dain, who hasn't contacted me since our pub meeting and another reason I have to do something active. If I sit around here reading about the Brontës, I'm going to be tempted to message him.

Collecting my book and phone, I head out of the dining room to get ready for my expedition. But in the doorway, I turn to Gareth. 'Actually ... you don't have a trowel, do you?'

***

Puffing, I reach the top of an incline, cross over a gushing stream, and check Gareth's map. All going well, if I follow the rutted dirt track to the left, I should reach Penistone Crag in a few minutes' time.

My walk up until now has been uneventful, though the sprawling stone estate of Ponden Hall provided an interesting diversion. The Brontë sisters apparently spent time in this home when they were young and played with the owner's children. Its interior reputedly provided inspiration for Thrushcross Grange, the Linton family home in *Wuthering Heights*, and also *The Tenant of Wildfell Hall*.

Not long after, I'm standing on a stone outcrop, looking down into a purple-heather-strewn valley, with Ponden Reservoir a silvery strip in the distance. A cold, blustery wind whips up tendrils of my chestnut hair like snakes; and I pull my beanie down further to protect my ears, which are starting to ache from the constant buffeting. Away from the confines of the hotel room, the moors, with their wild beauty and streaking black clouds, are affording an energising freedom, motivating me to keep pressing forward to my goal: Top Withens, the farmhouse that inspired *Wuthering Heights*.

I'm following Gareth's map faithfully, or so I think, until I realise I've strayed too far east and have to pick my way back over boggy ground. But still, I can't find the path. There's nothing for it but to go off-piste and climb up a ridge through knee-high bracken, in the general direction I'm meant to be going, until I come across it.

All this takes time under the dark watchful gaze of a threatening sky, which seems to be gathering momentum. Gareth wasn't joking when he said the weather forecast didn't look good. Panicking a little, I pick up the pace. But it takes me another twenty minutes to find the path, by which time I'm tired, sweaty, and ready to go back. But I've come this far, and a wooden signpost juddering against the wind says it's only another half a mile to Top Withens. Hopefully, I can get there and do what I need to do before the heavens open and that there's no one there to witness me doing it.

A cold, misty spray is falling as Top Withens, the remote ruined farmhouse with its two old trees nestled in the brow of the hill, comes into sight. By now, my short walk has turned into a persevering slog. The rain worsens and is persistent enough to make me pause and flip up the hood of my jacket as I locate the trowel in my backpack. The lower part of my jeans are soaked. I probably should be wearing proper hiking gear. No matter. Let's get this done. I can have a warm shower when I get back to the hotel.

Checking there's no one else around, I clamber over to the foot of the nearest tree and start digging ... and remembering ...

***

I first met Klint during a climate change protest in central London. I was wearing a green onesie and had 'Vote for Earth' written across my face in blue paint.

Four years ago, I was more assertive and ready to stand

up for my beliefs. If there was a march, I'd be on it. I suppose it's in my genes. I come from a family of strong female activists. My great-grandmother was a suffragette; and my mother, a supporter of the 'make love, not war' campaigns of the 1960s, took part in the famous protest against the Vietnam War in Grosvenor Square when she was a teenager.

There I was, marching along with my flatmate Petra, and a guy fell into step beside me. After a while, he leaned over and said, 'Hi, would you mind holding this? I need to tie my shoelace, but I can't stop walking in this crowd. I'm going off to the side, but I'll find you.'

'Uh, sure,' I replied, taking his sign, which said 'I SHOULD BE STUDYING, BUT I'M AGAINST THIS SHIT'. He took off into the crowd, and we kept walking.

Petra rolled her eyes. 'Doh, you shouldn't have agreed. That's the last you'll see of him. He's scarpered off to the pub. Now you're lumbered with two signs.'

'He'll be back,' I said, trusting that the cute intellectual-looking guy with the messy brown hair and glasses would keep his word.

Five minutes later, he was there again by my side.

'Told you I'd find you,' he said with a grin, taking back his sign.

I grinned back. Here was a guy that interested me,

someone who also wasn't afraid to stand up for his beliefs. Plus he had confidence in spades. With Klint, there was no pussyfooting around. We chatted throughout the march, much to Petra's annoyance. He got my number at the end and promptly called me the next day to ask me out on a date. I liked that. It showed he was mature and wasn't into playing games, which I hated. I'd been single for two years, and I was ready for a proper relationship. Klint Cooper—with his witty, sarcastic banter; dependable nature; and methodical research methods—was just what I wanted.

After that, we quickly became a thing. Our friends even called us Klizzy, and as much as I hated that nickname, it seemed to suit us. For quite a while, we were happy—and then we weren't.

***

The first tree yields no treasure even though I dig multiple deep holes, so I fill them back in and wipe my frozen, muddy fingers on the grass. The branches overhead shelter me from the worst of the rain, but the drops pelt disconcertingly against the back of my windbreaker. Refusing to give up until I've seen this through to the bitter end, I switch to the second tree, crouch down, and start digging again ...

***

The change in Klint's personality was gradual. I can't pinpoint it to a particular date or month, but it was happening around the time I was near the completion of my undergraduate English degree at UCL. I remember I was visiting him in Oxford only every other weekend and relieved to have essay deadlines as an escape from his dark mood.

He'd send me an apologetic message on the Monday following, saying sorry for being a grumpy bastard and that he was stressed about his dissertation and money, and I'd forgive him because isn't that what you do when you love someone?

I understood his situation too. He was deeply committed to his research on the Industrial Revolution, but it was mentally taxing. He was also paying off a Balliol short-term loan, which was an added pressure.

As I had an idea of my master's dissertation topic (nineteenth-century American feminist literature), he suggested I apply to Oxford and we rent a flat together. He also encouraged me to apply for any scholarships or funding I was eligible for. Ever the perpetual student, he knew the system pretty well by then since his parents weren't interested in funding his 'hobby', as they called it. If he'd been heading a tech start-up, like his brother, they would've gladly dipped into the coffers. But since they couldn't see any ROI on a degree in history, they kept the purse firmly closed. I felt for him then—I still do now. He wants to pursue his dreams like anyone else, and not having supportive parents makes it doubly difficult. I know what that's like.

So I applied, not expecting anything because the admission process is competitive; and to my utter astonishment, I got accepted and offered a partially funded studentship as well. We were over the moon and quickly set the wheels in motion to rent a flat.

Things were fine for a while. We were enjoying our study and living together, but Klint's 'bad days' started to turn into 'bad weeks'. He couldn't seem to get on top of it, so his mother got him an appointment with her psychiatrist. He was prescribed antidepression medication, which seemed to help. His moods evened out. We repaired the cracks in our relationship and continued on.

Then three months ago, we went to a midsummer party at his supervisor's house. I drank too many margaritas and royally fucked things up between us.

In essence, I dug my own muddy grave.

Chapter 13

The night is darkening round me,
The wild winds coldly blow;
But a tyrant spell has bound me
And I cannot, cannot go.

(Emily Brontë, 'Spellbound')

I've failed. Whatever Charlotte did with Emily's novel, it's not buried under the trees at Top Withens. I've got multiple blisters on my fingers and brown dirt smeared all over my clothes to prove it.

Currently, I'm holed up in one of the corners of the farmhouse and reluctant to set foot out into the turbulent gusts of wind and rain sweeping across the moors. Gareth warned me, but I had no idea the weather could get this violent. The sheer force of it is terrifying, but rather exciting to witness, at least from the safety of these sturdy stone walls. Luckily, the wind is driving the rain sideways, buffeting the farmhouse. So the fact it doesn't have a roof isn't directly affecting me—yet. But it's getting dark, and I'm cold. Am I going to be here all night? It's not a fun thought. I poke my head out the nearest window opening to see if it's clearing up, and my face is pelted with hailstones. Shit. That hurt.

I have to message Klint; he's going to freak—if he hasn't already. But upon extracting my phone from my backpack, I see a curt text message sent ten minutes ago: *Lizzy - Gareth. Klint said you're not back. Are you out in this?*

Me (feeling guilty): *Yes. I'm waiting until it clears.*

Gareth (no doubt muttering expletives): *It's not going to clear. Where are you?*

Me: *Top Withens. Sheltering in the ruins.*

Gareth: *Stay where you are. Don't move! I'll send help.*

Cringe, now he's organising a rescue party. How embarrassing. But it's better than staying out here on the moors all night since the temperature's dropped another five degrees. I blow into my cupped hands and stamp my frozen feet, but it does little to warm me up. I try not to think about how I'm going to walk an hour and a half back to Haworth when I can't feel my extremities. Hopefully, the team brings hot coffee or warm soup; even a packet of nuts would be good right about now. I've brought water with me, but I've forgotten the golden rule of hiking: always take snacks. *Stupid stupid stupid!*

There's a pause in the wind, and I perk up. But it simply changes direction, and sheets of cold rain start flinging through the top of the house. Within minutes, I'm drenched and seriously worried that I might freeze to death before help reaches me.

What feels like a painful and shivering amount of time later, I hear someone calling my name in the lower part of the farmhouse, though I can hardly hear them through the screaming wind.

'Up here!' I yell as loud as I can.

I've moved into the upper room of the farmhouse and piled some loose stones around me to try to shelter from the elements. But I'm chilled to the bone and feeling drowsy. That's not a good sign. I open my eyes woozily as a beam of light cuts through the darkness, almost blinding me. I raise a hand weakly to shield my eyes from the piercing light.

'Sorry, I'll take it off.' The person removes their headlamp and sits it on a ledge, and my heart almost gives out.

Oh god, it's Dain. In the light of the headlamp, I can see he's kitted out from head to foot in black waterproof hiking gear and wearing heavy-soled army boots. He hefts the full-sized backpack he's been carrying onto the ground. His black hair is plastered to his head, and his perfect features are dripping with rainwater. *No no no.* This is too humiliating.

Then he's looming, like a dark angel come to save me from the thundering storm. 'Can you move?' He helps me to stand up so I'm leaning against the wall, my muscles crying out after being huddled into a cramped space for so long. Our breath hangs in white puffs between us. Dain takes up the headlamp to peer at me, and I flinch away from the light. I can't even imagine what I look like—a haggard ghost with pale skin, matted hair, and blue lips.

He feels my sleeve. 'You're wet through. I thought you'd have a waterproof jacket at least. Can you feel your fingers or toes?'

'N-n-no.' My teeth are chattering so much it's difficult to form the word. Dain swears under his breath, and I try not to take it personally. He puts on his headlamp again.

'OK, I'll just be a minute. Flex your fingers and toes to get the blood moving.'

My head lolling on the stone wall, I do as he says, half watching as he kneels to open the backpack and extracts something rustling and orange out of it. What is that? Is he fetching me coffee? Why is he moving stones? I can't figure out what's happening.

There's a popping noise, and the fabric on the ground grows into an orange mushroom in front of my befuddled eyes. A tent. He's erected a pop-up tent.

'Come on, we need to get inside.'

Ooooh nooooo. This can't happen.

'D-D-Dain ...'

My objection falls on deaf ears as Dain hooks one of my arms over his shoulder, unzips the opening, and bundles us both inside with the backpack. He zips up the tent and extracts a couple of large cylinder-shaped items from the backpack along with his silver thermos.

'We need to stay here overnight. Take off your wet clothes.'

I kneel on the floor of the tent, looking at him blankly. *What?*

He takes my silence for scepticism about his search and rescue skills. But I'm not comprehending what he's suggesting.

'Don't worry. I'm fully trained. I know what I'm doing. You should be OK once you have some hot toddy.'

Hot toddy? I really hope he means whisky. And why am I taking off my clothes?

He unrolls the cylinder-shaped items to reveal a black padded sleeping mat and places the other, a khaki sleeping bag, on top.

'We need to get into the sleeping bag so I can raise your core temperature with my body heat,' he explains.

I gaze at it, not speaking. *Reader, it's not a double.*

Dain sees I'm staring at the sleeping bag and unmoving. He takes my hands and chafes them, but they're so numb I can't feel if his are warm or not. He starts unzipping my wet jacket, talking to me in a low, calm voice. Saying everything will be OK. That he just needs to get me warm.

He attempts to remove my jacket at the same time I try to hold on to it.

'N-n-no,' I protest. From the look on his face, I know he sees the panic in my eyes and understands exactly what I'm worried about.

'Lizzy, I'm sorry, but I have to. You're hypothermic. Do you want to die?'

I'm too exhausted to put up much of a fight, so I let him take off my jacket and then my damp hoodie and then unzip my sodden jeans. Well, I don't want to die ...

***

'Why are your mitts so dirty?'

'Hmmm?' I reply sleepily.

It's been half an hour in the Arctic-issue sleeping bag

with my frozen limbs entangled with Dain's toasty, warm ones. It's a tight fit in the sleeping bag due to his tall frame, but thank God, it's not as intimate a scenario as I thought it would be. I still have some clothing on: a T-shirt, bra, knickers, and the thick woollen socks he's pulled on to my feet. Dain's in black thermals. It's all very proper—apart from me snuggling against his chest and him rubbing his hands up and down my arms and thighs to get the circulation flowing.

We've shared several cups of hot toddy, which, on top of the drama of the day, is making me feel tiddly. My stomach is filled with home-made oat and honey flapjack things he's brought along. I'm beginning to thaw out. Or just melt into him.

His headlamp has been set up nearby 'so it's not so goddamn dark', and it's illuminating the tent like it's a glowing orange bubble. He's also 'checking my vitals', which involves taking my pulse and staring intently into my eyes, looking for signs of persistent wooziness. I'm pretty sure he'll find it. Being so close to him is making me feel dazed and confused.

On this latest check, he's also inspecting my hands. 'Your mitts, they're filthy.' He reaches over into the front pocket of his backpack and pulls out a packet of antiseptic wipes. Extracting a couple, he gently cleans the mud from my fingers. Now that I'm defrosted, the blood is flowing freely through my extremities, so I can feel every small cut and blister he touches.

'I was digging. For Emily's novel. Under the trees,' I say through gritted teeth, wincing at the stings. 'You know, Charlotte's passage in *Villette*.'

Dain silently scrubs at my palm before saying, 'And did you find anything?'

'No.'

'Well, there you go. Crazy novel search over.' He doesn't say anything else, but I know he was worried about how cold I was. Tucking the soiled wet wipes into the packet, he places it on the ground and snuggles back into the sleeping bag with me again.

'But it seemed logical. Where else would she hide it but at Top Withens, the proposed site of *Wuthering Heights*? I thought if there was something to what she wrote, I needed to take action. What if the novel still exists, and it's languishing somewhere?'

Dain shakes his head as if to say I'm nuts, but I feel one of his thigh muscles contract against mine. The wind, which had lessened, has picked up again, snuffling around the roofless rooms like a dog. The noise increases to a howling crescendo, making the sides of the tent flap. Afraid, I press closer to him.

'It's OK, it's just the wind. It can't hurt you,' he says comfortingly, putting an arm around me. Feeling like it's OK to do so, I snake one of mine round his waist.

'I don't like it. It sounds feral.' I shudder, glad that he's with me. I'm dreading the fallout with Klint tomorrow (he's been notified that I'm safe via message, but we haven't actually spoken).

'Thank you. I don't know what would have become of me if you hadn't shown up,' I say in a muffled voice, my face now smooshed against his thermal-covered hard chest. I breathe him in. He smells like vanilla and paper, like he's been browsing in a library; it's a heady cologne for a book lover.

'Let's not think about it. I'm glad you followed my advice and had a fully charged phone.' He strokes my back, and it feels nice—probably too nice. But I may as well enjoy this since it's the last time I'm going to see him.

'You're kind of the last person I expected to show up after our discussion the other day.'

'When I heard there was a girl with long curly hair and blue eyes stranded on the moors, I leapt into action,' he murmurs in my ear. 'Besides, I didn't like how we left things.'

His whisky breath tickles my neck, and I shiver. That sounds like he saw an opportunity to be alone with me—

something that both pleases and scares the dickens out of me.

'Me neither,' I say, trying to breathe evenly. But my heart thuds erratically, and I shift away from him. If Dain feels it beating against his chest, he might decide to take my pulse again, and I'm not sure how I'll explain a rate of 120 beats per minute.

He touches my damp hair, which has spread out on the top of the sleeping bag. I presume he's checking if it's dry yet. 'Well, since we're here now', he says, 'tell me something about you.'

'I'm a silly idiot who doesn't have a waterproof jacket,' I quip.

He huffs, 'Obvious. Something else.'

'I'm an Oxford graduate with a master's in nineteenth-century American feminist literature,' I say automatically.

'I know that already. Tell me something more personal.'

I'm not sure what to tell him, but all of a sudden, there's a burning need in me to confess. 'I'm not ... I'm not a good person,' I choke out.

God, I'm not sure why I said that. I must be delirious or drunk from the whisky in the hot toddy. But it's out now.

'I don't believe that for a second,' Dain replies softly.

Tears well up in my eyes before I can stop them.

'It's true, I'm not.'

'Why on earth would you think that?'

'I cheated on my boyfriend.'

Dain winds a ringlet of my hair around his finger. 'When?'

'Three months ago. It was at a faculty party ... with one of Klint's friends, August Titmeyer.'

Dain snickers. 'With a name like that, he was bound to be trouble. What happened? Don't tell me—Titmeyer waited until you were tiddly, and Klint was out of the room. Then he pounced.'

He's not far wrong, but I have to tell him the whole truth. 'Yes, but it was more complicated than that. August and I had an unspoken "thing" between us. I tried to ignore it. But it was problematic because he was one of Klint's closest friends, so he hung around at our flat a lot. But that night, it was mainly my fault. I drank too many cocktails.'

'I see.'

I take a deep breath, trying not to picture August's cornflower-blue eyes and his silky golden hair that fell perfectly into place, no matter how much he ran his hand through it. 'We always kind of flirted with each other, but jokingly. However, on this particular night ...' I take a deep breath. 'The flirting progressed to *more*.'

'So you slept with him?' Dain says bluntly.

'No!' I say, shocked. 'We were at Klint's supervisor's

house!'

He shrugs. 'Sorry, I assumed the worst. Go on.'

'Klint and I were going through a ...' I cough. 'Dry spell. I guess I was feeling lonely, unloved, and unattractive.'

'Mmmhmm,' says Dain, his tone emotionless, like he's heard this a thousand times before.

'August had cornered me in the lounge, and we were chatting next to the window. I'm not sure where Klint was. I'd had a few margaritas by that stage. I remember there was this green crushed velvet curtain, and we were flirting as usual. Next thing I knew, I was being pressed back into the curtain up against the window. August was kissing me, and he had his hand up my top.' I cringe in shame. 'I pushed him away. But apparently, quite a few people saw it, including Klint's supervisor. So I had to tell him. Since then, I've been in disgrace, and August was dropped as a friend. Luckily, Klint forgave me, but it's made things shaky between us. I'm hoping we can get past it.'

I'm expecting Dain to say a number of things, but 'Did you enjoy it?' isn't one of them.

'*What?*'

'Titmeyer kissing you and his hand squeezing your breast. Did you enjoy it?'

I swallow, feeling a trickle of hot desire run traitorously through my veins. I fantasised about it for weeks afterwards, wondering what would've happened if we'd been alone in the coatroom.

'No,' I say tersely. 'I didn't.'

'Truthfully?'

I slump against him and moan. 'I did. I did. That's why I'm not a good person. I should've tried harder to keep away from him.'

'Did Klint say that?'

'Well, yes.'

'What else did he say?'

'That I needed to talk to his priest, and if I did, he could move on.'

Dain blows out his cheeks. 'He made you go to confession?'

I nod. 'It was the most embarrassing thing ever. I was told to repent and do forty Hail Marys.'

He shakes his head. 'Wow, just wow.'

'I agreed to it. I didn't want to lose him because of a drunken fumble.'

'Did it help?'

'Not really. But I was desperate to try anything. Apologising wasn't working.'

'I get it. I know how it feels to love someone and not want to lose them because of a stupid mistake.'

Is he talking about Joelle? It's on the tip of my tongue to

ask why they broke up, but I bite it back.

Dain rubs my arm. 'For what it's worth, I don't think you're a bad person. You're human, and you're sorry. Deep down, Klint must know that.'

'I hope he does.'

'I assume this'—Dain gestures to us lying together in the sleeping bag—'isn't going to help your case, though?'

'Hopefully, he'll understand that it's a necessary evil.' Dain's mouth quirks at that. 'You know what I mean,' I say hurriedly.

'Speaking of evil, our backs are going to hurt like the devil tomorrow, thanks to this uneven ground. We should try to get some sleep if we can. You need your strength so we can hike back to Haworth.'

I agree, glad we're not talking about me anymore, and twist away from him over onto my side. But as soon as I close my eyes, I can picture the black gaping moors beyond the walls of Top Withens, and I quickly roll back.

'You all right?'

'I'm not used to sleeping on an open moor. Anything could be walking around out there, like the ghosts of Cathy and Heathcliff.'

'Would a rousing verse from Emily help?'

I nod, and he thinks for a minute, then murmurs in a low voice above the wind,

No coward soul is mine
No trembler in the world's storm-troubled sphere
I see Heaven's glories shine
And Faith shines equal arming me from Fear.

I sigh. Of course Dain can quote Emily Brontë by heart, and it's the right thing to say. 'I love her.'

He smiles at me. 'I do too.'

Chapter 14

I asked myself if I was wretched or terrified. I was neither.

(Charlotte Brontë, *Villette*)

As soon as it's dawn, Dain wriggles out of the sleeping bag like a lover making a quick escape. I watch dozily as he pulls on his hiking pants. Disappointment smarts—even though we bonded last night, now it seems he can't wait to get away from me. But perhaps he's being wise. If we linger in the warmth for too long, who knows what might happen.

The hike back is never-ending. We squelch down waterlogged tracks and across moorland fields, and I try not to fall over on my arse. Dain is a rock—encouraging me, feeding me snacks, and not minding if I want to take a break. I don't know how I would've coped alone. He delivers me to the entrance of the hotel and says his goodbyes.

'You're not coming in?' I ask, surprised. 'Gareth will still be serving breakfast. You could grab something to eat and a hot coffee. On me, of course.'

'No, best not.'

He looks tired; the restless wind never ceased last night. So we managed only a couple of hours' sleep, if that. Purple smudges mar the translucent skin under his eyes, there's a faint outline of stubble on his cheeks, and his hair is sticking up on one side from where he's lain on it. But after coming to my rescue, he's more attractive than ever, and I wish I could wrap my arms around him. But it doesn't feel right, not here in front of the hotel as Klint could appear at any moment.

'Well, take care,' he says, giving me a lopsided grin. 'No more wandering out on the moors by yourself, OK?'

'Definitely not,' I reply. 'Thank you. For everything. I'm not sure how I can repay you.'

'Knowing you're safe is all the repayment I need. Just send me an update later.'

'OK, I will.'

I open the door to go into the hotel, but Dain steps forward. 'Lizzy?'

I look up at him expectantly.

'About what you said last night ... I'm probably out of line saying this ...' He hesitates, chewing on his bottom lip. 'But if at any point you need another option, a place to figure things out, or some time to yourself, you're welcome to stay at mine—I have a spare room,' he adds when he sees my quizzical expression.

'Oh, er, thanks,' I say, feeling a stab of guilt that he's deemed my relationship problems the sort that require him to provide accommodation. 'That's kind of you, but I should be fine. I've ... we've ... got some issues. But we're working through them. It's all good.'

'OK, well, the offer's there. It's a bit of an unusual set-up, but I think you'd like it.'

He turns and strides up the road back towards the village, and I watch him go, feeling taken aback. That sounded very much like he asked me to move in with him, which is completely impossible under the circumstances. Or is he simply being a good Samaritan and offering me refuge because I clearly haven't got my shit together?

With a mix of emotions churning in my gut, I enter the hotel and head up to room 9. As predicted, Klint's joy at me turning up damp and rumpled, but alive and well, is short-lived and tempered with mistrust because he knows I spent the night in a tent with Dain. He hugs me, but I'm kept at an emotional distance. I'm hoping, once I explain, Klint will appreciate that it was an exceptional circumstance. Now all I want to do is have a hot shower, don some dry clothes, and have a large breakfast—only then will I be in the right mental state to deal with his suspicions.

However, shortly after breakfast, Klint pries it out of me that Dain and I were in the sleeping bag together; and he hits the roof despite my attempts to plead innocence. He strides back and forth in the limited space next to the bed, clenching his fists.

'*Nothing happened!* How many times do I have to say it?' I kneel on my bed, clutching a pillow to my chest in case he decides to use one of his fists as a battering ram.

'Why was he in there too? It wasn't necessary! You obviously have no respect for me!'

'It had nothing to do with you. It was purely a survival technique to get my core temperature up. Would you rather I'd died of hypothermia?'

Klint doesn't answer and looks like he's actually considering the pros of that.

I hug the pillow and slump against the headboard dejectedly. 'Well, that's wonderful! My own boyfriend wishes I were dead!'

'Of course not. Don't be silly. I just wish you'd survived without *him* being involved.'

'Dain saved my life. You should be thanking him, not acting like a jealous dimwit.'

Klint takes a deep breath. 'I'll ignore that insult. Anyway, it's pointless arguing. We're off tomorrow morning. My funding came through, so I've booked us on the 10.31 train from Keighley.'

'What? I'm not ready to go. I've got a solid idea for my thesis topic.' I've decided to give up on Emily's second novel and focus on the depression aspect instead. Reading about Charlotte's pain through her novel and letters has given me an insight into the Brontës' lives, and it's forged a bond. Things weren't easy at the parsonage. They all struggled with melancholy, poor health, and an uncertain future. Exploring the subject further and seeing how each of the sisters coped with it through their writing will be fascinating—and possibly cathartic for me. Last night, when I couldn't sleep in the tent, I even came up with a fitting title: 'Black Dog: Expression of Depression in the Brontë Novels'.

'What about your documents? Don't you need to stay for your meeting?' I ask, feeling panicked. He's going to ruin everything now that Dain and I are back on track.

Klint gives me a sly look. 'I'm getting them scanned and sent to me instead. I had a lot of time to arrange things yesterday evening while you were camping out on the moors with *lover boy*.'

I bite back a churlish reply. There's no point reiterating

my innocence. I know from experience it's like flogging a dead horse.

I take a deep breath. 'Why is it all about your research?'

'Because it's *my* funding. The fact that you've decided on a topic out of the blue is completely irrelevant.'

'But you encouraged me!'

However, Klint has made up his mind. 'You don't need to be in Haworth for your research, Lizzy, do you?' he says in a placating tone.

Silently, I shrug my shoulders and look away. He's right. I don't, but it feels like he's punishing me for something I haven't even done.

Klint leaves me to sulk and uses the bathroom. While he's in there, I take the opportunity to message Dain.

Me: *Hi, hope you're feeling more human after our adventure on the moors. I know I am. Just wanted to say thanks again. And to let you know that Klint has decided that we're going back to Oxford tomorrow. Yes, as you may surmise from that, I'm in the doghouse. Maybe I should take you up on that offer after all, haha.*

Dain (two minutes later): *Sorry Lizzy, I should've come in and explained the situation to him.*

Klint exits the bathroom as I'm typing out a perfectly innocuous reply.

'Who're you messaging?'

'No one.'

Before I can stop him, he swipes my phone out of my hand and speeds away to the other side of the room. He stands by the window, reading the message thread, and his face slowly turns puce. He jabs at the screen with his finger. 'What offer?' he splutters.

'Nothing. It was a joke.'

'So now the two of you are laughing at me?'

'Jesus, I was thanking him! Can I have my phone back please?'

'No, I don't want you messaging with him again.'

'Seriously? You're confiscating my phone?'

'You've done it to yourself.'

I watch in dread as Klint types something and sends it to Dain, smirking to himself. 'There, that should warn him off.'

'What the hell did you send to him?'

'Only what you should have said in the first place. You have weak boundaries, Lizzy, and you act ambiguously. Guys like him see it as an invitation to take advantage. But don't worry, he's got the message loud and clear that you're off-limits.'

Oh god, I can only imagine what he's said.

All through the afternoon, I'm desperate to have my phone back so I can do damage control. But Klint is adamant that he's holding on to it so I don't fall into "Dain's trap"— whatever that is.

'Stop treating me like a 3-year-old!'

'Well, if the cap fits!'

At dinner, we bicker in muted tones with our heads down so we don't disturb the other diners. But I'm sure they're aware we're having issues by the tension that's strung tight across the table like a rubber band. Not even Gareth, who comes over to congratulate me on arriving back safely, can dissipate the outrage that's brewing deep within me. Klint is obviously testing me, and I'm failing badly. But it's Dain's feelings I'm worrying about, and it's driving me mental thinking that he's been hurt by Klint's reply.

I roll my eyes at him. 'I can't imagine what wickedness I'll get up to between now and tomorrow. Just give it back.'

'I'm not taking any chances.' He pats his blazer pocket, where he's stashed my phone. Grrr, maybe I can tackle him on the stairs, kick him in the nuts, and grab it while he's bent over, clutching his goolies.

But even that satisfaction is denied me because he insists I go up the stairs first, as if he's cottoned on to my plan. In the room, he carries my phone with him into the bathroom and slides it under his butt cheek in bed. I assume he's going to lie on it all night like a guard dog. There's nothing I can do.

He makes no attempt to push the beds back together either, so there's no 'kiss and make up' sex for me. The atmosphere between us is chillier than a freezer; and for all his posturing about me running into the arms of another man, ironically, Klint is the one who's pushing me out into the cold.

***

It's not until we're on the train the next morning and I'm sitting glumly, looking out at the passers-by and wishing I had their lives, that Klint relents and places my phone on the table between us.

'There you go.' He looks at me expectantly, and I stare at him.

'If you want me to say "thank you", you'll be waiting a while.'

He shrugs. 'You may not like what I did, but you'll thank me later and realise it was for the best.'

If he's irreparably damaged my friendship with Dain, I will never thank him. Ever.

Clicking into my messages, I look for the one Klint sent. But he's deleted the whole thread, and there have been no further messages from Dain. My heart sinks. Now I'll never know. The train pulls away from the station, making things seem even more final. Cutting ties. Maybe Klint's right—it's for the best. In the light of day, I can see how it must look to him. But oh, to tear me away from Haworth like this!

I lean my hot forehead on the windowpane, feeling the motion of the train juddering through my body, and attempt to make sense of myself. Why am I still with Klint? Is it indeed masochistic tendencies? If I punish myself enough, will that prove I'm a good person even if I'm miserable for the rest of my life?

I can't help but think of Dain's offer: *If at any point you need another option, a place to figure things out, or some time to yourself, you're welcome to stay at mine ...*

It's looking more and more tempting. In fact, I should've grabbed my luggage and gone to his place rather than stay at the hotel. I would've saved myself from a night of being punished by old misery guts.

But Dain—he's such an unknown. I have no clue what his intentions are other than a strong feeling that he likes me as much as I like him, and given time and space, it could develop into something special—or cause me a lot of heartache in the process.

Then there's sticking with the devil I know. I look over at Klint, who has his nose in his laptop; he's frowning, his hair hanging in his eyes. I do know him. He's a hard worker, he's trying to pursue his passion, and he cares about me. I know he does. Otherwise, why would he be trying to protect me from myself?

Reaching over, I take Klint's hand in mine as a conciliatory gesture, and he lets it lie there for a moment before withdrawing it with his usual line: 'Sorry, you know how I feel about PDAs.'

I'm silent, thinking. Standing on the edge of a precipice.

What if I want PDAs? When do I get to feel happy? I can't remember the last time we had a laugh or enjoyed each other's company. It seems to be a continual round of fighting, patching things up, then more fighting. Even sex with me seems like a chore to him or a way to mark his territory.

The next station is announced: Crossflatts.

If I'm going to do it, it has to be now, before we're too far along. And I can't not do it. As soon as he confiscated my phone, it was the beginning of the end. I rise slowly from my seat and edge towards the aisle with my tote.

'You off to the loo?' Klint says absently, tapping away

on his laptop.

I nod, but he doesn't see me, just assumes I am.

The train is pulling into the station, and I walk down the aisle in a dreamlike state. Pulling my wheelie from the luggage rack, I wait in the corridor by the door for the train to inch in. Come *on*!

The train sits in the station for exactly five minutes. Five excruciating minutes. But the whistle blows, and I'm where I need to be, on the platform. Klint looks out the window and right through me, which I can hardly believe, but there it is.

With my heart thudding fit to burst, I send him the message I typed while I was waiting in the corridor:

Klint, I'm sorry, but I can't do this anymore. I know I broke your trust, but I don't think you'll ever forgive me, and I'm turning into a person I don't want to be. We're not happy together, so I think we're better off apart. PS: Please don't try to change my mind. It won't work.

Through the glass, I see him pick up his phone and read the message. He frowns, confused, and glances towards the corridor, like I might be standing back there.

I wait for him to notice me outside on the platform with my luggage. Eventually, he does, but it's too late. The train is pulling away. The last thing I see is Klint's shocked expression, realising he's been dumped via WhatsApp, quickly followed by his scowl of annoyance.

Then he's gone.

Afterwards, I have a panic attack. I turn off notifications on my phone (in case he lashes out with a barrage of hate-filled post-break-up messages), walk to the ticket machine in a daze, buy a ticket back to Keighley, and wait for the next train.

Sitting in the waiting area on the platform, my heart is pumping erratically in my chest. I can't believe I've done it—the thing that I know I should've done months ago. I try not to think about how Klint must be hating me right now. His shocked face keeps flashing before my eyes. But I can tell it's the right decision because I'm feeling a flood of relief and not the slightest bit tempted to apologise and beg him to take me back. The thought of grovelling to Klint for the indefinite future makes me feel ill. I care about him, but being his girlfriend is hard work. I know relationships aren't a walk in the park, but they're also meant to be fun too. His moods affect me, his controlling behaviour is just wrong, and that awful sleep biting... I can't see anything positive out of staying with him.

Deep down, I've been telling myself I wasn't to blame with August, that he was the one who instigated it. But that night, I flirted with him, smiled at him, and acted like I wanted more. I'm not surprised he kissed me. Come to think of it, I kissed him back for a good few minutes and enjoyed him feeling my boob before I pushed him off, feeling afraid and confused at what was going on, and not quite able to let Klint go.

But something's changed. Meeting Dain has shown me the old Lizzy is still there—the one that likes to laugh and have fun, the one that has a beating heart. He's offered me a lifeline, and it's too hard to refuse. He's seen what I couldn't see myself: That I do need a place to figure things out and some time to myself. That I need to learn how to be me again.

However, staying with Dain could complicate matters. On one hand, it's the best set-up for my thesis. What better situation could I ask for than living with a Brontë expert? He's the perfect person to bounce ideas off, review my chapters, and listen to me droning on without yawning with boredom. I *know* in my gut he'll be fully into it and will help me in whatever way he can.

Yet, I don't want to rebound onto him, and that's going to be difficult since I find him inordinately attractive. I'm going to be walking a risky line. But it's one that I think the Brontës would wholeheartedly approve of because Lizzy

Doyle will be able to (*a*) research their novels and bring a dark subject into the light and (*b*) get to know Dain better while figuring out her shit.

Surely, it's a win-win?

Chapter 15

Daylight began to forsake the red-room;
it was past four o'clock.

(Charlotte Brontë, *Jane Eyre*)

Upon arriving back in Haworth, I have to visit the parsonage to seek out Dain as I have no idea where he lives. I almost messaged him on the train to say I'm definitely taking him up on his offer if it still stands, but Klint's little trick yesterday could have been damaging. I need to explain what happened face to face.

So I pull my bulging tote bag higher up my shoulder and lug my wheelie up the flagstone steps and enter the Brontë home for the third time. Bridget is standing at the entrance to welcome visitors, and her face is bemused when she sees me trundling up the path with my bags.

'Hello again. Are you moving in?' she asks.

I feel the colour rise in my cheeks. 'Um, no, I was hoping to speak to Dain. Is he around?' I don't explain why I've got luggage with me, but Bridget doesn't pry.

'He's not, sorry. He's taken an unscheduled day off, which isn't like him. Did you have a meeting?'

I shake my head, feeling crestfallen. Damn, what am I going to do now? I'm going to have to call him.

'You'll probably find him down by the river at the Brontë Chair,' says Bridget helpfully. 'He usually heads there if it's a nice day or he wants to mull something over.'

That sounds ominous. Hopefully, Klint's message hasn't wounded him. I gaze at Bridget. She has kind eyes and seems like a nice person. She also appears to know Dain quite well. My initial notion that there is some kind of relationship between them resurfaces, causing my anxiety to spike. If I live with him, am I going to be a third wheel? But wouldn't he have said something about her if that were the case? This arrangement he's offered is starting to seem more complicated than I'd like.

'OK, thanks, I'll try that,' I say at last. I don't particularly want to go out on the moors again, especially after yesterday's palaver, but I have no choice. And it is sunny today at least. 'I don't suppose you'd be able to store my bags for me?' I ask hopefully.

'Since you're a friend of Dain's, I'll put them in the lockable broom closet. Just don't tell anyone, or they'll all want to use it.' Bridget zips a finger across her lips.

The Brontë Way is much pleasanter today with a clear blue sky and sunshine warming the top of my head. But the moorland grass quivers in a brisk, scooting wind; and mistrustful of the weather, I walk quickly, pulling my jacket sleeves down over my hands. It snows in Haworth. I've seen photos. If I do end up staying with Dain, I could be here all winter. I'm going to have to buy a thick coat.

Up until now, I've been running on adrenaline, and I haven't given any thought to my belongings in Oxford. But there's not much to consider: clothes, books, toiletries. It's all extraneous, and I don't need any of it. I've never been much into possessions. Klint's inevitably going to have to sort out my stuff—one more strike against me as the bad girlfriend. For now, I need to find Dain because the stress of not knowing if things are OK between us is starting to make my stomach twist into painful knots.

Approaching the wide sturdy seat-shaped stone, or 'the Brontë Chair', where the sisters used to sit and dream up stories, I feel sick with nerves. But he's nowhere in sight.

I walk on farther and discover him standing with his back to me on the riverbank with his hands in his pockets. He's wearing his long black overcoat and army boots.

I don't like to disturb him. He's staring intently at the rushing water, high after yesterday's storm, as if drawing energy from it. But he hears my footsteps on the track and turns around, hair lifting in the breeze; and I know instantly, by the way his brown eyes soften, that whatever Klint's said hasn't done any real damage.

'Don't you know you shouldn't be alone on the moors? I hope you've got a fully charged phone?' I say lightly.

'What are you doing here? I thought you'd left.' His tone is surprised rather than accusing.

'Klint's currently on a train heading towards Oxford—without me.'

Dain looks startled. 'You didn't?'

'I did,' I say simply.

We stare at each other for a moment, and I take a nervous breath. Now or never.

'Is it still OK for me to stay with you? I promise I'm an exemplary flatmate: quiet, tidy, a non-smoker. I also promise not to burn spaghetti on the cooker or overfeed your cat. Scout's honour.' I salute him, holding up three fingers of my right hand, and Dain's eyes crinkle.

'Of course it's still OK, though Tabby is woefully spoiled, I'm afraid. So you can't do too much damage there.' He gestures to the path. 'Shall we walk back?'

I nod, and we fall into step.

'Where's your stuff?'

'At the parsonage. I called in to find you, but Bridget said you might be out here.'

As we walk, Dain's unbuttoned coat billows behind him. He's wearing a loose-fitting white cotton shirt and black jeans tucked into his army boots. He looks like Mr Darcy out for a hike.

Dain shakes his head. 'I can't believe you broke up with Klint. How do you feel?'

'I'm OK. It's been a while coming, I think.' I don't elaborate on what went down. I'll leave it up to Dain's imagination.

He clears his throat. 'I gathered things weren't great from your message, and he sent that one afterwards.'

'Oh, so you knew it was him?'

'I suspected ... from the wording and the tone.'

'That's a relief. He confiscated my phone and wouldn't give it back. I was worried about what he'd sent you. What exactly did he say?'

'It was a thinly veiled threat to keep away from you. The wording isn't important.' Dain shrugs and looks out over the waving brown heather. After a moment, he glances down at me. 'At least you've got somewhere to lie low and take stock.' He squeezes my arm. 'I can't wait to show you my place.'

'I can't wait to see it,' I say, smiling at him. Phew, I didn't need to worry after all. This is turning out much better than I expected.

Dain leans on the wall outside in the lane while I collect my bags at the parsonage; he cites not wanting to answer questions on his day off as his excuse for not coming in with me. 'If someone throws me a curly one, I could be stuck there for half an hour at least. Brontë fans are intense.'

No kidding, I think.

It takes me a little while to locate Bridget, but I find her in the back garden in front of the bronze statue of the sisters. She's chatting with a couple of middle-aged men in Barbour jackets with expensive-looking DSLR cameras strung over their shoulders. I manage to catch her eye after hovering in the background, conscious of Dain waiting for me.

I wave at her discreetly. 'Hi, my bags?' I mouth from the doorway.

'Excuse me, I'll be back in a sec,' she says to the men and comes over to me.

'Sorry to disturb you.'

She laughs. 'Don't worry, you were rescuing me from being disturbed. They're paranormal fanatics, and they were quizzing me on whether I've seen or heard any of the Brontës walking around lately.'

'Oh. Have you?' I say conversationally as we walk up the stairs and back into the main house to reach the broom closet. Gosh, this village is ripe for ghost hunters.

'Dain and I stayed here overnight once,' she says breezily, taking out her keys to unlock the cupboard. 'But I'd never do it again. We didn't see anything, but we didn't get much sleep either. Did you manage to find him by the river?'

My gut twists, and I can barely give her my assent. They spent the night here together! He made it sound like he was alone. Was she the one who dared him to stay? Visions of Dain and Bridget snuggled up in Mr Brontë's bed are now assailing my mind, especially as I was snuggling with him myself only last night.

'Here you go.' She hands me my wheelie and tote, and I take them silently. 'Where are you off to now?' she asks curiously, staring at my bags.

I want to say 'I'm staying at Dain's' to gauge her reaction, but something stops me. 'Ah, just moving accommodation. Thanks a lot.'

'No bother.'

After she leaves, I check my WhatsApp messages because I can't keep avoiding them. Sure enough, there's an unread one sitting in there from Klint.

I groan silently, and Charlotte's ghostly admonishment drifts out from the parlour: *Well, Lizzy, you've done it now. You'd better read it at least.*

Klint: *I'm not going to try to change your mind or ask you to repay the £85 train ticket. Just let me know where you're staying.*

A needle of guilt pierces my heart. Well, if he wants to know …

Me: *I'm staying at Dain's. He has a spare room. I'm heading there now.*

He must be waiting for my reply because he's instantly online.

Klint: *Why am I not surprised?*

(Klint is typing. Klint is typing.)

Klint: *If you hadn't broken up with me, I'd feel obliged to warn you, but I guess you'll find out.*

I click out of the app quickly, feeling even more disconcerted than my conversation with Bridget. Warn me? About what? He doesn't know anything about Dain; they've barely spoken. I note there's nothing about him being upset about my decision. He sounds as belligerent as usual, and it steels my determination to not believe a word he says.

As I walk past the parlour on the way out, I pause in the doorway and listen, but there's no further advice forthcoming from Charlotte. I guess I'm on my own.

***

Dain's house is a five-minute walk from the parsonage, off the main street. It's a two-storey, semi-detached of butterscotch-coloured stone with a gabled roof at one end. A low stone fence encloses a paved front garden area. There aren't any plants in it, only a few wind-blown shrubs around the perimeter. I take it he isn't into gardening, or the weather permits only the hardiest species.

Dain unlocks the front door, which is a glossy black and has a gold door knocker. *Fancy.*

'Come in.'

He reaches down to take my wheelie off me, and I'm ushered through into an entranceway with a black-and-white-tiled floor. It contains an assortment of boots, shoes, and trainers all arranged neatly in a line. I feel a tiny thrill of privilege that he's invited me to stay at his house. Dain sheds his outdoor coat and hangs it up on a wooden coatrack. I decide to keep my jacket on until the central heating kicks in as it's a little chilly.

'I'll give you the tour. You can leave your bag there.'

I drop my tote onto the chair he points out and follow him curiously into a passageway with sombre grey walls. A flight of dark wooden stairs leads up to the first floor. The house seems a little dim, but I'm sure he'll turn the lights on as we go.

He walks through an arched doorway and states, 'So this is the parlour.'

I trail in after him, expecting a normal lounge set-up. But it's nothing like that. Silently, I survey the lounge or, should I say, *parlour* with its ruby-red flower-motif wallpaper and dark polished floorboards. There's no TV, stereo, or anything remotely resembling modern living. Just a large round mahogany table with a few stiff-backed red velvet chairs, a cast-iron fireplace, and an elegant antique couch with curved wooden legs, also in red velvet, placed in front of it. Thick black-and-gold brocade drapes hang on either side of the windows, and the far wall is inset with a floor-to-ceiling bookcase painted red to match the wallpaper. It's like stepping into 'Victorian Room of the Month' in the 1900s edition of *House Beautiful* magazine.

Really, knowing him as I do, I should've expected this. But it's still startling.

'What do you think?' Dain seems anxious to get my opinion.

'It's very cool,' I say, bemused.

And it is. But I assume this room is his passion project, that he's done an interior design course so he could create a Gothic reading room. But I'm not too bothered. *There's probably another more comfortable lounge elsewhere.*

'I thought you'd like it.' Dain looks pleased.

I go over to the bookshelf and peer at a few volumes. I was right about the Brontë box sets—and there are classics galore: Bram Stoker, Charles Dickens, George Eliot, Oscar Wilde, Mary Shelley.

'Wow, this is bordering on a library.'

The sun has gone, and the afternoon has turned gloomy, which is making it difficult to see in here. And the heating still hasn't come on yet. I shiver, pulling my jacket tighter around me.

'It's a little cold for reading, though.'

'I'll light the fires soon,' says Dain.

'Ah, OK.' *Fires? Does he mean fire up the boiler?*

I look around for a light switch by the door. But the wall is blank, and there's no fixture in the ceiling.

'Where's the light?'

'There isn't one. I use these.' He gestures to a couple of kerosene lamps sitting on a wooden sideboard, along with a collection of candles.

'Oh, I thought those were for show.'

He shakes his head, watching me carefully.

A worrying thought enters my head.

'Are there electric lights in any of the rooms?'

He shakes his head again.

'*What?*' I say, hardly believing it. Surely, he's joking! But it seems he isn't.

'The lamps throw out a surprising amount of light. It's quite bright and cosy if you have a few of them going at once, along with some candles ...' He trails off, seeing my dumbfounded face.

'But why?' I ask.

'My aunt didn't bother having the house wired, and I used to find it mysterious and romantic having the lamps and candles, so I continued with the tradition when I moved in.'

She didn't bother having the house wired. Another even more worrying thought enters my head. 'Does that mean there isn't *any* electricity?'

Dain shakes his head and chuckles darkly. 'If you've ever wondered what it's like to live in the nineteenth century, you're about to find out.'

'But how do you cook? And what about heating?'

'There's a wood-burning stove in the kitchen. It's pretty efficient, and the fires are good for heating the place. If I can't be bothered lighting them, I put on more clothes or have a jug bath.'

The words 'jug bath' nearly set me off into a full-blown panic. The Victorian era wasn't exactly known for its mod cons.

'Please tell me there's plumbing at least?' *Please, please, please don't make me use an outdoor toilet,* I pray silently.

Dain shrugs. 'Kind of. It's the full-immersion experience. As I said, I don't do things by halves.'

I gulp. *Oh my god.* He's a total eccentric born in the wrong era. 'You'd better give me the rest of the tour,' I say in a deadly quiet voice.

Chapter 16

No study, however interesting, interfered with [Emily's] bread,
which was always light and excellent.

(Elizabeth Gaskell, *The Life of Charlotte Brontë*)

A little while later, after the tour, I sit alone in my bedroom, trying to keep calm. To say I'm processing what I've seen is an understatement.

Dain showed me his kitchen. It looked like it was out of a Dickens novel: a scrubbed wooden table and a fully functional old Aga. No microwave, fridge, dishwasher, or washing machine in sight. I was relieved to see there was a large enamelled cast-iron sink but immediately noticed there were no taps. He told me that he gets his water from a tap outside in the garden, boils a kettle on the stove, and pours hot water into the sink for washing dishes or clothes. 'The stove is quite efficient. It only takes ten minutes to boil the kettle.'

More efficient than turning on a hot tap? I think not.

But I didn't say anything, wanting to get the lie of the land before I blew a gasket, so to speak.

The upstairs bathroom was … interesting. It contained nothing but a free-standing roll-top copper bathtub placed in the middle of the room on a black-and-white-tiled floor. Surrounding it were black walls, and upon one hung an ornate full-length gold-framed mirror. The aesthetic was undeniably edgy, if impractical, since, again, there were no taps.

I went into the room and touched the top of the tub. 'Is this a nineteenth-century original? It looks too shiny.'

Dain leaned against the doorframe. 'Sadly, no. I tried to bid for one in a local auction, but I got out of my depth pretty early on. It went for over 2,000 quid.'

I raised an eyebrow.

'This one is faux copper, much cheaper.'

'Ah. And how does one *bathe*, may I ask?'

'It's a bit of a process heating the water for a full bath, as you can imagine. So I only do that once a month, like they used to back in those days.'

'Right. And how do you wash for the rest of the time?'

He gestured to the bath. 'Stand in there, wet a flannel, and soap up, then pour a jug of warm water over my head. Does the trick. It's connected to a drain, so at least I don't have to bail the water out.'

I tried not to react in visible horror and said through gritted teeth, 'I think I might need more than one jug.'

I didn't get to see where Dain slept. We passed a closed door on the way back downstairs, and he mentioned that it was his room, but he didn't open it. So of course, now I'm imagining it to look like a vampire's lair. The way he's choosing to live is both amazing and crazy, so I wouldn't be surprised if it was.

My room is off the kitchen. It's not large, but big enough to fit a double bed against one wall and a free-standing antique wardrobe against another. Dain nodded when I remarked this was probably where a servant slept, but as he said, it is cosy because it gets the residual warmth from the Aga. There are no black-and-gold drapes or copper in here. The theme is lighter with white walls, pinewood furniture, and cream curtains.

Not that I can see it now as it's dark, but there's also apparently a view out to the back garden, and it gets the morning sun. Dain lit me a kerosene lamp, and it's flickering and throwing up eerie shadows on the wall. I shudder at the thought of the long night ahead with no proper lighting.

I'm having to quickly adjust to the fact that if I live here, all the home comforts I'm used to won't exist. Heating food in three minutes flat in a microwave—nada. Hot showers—nada.

I stare at a washstand next to the wardrobe, which holds a blue-flowered jug of cold water nestled in its matching bowl, a towel, and a cake of soap ... And—I'm not joking (reader, I wish I was)—there's a chamber pot with the same flower design under the bed!

Dain is used to living this way and obviously thrives on it; he's got one foot firmly in the past and embraces it wholeheartedly without any qualms. But I feel like I've been thrown in the deep end. Noticing the tight expression on my face when he told me there was indeed an outdoor toilet, he said I should 'think of it as an alternative lifestyle experiment'. But apart from non-existent plumbing, how am I going to charge my laptop or my phone? (How does he, for that matter?)

I'm sitting on the bed, an embroidered pillow propped behind my back, feeling completely bewildered and thinking maybe I should do a runner, when a folded piece of paper is hesitantly pushed in stages underneath the door, as if the person who's pushing it isn't sure how it will be received.

I get off the bed, pick up the paper, and unfold it. It's a note addressed to me—written in black ink with a quill pen. I sigh. Is he trying to be funny?

I have to use my phone torch to read his handwriting because it's in Gothic cursive.

Dear Lizzy,

Sorry if this is a lot to take in. I told you it was an unusual set-up! I know it doesn't seem like it now, but you will get used to it. It's not an uncomfortable way to live, just different. And there are benefits. At least I've found there are. Anyway, I hope you'll stay and give it a try. I promise it will be nothing like you imagine it will be.

Yours,
Dain

Huh, how does he know what I'm imagining? I scrabble in my tote for a pen and write on the back of the notepaper in my best handwriting,

I feel a little tricked. You could've told me how you lived before I decided to move in so I knew what I was getting myself into!

I fold the paper and push the note smartly back under the door. There's silence, then a scratching noise that goes on for a few minutes. The note appears again, this time more abruptly.

You broke up with Klint and showed up with your bags before I had a chance to explain! Not that I'm criticising your decision, but you have to admit it was a quick turnaround.

That is true—things did move fast today. I can't blame him for my own impulsive behaviour. I write underneath his sentence,

You're right. I didn't give you a chance to explain. I know I don't seem it, but I am very grateful that you've offered me a place to stay. But I'm also a teensy bit worried about how I'll cope. I might need some time to adjust. PS: Your cursive handwriting is really cool.

I post the note under the door. This is kind of fun. There are further scratching noises, and the note pokes out again.

Thanks! Since there's no TV, I've had to take up a few hobbies. Practising cursive handwriting is one of them. Btw, Tabby is here and wants to say hello. Can she come in?

I post back,

Yes she can.

The door opens a crack, and a fluffy white cat with big green eyes and a cute pink button nose pushes into the room with her tail in the air and a haughty expression on her whiskered face. She jumps up on the bed, stretches out on the flower duvet cover, and looks at me as if to say 'You may pet me now'.

Dain pokes his head in after her and grins at me. 'Meet Tabitha, but she doesn't mind if you call her Tabby.'

I stroke her soft fur, and Tabby's tail flicks lazily. 'What is she?'

'A Turkish angora.'

'She's lovely. I always wanted a cat. But Klint is or, should I say, *was* allergic.' It's the first time I've thought of him since I stepped foot inside the house. I've been too distracted.

At the mention of Klint, Dain's smile wavers. 'Well, I'll leave you two to get acquainted. Come out to the kitchen when you're ready. I'm going to make some bread.'

I look at him. 'I assume by hand?'

'Yes, it's pretty easy.'

He shuts the door, and I breathe out in relief. I have so many questions bouncing around in my head that I need a moment to sort them into logical order. I scratch Tabby's head, and she closes her eyes, purring. 'I think your owner is a bit cuckoo,' I tell her. She butts her head against my hand, and it feels like a nod, but I don't think she's agreeing with me. Despite my misgivings, Dain's dedication to the Victorian era has my curiosity piqued as to what else this lifestyle entails. Perhaps he has a house manual quilled in Gothic cursive he can give me?

After I've freshened up, I leave Tabby sleeping on my bed and go out to the kitchen. Splashing ice-cold water on my face was tantamount to a slap on both cheeks, so I feel wide awake now.

Thanks to the Aga, the kitchen is warm and lit by half a dozen kerosene lamps, and I feel like I have indeed time-travelled into the past.

Dain is standing at the kitchen table, wearing a dark-blue baker's apron and levering a lump of pale dough out of a yellow ceramic bowl onto the floured surface. In his white blousy shirt with the sleeves rolled up, he could have stepped out of the pages of *Wuthering Heights*. However, I can't imagine any of the male characters choosing to make bread. That was definitely women's work.

Dain nods at the wooden chair opposite him. 'Take a seat.'

If you'd told me this morning that I'd be sitting in Dain's kitchen, watching him knead dough by lamplight, I would've said you were crazy. But here I am. And it is quite soothing to watch, as he continually folds and pushes it with his palms. He has nice hands, large and smooth with long blunt-tipped fingers slightly stained with ink.

'Are you feeling better about things?' he asks, sprinkling more flour on the table from a paper bag.

'Strangely, yes,' I say. 'I think Tabby helped. And your note, of course. Where is that, by the way?'

'In here.' He taps his apron's front pocket.

'Can I have it?'

'Sure.' He wipes one of his floury hands on a tea towel, plucks out the note, and hands it over, looking at me quizzically. But I tuck it into the back pocket of my jeans without saying why I want it. I guess if I had to explain, it would be that I need something real to ground me. But really, I want to look over what he wrote again. Is this why women back then kept letters, to pore over in private, analysing each word? Not that I'm going to do that exactly, but it's nice to have a keepsake.

'Does your mum visit you?' I ask, picking up a thread from our meeting in the pub.

'Sometimes, yes. And she doesn't mind the set-up, for a few days anyway.'

'What about your dad? Does he come?'

Dain's dough kneading starts again briskly. 'My parents

are divorced. Mum's happily remarried, living in Chester and bringing up another man's kids from his third marriage. My father and I are … estranged. He doesn't have a part to play in my life, or more that he chooses not to have a part to play.' Dain punches the spongy dough with his fist as if he's seeing someone's face in his mind's eye. I know how he feels.

'My dad isn't in the picture either.' *Klint took up the father figure mantle, and look how that turned out.*

'Tell me more about living here.' I eye the ancient-looking bone-handled knife that he's using to score the top of the dough. 'That knife looks authentic.'

He grins at me. 'It is.'

Fashioning the dough into a neat oblong, Dain places it on a greased and floured tray while telling me about his fascination for antique shops and the thrill of discovering a knife or razor or fountain pen from the period. 'This area is full of Victorian artefacts. Things get passed down through the generations and end up being sold for a quick buck when people have a cleanout of their relatives' possessions. Someone like me is much more appreciative than they are, and the quality and workmanship of the artefacts is so much better than today's cheap knock-offs.'

'However, you do use a mobile phone,' I point out. 'So you're not completely denying yourself the perks of twenty-first century living.'

'That's for no other reason than I don't want to completely cut myself off from society. I'm not that perverse. The parsonage needs to contact me about shifts, and my mum messages me. I sent her a letter once, and she complained she couldn't read it. She prefers to WhatsApp.'

He opens the oven door and quickly closes it again. 'That's hot enough.' But I'm not sure how he knows as there's no temperature gauge. Maybe feeling your eyebrows singe is indication enough?

'How do you charge your phone, though?' I persist. 'I don't want to be completely cut off from society either, and I need my laptop.'

'I've got a few power banks. I charge them at the parsonage and bring them back here. They don't mind. You're welcome to use one.'

'Right.'

Ironically, he's charging them at the Brontë home, which is now more modern than his. Sigh. But I understand why he volunteers there. It's like an extension of his lifestyle to keep fully immersed in the period. But what does he do for money?

'So your power bills are non-existent, of course. But what about council tax, insurance, and maintenance? And antique buying ... How do you pay for all that?'

'I have a side gig.' He picks up the tray with the bread and pops it into the oven without elaborating. But by now, I'm extremely curious.

'Are you an secret agent or something?' Well, he is well groomed. It's not unfeasible.

Dain lets out a bark of laughter and turns to face me, merriment dancing across his face. 'A secret agent! I wish! I'd probably get paid more. But no, I'm not a secret agent.' He gazes at me and presses his lips together.

'You're not going to tell me, are you?' I say, feeling disappointed.

'I will, but not right this minute. It's a long complicated story, and I'm hungry.'

'Me too. Are we waiting for the bread to cook?'

'No, that's for the next few days.' Dain goes over to an old-fashioned bread bin and pulls out half a loaf of bread. 'Something I prepared earlier,' he says. 'It's all about forward planning when you're not relying on modern conveniences.'

He hands me the loaf and a bread knife. 'Can you hack off a few doorsteps from that please? And there's some butter there to spread on it.'

'Ah, I now see why you make such man-sized sandwiches.'

'Exactly.' He turns his attention to the stove and lifts the lid on a cast-iron pot that's been bubbling on the stove. 'We can have this leftover meat stew with it.'

A delicious aroma wafts from the pot, and my stomach rumbles. I hastily start sawing into the bread in anticipation. This Victorian cooking lark might not be so bad after all, and Dain seems to know what he's doing. He also visits Joelle's café for lunch, so I know he doesn't entirely rely on rustic home cooking.

I lather a slice of bread with butter and think about Joelle. His insistence on living in a bygone era *must* be why they broke up. She couldn't handle it. Can't say I blame her, but it's a pity they couldn't find a workaround.

'Don't you get lonely living like this?' I ask before I can stop myself.

Dain keeps stirring, and I think he's not going to reply. Then he says in a flat tone, 'I did have someone, but we parted ways a couple of years ago.'

'I know. Joelle, I met her in the café. She said she was your ex.'

'Oh, yes,' he says, but I can tell by his shoulders hunching that he doesn't want to talk about it.

Gosh, it must have been a bad break-up if he can hardly bear the mention of her name. Does he still have feelings for her?

Silently, he reaches into the dresser next to the stove and

brings a couple of plates over to the table. I gather the subject of his ex-girlfriend is now also closed. I got too close to the bone. It's strange—he's so open about some things and locked up tight about others, though I suppose I am being nosey.

'Are you OK eating in here? It's warmer than the parlour since I haven't lit the fire in there yet,' he says.

'Sure.'

He starts wiping the table down, and I move a thin book out of the way. Its light-blue cover is sprinkled with flour.

'Don't tell me you're learning German like Emily did while baking bread?' I joke.

'No.'

'I don't believe you.' I check the inside of it, and it's an exercise book of German verb conjugations. Dain looks at me sheepishly, and I can't help laughing, albeit with a tinge of hysteria. Oh my god, he's in full Brontë immersion!

Chapter 17

The difference between Miss Brontë and me is that
she puts all her naughtiness into her books.

(Elizabeth Gaskell, *The Life of Charlotte Brontë*)

Hours turn into days. Days turn into weeks, and before I know it, I've been living at Dain's for six of them. Going from a hotel to a house with amenities from the dark ages takes some getting used to. But surprisingly, Dain was right. Once I got my head around it and gave myself permission to embrace the full-immersion experience, I started enjoying it a little. When else am I going to get the chance to live in the same conditions that the Brontës would have (albeit with a laptop and mobile phone)?

But I can't lie. I miss the convenience of stepping into a hot shower. Washing now involves stripping first thing after I get up, a quick going-over with a wet washcloth and soap, another rinse with the washcloth, and rubbing myself down briskly with a towel, trying not to freeze to death. I haven't been brave enough to get naked, soap up, and rinse with a jug of warm water in the bath as Dain does because I discovered the door doesn't have a lock; and although I mostly trust him to knock before he waltzes in, I'm not prepared to risk it.

Some days, my washing routine is more thorough than others. Let's just say I've come to appreciate my 'natural oils'. However, my hair is getting ratty, so I probably need to do the full bath ritual soon. Neither Dain nor I have had one yet due to the hassle of heating the water and filling the tub. But I'm determined to try it, even if my arms fall off from lugging buckets of water upstairs. Meanwhile, I'm putting my hair into a messy bun and using dry shampoo. As for clothes, I'm using the launderette in town as I can't face handwashing. Sometimes Dain asks me if he can add a few shirts too, which makes me smile. I don't think it's high on his list of favourite chores.

He much prefers cooking and has shown me how to make the bread. We take turns. I'm much slower than he is, and my bread-making skills leave much to be desired. My first attempt almost caused him to crack a tooth. He said it was 'delightfully crunchy, but perhaps best dipped in soup'.

Cooking has never been one of my strengths, and Klint hated it too, so we ate out a lot or existed on Pot Noodles if funds were low. I'm jealous of Dain's ability to whip up all sorts of things on the temperamental Aga. The other day, he made a soufflé since he's rather into French cooking. It was so delicious and, most importantly, edible that I'm seriously tempted to let him do it all. But I don't want him to think I'm a shirker, so I'll persevere.

For his part, Dain is being careful not to ask too many probing questions about Klint or how I'm feeling. He knows I've been fielding messages from him, but wisely, he's letting me work through things at my own pace and not doling out manly advice. I've noticed mentioning Klint's name causes Dain's jaw to clench, so he may not be his favourite person, though he's never said as such to me. The only reference he made was a few nights ago as I was sighing at the kitchen table over an annoying 'woe is me' message Klint had sent.

'Lizzy, you know that if you want to talk about stuff, I'm here. But I'm not going to tell you what to do,' he said.

'I'm open to opinions,' I replied.

He shook his head. 'You're smart. You know what you need to do.'

'Well, I wish someone would tell smart Lizzy because dumb Lizzy is in danger of being emotionally blackmailed.'

But still, I haven't caved and gone back to Klint, which is perhaps what he's thinking I'll do and why he's keeping out of it.

I ponder a lot on how things might have turned out if I'd been single when I met Dain. Our pub lunch maybe would've turned into dinner and something more that evening; our sandwich and hot chocolate meetup on the bench would've been a romantic tête-à-tête, where we *did* touch fingers over the thermos cup. And don't get me started on the number of times I've reimagined us getting it on in the sleeping bag.

Not that it does me any good—Dain hasn't made a move even though I know by now that there's nothing going on with him and Bridget; from what he's said, they're just friends.

I get the impression he does like me but thinks I'm in mourning over Klint. Though I was sad for a few weeks, the old Lizzy has bounced back remarkably quickly, and I'm not upset anymore. Yet I have no idea how to convey that to Dain. Announcing 'I'm over Klint, let's have sex' might shock him into kicking me out. He seems kind of shy in that regard. So even though I'm in the friend zone with him, it doesn't stop me from freely fantasising about what could be. It's not easy living with someone who's so inherently, yet modestly sexy, and the fact that he walks around looking like a Victorian rake but is an exceedingly *kind* person makes it even more difficult. It's a potent mix of pleasure for my eyes, solace for my soul, and yearning from my loins.

But whatever feelings I have for Dain, I suppose I should keep a lid on them. I don't want to drag him into the emotional whirlpool that Klint is stirring up. The theme of his constant messaging is that he can't (or won't) let go of our relationship and wants me back. He says he's depressed and can't work and that he misses me (finally). Of course, I get sick of it and snap, sending something to reiterate that we're over and to take his medication, which I think is cruel to be kind. But it simply adds fuel to the fire. He gets shitty and goes away. A few days later, he's back again, trying to wheedle his way into my affections with the same messages but worded differently. Then there are the cryptic jibes asking if I've discovered Dain's 'secret' punctuated with laughing emojis, which I ignore. Yes, Dain has an alternative lifestyle. It's no business of his. And how did he find out about it anyway?

Worst of all, his mother, Lydia, rang the other morning and left a long, rambling message accusing me of making her Klinty miss out on his award because he's not going to get his thesis in on time to apply for the research prize, which is rubbish. He has plenty of time if he knuckles down. I quickly deleted her message.

Smart Lizzy knows she needs to block Klint to get him out of her life for good. However, he has all my stuff in our Oxford flat; and on reflection, I would like to keep some of it. I just have to figure out how to extract it without dumb Lizzy being sucked into his drama.

One silver lining from breaking up with Klint is the renewed determination to pursue my own doctorate at Leeds University. After years of suffering from imposter syndrome, I no longer have to worry about the fear of failure. Klint made it clear what he thought; attaining a degree with distinction was the only acceptable outcome, and it was a lot of pressure during my master's.

However, it's my fear of not being accepted into the programme that's making it difficult for me to start the application process. But after mulling it over for days, I mention it to Dain, and he says instantly, 'Do it, Lizzy. You're an Oxford graduate, and you're researching the Brontës. They'll snap you up!'

So I pluck up my courage and fill in the online form, attaching my Brontë research proposal. After a nerve-racking on-site interview, an electronic letter is sent saying I've been unconditionally accepted for a PhD in English at Leeds University.

'I told you!' exclaims Dain when I break the good news to him. He surprises me by pulling me into a warm hug, which I enjoy immensely before he quickly releases me. 'Congrats! Now you can start researching and writing with a purpose.'

'I know. I can't believe it.' I do a little jig on the spot. Dain takes my hands, and we caper around the kitchen, where we seem to spend the majority of our time because it's the warmest room in the house.

'This calls for my best bottle of red wine!' he pants, which makes me laugh since I've never seen him drink anything.

'I thought you were a teetotaller?'

'No, there are several bottles in the dresser. I don't like drinking by myself. But now there's a reason to celebrate: you and your thesis.'

It's a sobering thought, and I stop capering and sit down on the nearest kitchen chair as the realisation sinks in.

Dain looks at me. 'What's wrong?'

'I'm going to have to write a 100,000-word thesis.'

'Don't worry about that. You can do it,' he says reassuringly. 'I'll be here to provide unwavering encouragement, chapter critique, and late-night cups of hot chocolate.'

It's a comforting thought that he has complete confidence in me that I can produce the thing. Even if we can't be more, he's proving to be a caring friend, and I'm coming to appreciate that the longer I live here.

***

One evening, not long afterwards, I visit the supermarket to get some provisions. Upon returning, a blast of warmth and light emanate from the parlour, causing me stop short in the doorway with my Sainsbury's bag. The kerosene lamps are lit, the fire is crackling, and Dain is sitting at the table, which is stocked with paper and an inkpot. He's scratching away on an old-fashioned sloped writing desk with a quill. I gawp. This is next-level Brontëmania.

'What are you doing?'

He looks up. 'Just some writing. Join me if you want. There's a charged power bank.' He nods to it on the table.

'Er, OK.'

Depositing my bits and pieces in the kitchen, I grab my laptop from my bedroom. I need to meet with my supervisor shortly to talk about the structure of my thesis, so I do need to write up some notes of different ideas I've had.

Dain and I work quietly, with only the sound of my tapping fingers and the scratch of his quill pen, along with an occasional shifting log causing sparks to fly in the grate. He's writing rapidly, filling sheet after sheet with his Gothic cursive, and totally absorbed in what's doing, which is making me extremely curious.

Eventually, he sighs, and rolls his shoulders, easing out the stiffness. 'I'm going to make some ginger tea. Do you want some?'

'Yes please.'

After he's gone, I pull the edge of one of the sheets of paper towards me, but I can't read it upside down. With one ear on the door, I swivel the paper around and glance at a random paragraph. It seems to be the description of a bedroom in a historical home. There's dialogue between a woman, Azalea, and a guy called Nathaniel. They're engaging in banter about her dress. I finish that page and start on its neighbour; there's more banter, and the dress seems to have been removed. Nathaniel is unlacing Azalea's corset. He slips a hand down the front and pinches her nipple hard and runs soft kisses down her neck. By her enthusiastic gasps, she seems to be enjoying it a lot. I'm absorbed in Nathaniel trying to remove Azalea's corset and her half-hearted protests when Dain's amused voice sounds from the doorway.

'Do you like it?'

I push the paper away and return to my laptop, my face flaming. What the hell is he writing? And what happens with Azalea and Nathaniel? Do they get it on?

Dain comes in with a tray laden with a teapot, a couple of cups, and a plate of oat and honey flapjacks.

I can't look him in the eye. 'Sorry,' I mumble. 'It was there in my line of sight ... I only read a tiny bit.'

'Mmhmm.' Dain pours the tea and hands one to me, but my hand shakes so much the cup rattles in its saucer and slops tea over the side. 'Lizzy, it's fine. I don't mind.'

I take a deep breath and try to control myself.

Dain looks at me slyly. 'Are you shocked?'

'Uh, a little. I was expecting an essay on nineteenth-century razors, not a spicy short story.'

'It's a novel actually,' says Dain, sipping his tea nonchalantly. 'I've just started. I'm glad to see the first chapter kept your interest.' He smirks.

My eyes widen. 'You're writing a spicy novel?'

Without answering my question, Dain saunters over to the bookshelf and extracts a paperback from the lowest shelf. 'Have a read of this one.'

He hands me a book with a blood-red cover and a title in spiky black font: *Desired by the Yorkshire Libertines*. There's a woman in a black corset and fishnet stockings with long flowing red hair sandwiched between two men in white ruffled shirts and tight black trousers. As they're slightly taller than her, the illustration shows only their lips and chins. She's gazing up at one man amorously, and her hand with red-painted nails is resting behind on the other's thigh. A four-poster bed with black velvet curtains is in the background. The author is Tabitha Lavish. Huh, she sounds kinky. This must be who he's using for inspiration, how funny.

I turn the book over, and there's a small blurb and

author bio, but no photo. It says Tabitha Lavish lives in a Yorkshire village with her cat. She likes reading historical fiction, cooking up a storm on her Aga, and hiking on the moors ...

My hand flies to my mouth as I click. 'Oh my god, don't tell me *you're* Tabitha Lavish?'

Dain smiles and gives a little bow.

I can't believe this! Quickly, I flip to the first chapter.

Sophronia Milton was decidedly fed up with her life. What was the point of it all? She was utterly sick of being paraded around like a cow in a livestock sale, simply to be handed off to the highest bidder. And the thought of marriage and babies made her feel ill. If she had her way, she'd choose a man who'd go walking with her in the woods, teach her to shoot and the various ways of intimate pleasure. She wanted a lover she could experiment with. She couldn't do that with a husband. But all was not lost. Little did her parents know that Sophronia had written to her cousin Rayne, bemoaning her fate, and her bewitchingly beautiful naughty cousin hadn't found her such a man. Oh no, she'd found her two ...

I stare at Dain in disbelief, who shifts awkwardly under the weight of my stare.

'It's a spicy MFM historical romance in case you're

wondering,' he says.

'What. The. Hell!'

He shrugs and moves to stand in front of the fire with his hands clasped behind his back. From this position, his face is in the shadow, so I can't tell if he's highly embarrassed or not.

'It started out as a fun hobby, but now I've got a loyal fan base, and it's starting to pay a decent amount of royalties each month,' he says. 'Plus spicy historical romances are popular, so there's a ready market of ravenous readers.'

From the calm and even tone of his voice, he doesn't seem fazed in the slightest. I'm the one who's losing it.

Still holding the book, I gaze at the table spread with pages that sport his flowery handwriting.

'Don't tell me you write them by hand? That must take ages.'

'I was slow to start with, but now I can write quite fast,' he says. 'I average around 700 to 800 words a night.'

I still can't quite believe it.

'Surely, you don't package them up in brown paper and send them off to a publisher?'

Dain shakes his head, laughing. 'Can you imagine? No, I give the pages to Bridget to type up as I go. She prints the whole thing out, and I edit it. She makes the changes, gives it a final proofread, and publishes it for me on Amazon under my pen name. She sourced a great cover designer who isn't too expensive.'

'Do you pay Bridget?'

'Of course, I wouldn't expect her to do all that for free.'

I peer over at the lower shelf; there seems to be at least half a dozen titles sitting there. 'Is it a series? With the same character?'

'There's a three-book series about Sophronia and another three-book series featuring her cousin Rayne.'

'And … and is it all the same theme … sexually?'

He shakes his head. 'No, Sophronia is into threesomes, and Rayne is a lesbian.'

My eyebrows shoot up. 'Diverse! And the one you're writing?'

'It's a stand-alone featuring Sophronia's younger sister, Azalea, who's into BDSM,' Dain explains. 'If my fans like it, I might make it a duology.'

My head is spinning that he's doing this. Publishing books. Spicy, kinky books! And making money from them too!

This must be the secret that Klint keeps going on about. How on earth did he find out?

'Does anyone know you're Tabitha Lavish? Apart from Bridget?'

'Only a few people. It's a strict secret punishable by death. Since you've found out, you'll need to take the blood oath tomorrow.'

'What does that entail?' I have visions of him cutting our palms until they bleed and pressing them together in a candlelit ceremony.

He grins at my concerned expression. 'Don't look so worried. It's only signing an NDA.'

I let out a breath.

He sits back down at the table and picks up the quill with his ink-stained fingers. 'Anyway, feel free to have a read. I won't be offended if you don't like it. What I write isn't everyone's cup of tea.'

With Dain's parting words, 'happy bedtime reading', ringing in my ears, I head off to my room, clutching book 1 of the Sophronia's Secret Life series and feeling apprehensive about what it contains.

As I suspected from the pages I read on the table, there's a lot of spice in this book, more than I would normally be comfortable with. But I still devour it at a feverish pace by the light of my kerosene lamp. There's everything from corset ripping, smutty talk, and heaving bosoms to open-door scenes featuring Sophronia and each of the two gentlemen as she gears up for her ultimate fantasy of a threesome (however, 'gentlemen' is too nice a word—these guys are hot, horny, and up for anything!). I'm trying not to imagine Dain as one of the main characters, but it's difficult, especially as the men dress like him and wear fob watches.

Halfway in, the threesome scene occurs, and my eyes widen. Reader, it's graphic—so much so that I have to close the book momentarily. I stretch out in bed, close my eyes, and press my hands to my hot cheeks. Oh my lord, I need a fan to cool down. *Dain Whitmore or, should I say, Tabitha Lavish, you have a dirty little quill!*

God knows what Bridget thinks about his books. Or maybe she's used to it by now?

After five minutes, I sit up and flip open the book again, craving to know what happens next. Damn him and his cliffhanger chapter endings!

***

The next morning, I'm up at the crack of 9.30 and in the kitchen waiting for the kettle to boil when Dain appears, hair mussed and damp from a jug bath. Oh god. Feeling unprepared to see him quite so soon after last night's tumultuous reading experience, I turn away quickly, pull out the grill, place two slices of bread on it, and pop them back in the oven to brown.

'Well, Lizzy?' Dain says gruffly from behind me. 'Don't keep me on tenterhooks. What did you think?' He sounds truly concerned about my opinion of his book, which, judging from the subject matter, isn't surprising. Maybe he's been lying awake all night, regretting telling me about his side gig.

'Why do you want to know?' I say slowly, still not brave enough to look him in the eye.

'Well, you're my target audience: female, between 20 and 50 with an interest in historical novels, and hopefully not averse to R18 content.'

There's a pause as I deliberate over what to say. I settle on 'It was good'.

'I need more feedback than that!' Dain sounds agitated. Does he care that much about what I think?

I sigh and turn to face him. 'It was fantastic, OK? I read the whole thing.'

'The whole thing in one night?' Dain's dark-brown eyes narrow as if he thinks I'm fibbing. 'It's nearly 400 pages.'

I nod, quelling a yawn in case he takes it as a sign I was bored with his book. 'Trust me, I didn't get much sleep. It's definitely a page-turner.'

Dain's worried expression relaxes. 'Wow, OK. Thanks. Good to know.' He takes an apple from the wooden bowl on the table and bites into it, chewing thoughtfully. 'So on a scale of 1 to 10, how aroused were you?' he asks coolly.

'Er ... um,' I mutter. I'm so flustered my hand knocks against my recently poured cup of tea. It goes flying, and milky brown liquid spills all over the table. To my embarrassment, I'm blushing fiery red to the roots of my unwashed hair. Hastily, I grab a sponge and start mopping up the tea spillage while Dain looks on with an amused expression.

'Is that your toast I can smell burning?' he asks.

I hurry to the grill in a flap. *Forget my toast—it's my body that's on fire!*

'Hmm, I'll take that as a 10 for the arousal. Note to self: keep with that level of detail for the spice,' Dain murmurs, walking out of the room.

I tip out the dregs of my tea and boil the kettle again, deciding I need a strong cup of coffee instead. So much for him being shy about sex! Dain's not the prim and proper gentleman he's been making himself out to be.

Chapter 18

The young man had been washing himself,
as was visible by the glow on his cheeks and his wetted hair.

(Emily Brontë, *Wuthering Heights*)

With all the reading and note-taking I'm doing for my thesis, I'm keeping pretty busy. But in between all the Brontë books, biographies, and research essays, I've managed to fit in books 2 and 3 of Sophronia's Secret Life, as well as book 1 of the second series about her lesbian cousin.

Dain doesn't remark on it, but every time I abashedly return a book to the shelf and take another, a satisfied expression comes over his face. If I didn't know how modest he is, I would even go as far to say that it's bordering on smug. I guess having your target audience living with you and devouring your books must be quite an ego boost. Either that, or it's vindication that what he's writing is hitting the mark. I'm glad he hasn't wanted to engage in an in-depth discussion about them. It's one thing to discuss *The Tenant of Wildfell Hall*, but quite another to be put on the spot about critiquing Sophronia Milton's sexual escapades, and I get the feeling that Dain liked seeing me unnerved.

Our living arrangement is still going surprisingly well, better than I thought it would since I've been stripped of twenty-first-century luxuries and had to learn a whole new set of skills. My bread making is slowly improving, and I can now light a fire that catches on the first take. But despite my acquiescence to Dain's lifestyle choice, every morning that my warm toes hit the cold wooden floorboards, I crave central heating and a hot shower like a lost child yearning for its mother. And the outhouse is a nightmare I don't even want to get into.

As soon as my postgraduate research funding comes through, I mention that I'd feel better paying him rent and contributing to bills (whatever those are). After some protestation, he concedes that I can and tells me a low figure, which I bump up by another £100, causing more protestation. But I stand my ground, and he caves under much duress. Before he changes his mind, I set up a monthly payment to go into his bank account. Apparently, he does have one and doesn't keep cash under his mattress or anything.

But this conversation obviously sparks something in him;

and a few nights later, he announces during dinner that he's arranged for plumbing and a boiler to be installed and that, once they are, there will be (and, reader, these words are music to my ears) 'central heating, taps with running water, an indoor toilet, and a shower'.

I'm more than a little joyful at this news, as you can imagine. 'But ... why?' I ask, astonished at his unexpected change of heart. 'Don't you want the full-immersion experience anymore?'

'I'm going to keep the lighting like it is as it helps me get into a historical mindset for writing. But I can appreciate it's difficult to live with certain aspects of the house. Plus winter's coming, so I thought a compromise was in order.'

'Can you afford it?'

He nods. 'My books are doing well, and if you're helping out with bills ...'

'Oh my god, thank you!' Unable to contain my glee, I jump up, run around the table, and plant a swift chaste kiss on his cheek. Come to think of it, this is the first time I've shown him anything resembling affection since I broke up with Klint. I've been waiting for him to make a move, but maybe I'm the one who hasn't been giving off come-hither vibes. As well as living like Victorians, we've been unwittingly acting like we're in a period novel—the unspicy kind.

Whatever Dain thinks of me kissing him, I can't tell. But a rouge of colour appears on his cheekbones, and a small smile plays on his lips. 'I knew it would make you happy,' he says quietly.

'You have *no idea* how happy you've made me.' I go back to my seat, feeling a bit shocked I did that. The nerve ends in my lips are on fire. Bloody hell, that was only his cheek—imagine what it would be like to kiss him properly.

Dain flicks me a heated glance as if he's wondering too. I pick up my knife and fork and swallow nervously.

'Obviously, I did *attempt* to wash my hair by hanging my head over the side of the bath. But it was difficult to rinse out the shampoo. I needed four jugs of warm water, and I had to wait for the kettle to boil each time, with my sudsy hair wrapped in a towel. So I haven't bothered washing it lately, and it's a greasy mess ...' I trail off, realising I'm rambling on about nothing and making it worse by drawing his attention to my lack of personal grooming.

'Ah,' Dain says politely but doesn't comment on my hair. If that were Klint, he'd screw up his nose and say he'd noticed. 'Well, I've booked the contractor in for Monday, and they said it will take about a week. It might be a little disruptive, though.'

I nod and cut into my piece of corned beef and mustard (Dain's latest craze is boiling salted meat and vegetables).

'That's perfect timing actually. I have to be in Leeds next Wednesday for a couple of things. I might book into a hotel rather than coming back to keep out of the way.'

'Oh?' Dain quirks an eyebrow.

'A meeting with my supervisor and a faculty function later on at a hotel,' I explain.

'Sounds fun.' He spears a boiled carrot and pops it in his mouth. 'Hmm, this is tasty. I think I might try a chicken and veggies next.'

I roll my eyes. 'Please tell me you're not going to turn up with a live one. I'm not interested in helping you kill and pluck a chicken.' Honestly, anything is possible with him.

'We could use the feathers to make a cushion?'

'No!'

Dain chuckles, and we continue eating by candlelight. My thoughts wander off. *I really hope he doesn't show up with a live chicken to prove a point. I should attempt to wash my hair before I go to Leeds. I need to book the hotel too.*

I glance at my phone on the table with its blank screen. Still no 'woe is me' messages from Klint. He hasn't been in contact for a week, and his silence is worrying. *I hope he's not doing anything stupid.*

* * *

On Sunday morning, before the plumbing works commence, I heat up the kettle and collect my towel, shampoo, and conditioner and put them in my tote. My hair is in a right state, and I can't meet my supervisor with a head full of greasy rats' tails. Even if I manage to give it only a cursory wash, it's better than nothing. I found a sturdy tin bucket in the shed outside, so I'm going to fill it with hot water and dip into it with the wash jug that's kept in the bathroom. I figure I should be able to get at least three, maybe four rinses.

Tabby follows me, purring, and tries to push in front as I lug the steaming bucket up the stairs. I stop to let her go past, adjusting my tote on my shoulder, wondering what her hurry is. Reaching the landing, I pause for a breather, my hands on my hips. Imagine doing this twenty or more times to fill the bath—ridiculous! I pick up the bucket again with both hands and stagger down the hallway. Tabby pads ahead of me towards the bathroom door. However, when I reach it, I hear a splash and clink from within. *Damn, I thought Dain had gone to the parsonage. I'll have to wait until he's finished.* But my water will get cold. How annoying. Maybe I can use the kitchen sink instead. I'm about to turn around and go back downstairs, but Tabby nudges the bathroom door open with her paw, slips in through the crack ... and I catch sight of a soapy penis.

Oh dear God. I press back tightly against the wall, my heart pounding fit to burst. Closing my eyes so tight I see stars, my common sense tells me I should inch slowly towards the hallway with my bucket. But curiosity takes over, and I jut my eye into the crack like a Peeping Tom to get a better view. And whoa, what a view it is.

Dain, in all his pale naked glory, is standing in the bathtub, slowly stroking said soapy penis. His eyes are closed, and a smile flits across his lips as if he's enjoying the sensation or thinking of a scene in his new smutty novel.

My throat constricts, and heat rushes to my cheeks. I should not be watching this! But my eye is glued. At this point, a ten-tonne truck couldn't drag me away.

The stroking gets faster and firmer, and Dain emits a low guttural moan. OK, definitely thinking of a scene in his new smutty novel! An echoing arousal blooms in the base of my belly, and the back of my neck starts sweating. Oh lord, he's going to ... My pussy clenches in joyous anticipation.

Maybe it's instinctive from being watched, or he's distracted, but Dain suddenly removes his hand (much to my acute disappointment) and finishes soaping the rest of his body—a treat in itself. He twists to grab the flowered water jug sitting on a nearby stand, displaying a lean, but muscular back and the curve of a delectable twitching buttock. Standing upright, he tips the steaming jug over his head. Hot water sluices down his sculpted chest, washing away the white suds, his long pink member bobbing merrily in its thatch of dark hair under the cascade. It's the most erotic thing I think I've ever seen and definitely worthy of a mention in any spicy novel. I lick my dry trembling lips. Wiping his eyes, Dain reaches for a towel folded on the side of the tub, glancing up as he does so, and I jerk back from the door.

'Hey, what are you doing in here?'

My heart leaps into my throat and does the Macarena. *Shit, he's seen me.* But Tabby mews in reply, and I breathe out in relief. He's talking to the cat. There's a sound of wet flesh slipping against copper as Dain gets out of the bath. He's chatting with Tabby, some kitty cat nonsense. I need to leave *now*. If he comes out and discovers I've been watching him jerk off ... *The shame will be unendurable.*

Hardly daring to breathe, I creep down the stairs, one step at a time, with my bucket and tote. My foot slips halfway, and I almost go careening down them on my backside but manage to right myself at the last minute. Bloody hell, there'd be no way I could hide that commotion. Dain would find me at the bottom of the stairs, soaked, with a bucket on my head.

Scurrying as fast as I can to the kitchen, I heave the

bucket up to the sink to pour the hot water down the drain. But it's taken me so long to boil I'm reluctant to get rid of it. I can't think straight. Dain's naked body keeps flashing into my mind.

I can hear his footsteps running down the stairs. So I grab a clean mug from the draining board, scoop it into the bucket, and plonk in a teabag. Dain strides into the kitchen, jiggling a finger in his ear to get the water out. His white flowy shirt is half unbuttoned, showing off that lovely smooth chest, which is glistening with droplets of water; his dark hair is damp and brushed back. He looks heart-stoppingly handsome. My glance flicks to his crotch, and I note that his black trousers are tented. He's still erect. I swallow hard as desire floods my body. *We could do it, right here in the kitchen, if he wanted to ...*

'You all right?' he asks, noticing that I'm staring at him wordlessly.

'Y-yes. I'm making tea.'

Dain looks confused. 'Why are you using a bucket and not the kettle?'

'Oh, er, I boiled extra water 'cause I was thirsty.'

Dain brightens. 'Good idea! I'm in the mood for a big cuppa.' He reaches into the cupboard and grabs the largest mug.

'Uh, I just have to go and do something,' I mutter.

Stumbling dazedly to my bedroom, I close and lock the door.

Father, forgive me for what I'm about to ... Helplessly, I fall to my knees in a praying position. But this time, I have no rosary beads, and I'm definitely not saying any Hail Marys. Unzipping my jeans, I dive a hand into my knickers and start rubbing, envisioning Dain slipping in and out of me with his amazing-looking cock. *Oh yes, like that, like that*, I moan silently; and within seconds, I come without warning, collapsing against the bedframe, my hand still wedged in my jeans.

A little shocked at the violence of my orgasm, I freshen up with a washcloth soaked in cold water and go back out, only to find Dain still in the kitchen, leaning against the counter and sipping his tea.

'What were you doing?' he asks. 'Exercising?'

I press a hand to my forehead to discover it's hot and bathed in sweat.

'Um, no, some last-minute tweaking to my thesis structure. It's causing me a bit of stress.'

'I'm happy to look at it if you want.'

'Uh, thanks, but I think I've managed to tame the beast.' I laugh, but it sounds unnatural to my ears.

Dain finishes his tea and places his mug in the sink.

'Speaking of beasts, I think I might go and buy some

steak for tonight, to celebrate our new plumbing. Tell me, how do you like your meat?'

My cheeks flush as I remember him standing in the bath. *I like it erect and soapy ...*

I cough. 'Oh, uh, m-medium rare, thanks,' I stutter.

Dain grins at me. Oh no, he's not stupid. Does he know I spied on him?

Chapter 19

She put up her hand to clasp his neck,
and bring her cheek to his as he held her.

(Emily Brontë, *Wuthering Heights*)

Two mornings later, I manage to wash my hair. It's a hash job in the kitchen sink as the plumber and his cohorts have taken over the upstairs bathroom.

I haven't seen Dain since the night of our steak dinner, which I stuttered and blushed through. Yes, my conscience made an appearance. I felt wholly ashamed of myself—first, for spying on him; second, for having the audacity to pleasure myself like a brazen hussy while he was in the Very. Next. Room. What on earth was I thinking? I need to stop reading his books!

Dain, bless him, attempted to keep the conversation going. But it kept sputtering out like a candle in a draft, thanks to my embarrassment. After dinner, I said I'd do the dishes, and he vacated to the parlour without a word. Now there's a weird, strained atmosphere between us, and he's obviously avoiding me. He must've somehow guessed I saw him naked in a compromising position because I'm acting so weird. Unless Tabby told him—that snitch!

The hammering, grunting, and general noise pollution in the house is making it difficult to work. So in the afternoon, I take myself off into Haworth to go shopping. I'm desperately in need of something to wear to this faculty function tomorrow night. It's not a flash event, only a postgraduate meet and greet for students, lecturers, and various other stakeholders. But still, I can't turn up in jeans and a hoodie as it's being held in a fancy art deco hotel.

Haworth doesn't have a huge selection of clothing shops, but there is one selling vintage items on the high street that is eclectic and quirky, so I head there first. While I'm browsing through the racks and idly wondering if Dain shops here, the door dings open; and Joelle breezes in, holding a cake box. She greets the shop owner cheerfully and lingers, chatting with her at the counter. Great, just what I need—Dain's beautiful ex-girlfriend making me feel inferior. I swivel and pretend to inspect a real fur coat that smells like mothballs. But I'm the only customer in the shop; and my chestnut hair—now that I've washed it—is long, curly, and conspicuous.

'Lizzy? Is that you?' Joelle's voice sounds from behind

my hunched right shoulder.

I turn and feign surprise. 'Oh, hi!' I say, smiling at her a bit too brightly. This is the first time I've seen Joelle out from behind the counter, and I note we're face to face, so we must be about the same height. She looks as willowy and pretty as ever and somewhat witchy due to silver hoop earrings and a black bat-winged jersey top that matches her perfectly applied inky eyeliner.

'You didn't come back into the café, so I thought you'd left to go back to Oxford. How're things? I was dropping off a birthday cake.' She nods towards the owner, who's lifted the lid on the box and is checking the contents.

I finger the coat, wondering how much to divulge, and decide to keep it brief. As Gareth said, Haworth is a small town.

'Nope, still here. I've enrolled in a PhD at Leeds Uni. So I'm staying here while I research my thesis.'

'Ooh, I take it you're doing it on the Brontës?'

I nod, and Joelle claps her hands together. 'Fantastic! You and your boyfriend are so clever.'

Great. Even though I haven't mentioned Klint, she's assumed he's here too. I wonder what she'd say if she knew I was living with Dain.

I mutter something non-committal and randomly pull out what I think is a dress. But it's a black lace-up satin corset.

Joelle giggles. 'Oo-er, looking for something to spice things up in the bedroom?'

'No.' I shove it hastily back into the rack.

'Hang on a sec.' She plucks it out again and peers at it, fingering the boning. 'This is mine. I dropped it off ages ago.'

'No takers?' she calls out to the woman at the counter and holds up the corset for her to see. The woman shakes her head and plumps up her bosoms like she's a saucy wench. Joelle laughs. 'I guess it is a little too racy for the locals. Anyway, I'd best get back. See you later.'

I say goodbye; and she exits the shop, leaving me to stare suspiciously at the corset. Sophronia has long red hair, green eyes, and wears a corset like this—albeit it gets ripped off her during the threesome scene and is unsalvageable. But ... was Dain drawing from something other than his imagination for the story, namely his ex wearing it? They say that jealousy is a green-eyed monster, but the colour of the feeling that rips through me at that moment is nothing but white-hot. I place the corset carefully back in the rack. But if I had a flamethrower, so help me God, I'd light the thing and gleefully watch it burn.

** * **

'But don't you think all the characters in *Wuthering Heights* are so one-dimensional?' The guy opposite sips from his glass of complimentary white wine and studies me intently through his horn-rimmed glasses. Disturbingly, he reminds me of a blond-haired version of Klint, except he's studying English, not history. He's got that same superior vibe going on.

'No, not really,' I reply, refusing to get drawn into his line of argument.

'I mean, take the male ones for a start. They're basically clones: Heathcliff, Hindley, Hareton.' He snickers. 'And don't get me started on the Cathy/Catherine issue.'

I inhale a slow, deep breath. If he can't grasp Emily's brilliance, I'm not going waste my time explaining it to him.

'What's your thesis topic again?' I ask.

'Environmental literature and ecocriticism. I'm looking at the relationship between literature and the natural world and how literature can help us understand environmental issues ...'

'Ah, fascinating.'

'Yes, isn't it?'

He starts telling me about his research in great depth, but I tune out, wondering how I can escape. I take a large gulp of chilled white wine to dull my senses and cool down. It's super heated in this crowded ballroom, and I'm wearing a tight-fitting black wool dress. It reaches to mid-thigh and has long split sleeves and a scoop neck. I've paired it with rose-gold twist earrings and white Converse trainers. The dress felt right when I tried it on at the vintage shop, but now I'm thinking I should've chosen something with more airflow. Living at Dain's, I've acclimatised to cooler room temperatures. I'm not used to central heating or so much body heat and noise.

At least I didn't have time to be too nervous or feel like Nancy No-Mates because my supervisor, Dr Flintoff, handed me a glass of wine and shepherded me over to a group with the brief intro 'Lizzy Doyle, PhD, Brontës' before scurrying off to greet the next newcomer. So I've been fielding interested enquiries about the nature of my research, apart from Mr Environmental Literature and Ecocriticism, who seems determined to irk me.

'Excuse me for a minute,' I say to him, tapping my empty glass. 'I need a refill.' He nods and turns to the guy next to him without batting an eyelid, dismissing me. Why are intellectual men sexy, but also soooo annoying?

Dain's not like that, I think. We'd find a secluded corner and privately discuss *Wuthering Heights* 'til the cows came home.

Acute need for him invades my gut. We're going to have

to have a talk when I get back, clear the air a little. I hate this awkward tension between us when we were getting on so well before.

So you'll tell him how you feel, Lizzy? enquires a ghostly Charlotte. I gulp. OK, maybe not *that* conversation.

I make my way over to the bar on the far side of the room and ask the bartender for a cappuccino instead of a wine. Thanks to the plumbing work starting at 6 a.m., I've had a couple of early starts. Maybe the caffeine will perk me up. I wonder how long I have to stay? And if my supervisor will mind if I take off? With all these people, I can't imagine me not being here will make much of a difference. At Oxford, I was never a big one for social events, only the odd drink with friends. But after Klint disapproved of that, I just spent time alone reading or watching TV with him.

I perch sideways on a bar stool to wait for my coffee, easing my black dress down to knee level and surveying the room. Everyone is talking animatedly—everyone except me.

Someone comes up behind me and takes the other bar stool, and I pray it's not the anti-Brontë guy. Nicholas, I think his name was. I don't turn around, but he leans towards me anyway, so close that I can feel warmth emanating from him. He's got a nerve! Probably thinks he can hit on me since I'm not wearing a wedding ring or didn't mention a boyfriend.

I'm about to hop down, but a familiar voice says, 'Hello.'

My head whips around so fast I nearly break my neck.

Dain grins at me lazily, larger than life. My mouth hangs ajar. Slowly, I take in his steampunk coat and starched white shirt, no waistcoat. He's also had a haircut, and the shorter style emphasises his classic bone structure. My heart starts thumping; he looks super hot.

'What are you doing here?'

Dain sips his white wine, unruffled. 'I was invited. I wasn't going to come as I didn't want to crowd you, but the house is unliveable at the moment with all the banging going on. Bridget said she'd look after Tabby for a few days, so I decided to take a leaf out of your book and stay in Leeds for the night ... Surprise!' He gives me a wry smile.

'But why were you invited in the first place?'

'I'm a stakeholder. When my aunt died, she left me some money, so I set up a nineteenth-century fiction scholarship. They have these functions each year, but this is the first time I've met the recipient. The wine isn't too bad.' He takes another sip and avoids my eyes.

'Well, it certainly *is* a surprise, seeing as you didn't mention a word of it to me,' I say, attempting to regain control of my senses. 'Are you staying at the hotel too?'

He nods. 'Don't mind me. I'll be ... around. I won't cramp your style if you want to pull.' He grins and nods over at Nicholas, who's walking past with his nose in the air.

I snort. 'I was actually going to leave after I'd had my coffee.'

'Oh, stay for a bit. I need to talk to a few more people, but I'll come back, and we can have a chat. Overdue, I think.'

He reaches for my hand and squeezes it, and my heart nearly shoots out of my chest.

'OK,' I say, feeling a little breathless. 'I'll sit here quietly and finish this.'

Dain smiles at me and heads off to talk to a group of men and women who all seem to know him. There are welcoming smiles and handshakes. Wow, OK, he's popular. I sip my coffee, watching him as he flits around the room like a social butterfly. After finishing my coffee, I order a G and T to have something else to drink. But I can't take my eyes off him—and neither, I notice, can most of the ovulating females in the room. At one point, he's talking intently to my supervisor, and they look over at me. I cringe. God, what is he saying? Something good hopefully and not 'Watch out for Lizzy. She likes to perv at naked men'.

After polishing off my G and T, I can't wait for Dain any longer. My bladder is fit to burst. Making my way back from the loo, which is at the end of a long empty corridor inset with curtained alcoves, I spot Dain leaning next to one.

As I approach, his dark-brown eyes trace the curves of my body, leaving a trail of fire in their wake.

'Waiting for the men's?' I ask, trying to ignore the shiver of anticipation I feel at being alone with him.

'No, waiting for you, for our chat. I haven't seen you much lately.'

Dain grabs my hand and pulls me into the alcove behind the purple velvet curtain. Oh no, what is it with me and crushed velvet curtains at faculty functions? But I'm drawn to him, relishing the chance to be up close and personal. Pressed against the wall, I look up at him, and confusion or apprehension or a mixture of both must be showing in my eyes because he whispers, 'Are you thinking about August Titmeyer?'

'N-no. M-maybe,' I stutter, surprised that he's remembered our conversation from the sleeping bag.

'Do you still feel like a bad person?'

'For ... for what?' I can't think straight with him being so close to me.

'You know.' He brushes a hand over the front of my dress, briefly touching my left breast. It happens so quickly I think I've imagined it. But my nipple hardens, followed by a quick pulse between my legs.

I suck in my breath and stare into his eyes; they're liquid, timeless, heated. His gaze lowers to my mouth.

I breathe out, knowing that whatever he's thinking, it doesn't involve chatting. 'Is this wise?'

'Probably not.' He cups his large cool hand around my hot cheek, and I close my eyes, relishing the feel of it. 'But don't tell me you haven't been thinking about it,' he whispers.

'OK, I won't,' I whisper back.

'But you have?'

My head nods of its own volition; and he releases my cheek with a small sigh, dropping his hand to my hip region, where his index finger draws small pleasurable circles on my upper thigh. I shiver in response. 'To answer your question, no, I don't feel like a bad person anymore. I think you've cured me of that,' I say in a low voice.

'Oh?'

'Definitely. Whatever I did is nothing compared to the utterly shameless women in your books.'

Dain chuckles and moves closer, his weight pressing me into the wall so I'm pleasantly trapped beneath him. Our bodies snake together, my arms looping around his neck. I can't resist threading my fingers through his hair and feeling the warm skin of his scalp. He closes his eyes with a hum of pleasure, bends his head, and brushes his lips down the side of my cheek, reaching the sensitive spot below my ear. He licks it, then blows softly, and my stomach does a slow somersault. I turn my head and seek out his lips; and they yield to mine—soft, pliable, yet instantly addictive. I can taste the wine on his breath and figure, since he's acting so uninhibited, he must've drunk a lot more of it than I have. Our small soft kisses turn deeper, open-mouthed, tongues twining and igniting multiple fires all over my body. I press my hips against his, feeling the hard outline in his trousers, and rub against him wantonly.

He palms my breasts, rolling my hard nipples between his fingers, and a low groan emits from the back of my throat. 'We shouldn't do this here.'

'As reluctant as I am to stop ... agreed,' he whispers, kissing the side of my mouth.

'I'm glad you're reluctantly in agreement,' I say and suck on his bottom lip, which sets off another bout of fervid kissing.

'Mmm.' Dain pulls away and looks at me, panting, his hair sticking up, eyes glazed. 'Which room are you in?'

'I'm in 612,' I say in a husky voice.

Dain visibly swallows. 'OK, I'll meet you there shortly.'

He takes my hand, kisses it, stares into my eyes with a half-lidded gaze of lustful intent, then melts away around the other side of the curtain.

I roll sideways, a burning cheek placed against the cool

plaster wall, my thoughts scattered to the wind. I'm struggling to comprehend what just happened. My lips feel bruised from his kisses, and my clit is throbbing. Weakly, I pull down my ruched-up dress. *Breathe, Lizzy.*

Chapter 20

I trust, I might one day become better, far better,
than my evil wandering thoughts.

(Charlotte Brontë, letter to Ellen Nussey)

I'm waiting at the lifts, smoothing my dress distractedly, when the Nicholas guy comes sauntering past. 'Oh, there you are. I was looking forward to chatting again, but you never came back. Hopefully, it wasn't anything I said? I can get a little confrontational after a few wines.'

He quirks an eyebrow and manages to look suitably cute and apologetic but also like he's on the prowl. It's scary to think that if Dain wasn't here, I may well have ended up with him. He's my type: intellectual and smarmy. Correction: *was* my type. It hardly bears thinking about. I stab the lift button again—twice.

'You're not leaving, are you?'

'Yes, I have a headache. Sorry.'

The lift arrives, and I'm so grateful I nearly fall into it.

The doors close on smarmy Nicholas's petulant face, who, I'm sure, will get over the rejection. Upon reaching the sixth floor, I speedwalk to my room and burst through the door in a panic. How is this going to work? Dain will knock on the door. I will open it. We'll fall onto the bed and start having sex like we're in a C-grade romcom? It seems unbelievable. But the way I'm feeling at the moment, not wholly impossible.

The caffeine is making me jittery, and my body is a hot mess thinking about the way he kisses ... My eyelids flutter shut, and my breath catches as I remember his mouth on mine ... *Perfection.* Better than I even dreamt it would be. And he smelled soooo good. I groan, imagining us rolling around on the king-sized bed half naked, Dain slowly taking off my underwear.

My eyes fly open again. Underwear. Shit. I'm not wearing my good underwear. But I can't do anything about that except fix the lighting. I twist the dimmer switch, plunging the room into semi-darkness. Perhaps I should get changed—into what, though? A T-shirt and jeans isn't romantic. Perhaps I should lie under the sheets wearing nothing? That's presumptuous. Damn, how could I not bring my good underwear to a fancy hotel! *Breathe, Lizzy. Dain isn't going to care. He wants you.*

The night and my imagination yawn wide with

possibility, yet the future is a mystery. I can't predict what might occur.

Everything might happen ...

Or nothing.

Half an hour later, I'm lying on the bed with my shoes off, bare feet crossed at the ankle, and nibbling on a complimentary shortbread. I'm seriously contemplating watching some TV. The caffeine has worn off, and so has my euphoric mood. I'll give Dain five more minutes. Then I'm going to bed—without him.

Five minutes trundles painfully past, and there's still no knock at the door. Did he get caught chatting with someone? Forget my room number? Or did the wine wear off, and he changed his mind?

I'm sorely tempted to pleasure myself, but it's Murphy's Law that he'll appear immediately after I've finished. After another ten minutes, my patience evaporates entirely, even if my libido is still on high alert. I drag myself to the bathroom, wet a flannel, and press it between my legs to cool down. For all the lack of plumbing in the nineteenth century, cold water and washcloths do come in handy in situations like this.

I shouldn't take Dain's no-show personally. Any number of things could have happened. It's probably not my main overriding fear—namely that he decided he didn't want me. But oh, I wish I knew what was going on in his head!

***

The next morning, I'm standing under a rainfall shower, washing my hair properly and generally enjoying the powerful surge of hot water tumbling over my body—hot water that I haven't had to boil up on the Aga. It's pure bliss, and I'm hoping the plumbing work is well on its way to being completed at the house.

In the cold, sober light of day, my sulkiness about Dain not visiting seems a bit immature. Yes, there's no denying a part of me wanted something to happen rather badly. But the other part isn't truly sure what I'm getting myself into with him. He's still so much of a mystery.

It's late by the time I head downstairs to the breakfast room. But there's fifteen minutes before they close it down, so I can still grab a cup of coffee and a piece of toast. I'm not expecting to see Dain, but he's sitting at a table with his back to me, finishing off a plate of bacon and eggs. My heart sinks.

There's nothing for it. I have to talk to him since he's right by the coffee machine and will see me anyway.

'Morning. Sleep well?' I say. My greeting comes out

sounding clipped and defensive. I take a coffee cup and place it under the machine and jab the espresso button.

Dain looks round, and momentary panic flashes across his face. Did he think by coming to breakfast late he was going to avoid me? Got that wrong, buddy.

'Not really,' he says, sounding tired. I'm tempted to give him some snark, like 'Well, that's what happens when you stand someone up', but I bite it back.

Putting on some toast, I bring my coffee over to his table and sit down.

'So what happened to you last night?' I ask snippily, taking a sip. It's too hot and burns my tongue. I place it back on the table and wait, trying to radiate understanding but not succeeding.

Dain plays with a crust of toast and doesn't look at me. 'I did plan to visit you, but—'

'The wine wore off,' I finish for him. *Just as I thought.*

'More like my common sense kicked in. I'm sorry, I totally overstepped the mark. You must think I'm an animal.'

I stare at him. 'Huh?'

He pushes his empty plate away impatiently. 'I hate myself right now. I drank too much and totally lost control. I hope you can forgive me.' He shakes his head. 'I know you're still getting over Klint, and I hope I haven't disturbed the equilibrium.'

He looks at me with a beseeching expression.

What is he going on about?

He fiddles nervously with his antique cufflink, which is shaped like a tiny book, and I get it. He's trying to live up to a quaint moral standard that has no place in the twenty-first century—a time when gentlemen were supposed to post women a letter expressing their admiration, not pull them behind a curtain and ravage them.

If it wasn't so ludicrous, I'd scoff out loud. So does that mean we're friends, or are we courting? I have no idea. All I know is that his fake chastity is making me a tad angry. I go and collect my toast and sit down and start buttering it.

'Lizzy, it's not that I didn't want to come to your room. Believe me, I did. But I didn't want to do something we'd both regret later,' Dain says in a placating tone.

I nod. But internally, I'm screaming, *Whaaat?*

The sachet of liquid honey I'm struggling to open doesn't budge, and I stab it with a fork. Dain watches me warily. A spurt of honey lands on my toast; the rest of it goes on my fingers. Maybe it's because I've been dealing with weeks of sexual frustration and less-than-ideal living conditions. But frankly, reader, I'm pissed off.

Dain reaches over and pats my sticky hand, and I almost snarl. 'It's important to me that you understand where I'm coming from,' he says.

'Yeah, sure, equilibrium,' I reply grumpily, moving my hand out of his reach and licking my fingers.

'I hope my slip-up won't make you move out. I like living with you.'

'I'm not going to move out …' I say.

'Oh, that's good.' Dain looks relieved and wipes honey off his hand on a napkin.

'But don't you think you're being old-fashioned to the extreme?' I continue. 'I know you're into this full-immersion thing. But now that you're getting a boiler, can't you shift some of your Victorian social mores to the present as well?'

Dain shakes his head. 'I think it's important to have solid boundaries if we're going to continue living together.'

I can't believe my ears. So that's it. A drunken fumble in an alcove—that's my lot? The worst thing is that although he's trying to be a perfect gentleman, I know damn well from reading his smutty books that he's not. He's being a hypocrite. I can't do this, sit across from him and eat toast like I'm not feeling rejected.

Getting up from the table, I say, 'Dain, I appreciate what you're trying to achieve, but here's my take on it for what it's worth. You're not a country squire, and I'm definitely not a virginal young lady. This is you and me, in real life. We're two consenting adults who are obviously attracted to each other, wine or no wine. Oh, and here's the thing in case I haven't made it clear to you: I'm really, really, *really* over Klint!'

With each 'really', I move closer and closer to his face until our noses are almost touching. I draw back, and he stares at me with wide eyes and dilated pupils. His mouth opens, but nothing comes out. He seems floored by my speech and, to my delight, a little turned on. Without saying anything else, I flounce off from the table and head upstairs to wash my sticky fingers.

After that conversation, I can now see exactly what the future holds. It's no longer a mystery. Dain is going to deny our attraction out of some misplaced sense of propriety, and I will be running to my room and touching myself every time he glances sideways at me. Maybe I *should* move out.

* * *

After 'the confrontation', things are strained between us at the house but slowly revert back to normal over the next week, basically because Dain's pretending nothing happened and I'm not sure how to change the status quo. But at least we're on speaking terms, and my notion of moving out is forgotten for the meantime.

Then strangely, items begin appearing. The first is a

potted plant on my windowsill along with a small tin watering can. It's innocuous enough that I don't think much of it. Dain has a few plants around the house, so he's probably bought it and put it there because my bedroom gets the morning sun. No biggie, I'm happy to water it if he wants me to.

A few days later, the old pink towel I borrowed from him has been replaced by a new fluffy white one with green embroidered flowers around the edge. OK, we've got a shower now (thank the Lord), so I guess he's updating the towels?

The next week, I come in from a cold afternoon walk to find three objects sitting on my bed, unwrapped: a Brontë mug featuring characters from their books; a wooden wall hanging with a *Wuthering Heights* quote, 'Whatever our souls are made of, his and mine are the same'; and an illustrated bookmark of the sisters standing in front of the parsonage.

I pick each up in turn to examine them, feeling confused. They're lovely things. But are these special gifts Dain's chosen for me, or are they having a cleanout at the parsonage shop? I thank him later on, and he looks pleased but doesn't mention a cleanout or anything. I still don't know what to make of them but decide not to press it.

A few nights afterwards, when the fire's been lit and

we're at the table in the parlour working on our respective projects, he goes out to the kitchen to make tea. Upon coming back, he places my new Brontë mug on the table next to my right elbow.

'Thanks,' I say distractedly, continuing to type. A few minutes later, I reach for the mug and see a square cream-coloured envelope propped against it with a curly Gothic *L* on the front.

'What's this?' I ask him.

'Open it and see.' He sits down with his own tea and a little smile.

I sip my tea and continue typing, feeling oddly nervous about whatever that envelope contains. He keeps glancing at me and at the envelope, and I know I'm stalling. I'm about to say I'll open it later in my room, but my phone buzzes. I read the message and grunt in annoyance.

Dain looks up from his manuscript, inky quill paused. 'What is it?'

I click out of the curt message. 'Klint. He says he's going to give my stuff to charity if I don't come and collect it by next week.'

Dain's fingers tighten on his quill. 'That's a bit extreme.'

'This is Klint—he only operates in extremes.'

'So I guess you're going to Oxford?'

I sigh. 'I don't want to, but it looks like I'll have to.

There are books I don't particularly want him donating and clothes I want to keep too.'

I know I should've sorted this out before, but I've been enjoying Klint going AWOL and not messaging me.

'There's space in the bookcase if you want to put your books in there,' says Dain.

I look over at the floor-to-ceiling bookcase stuffed to the gills with classics and his own novels.

'Are you sure? There doesn't look like a lot of room ...'

'I'll make room. I want you to feel like this is your home too.'

Warmth spreads throughout my solar plexus. Dain sharing his bookcase means a lot, especially as I know he treasures every book in it.

'Thanks, that's nice of you. It's all nineteenth-century fiction, so at least it will be on brand.'

He smiles. 'When will you go?

'As soon as possible, I guess. Once I've booked my train.'

He nods. I bring up Trainline and start planning how I'm going to transport my stuff back. I'll take a change of clothes in my tote, go with my empty suitcase, and fill it as full as I can. Whatever's left over, Klint can give to charity. I want to get in and get out of the flat and make the visit as painless as possible.

Dain clears his throat and looks pointedly at the cream-coloured envelope. *Oh yes, that.*

My gut clenches and unclenches in quick succession. But with him watching expectantly, there's nothing for it but to open the envelope. I draw out a small piece of blank card of the same colour.

'Other side,' he says.

I turn it over, and whatever I've been expecting, it's not this.

It's a tiny pen-and-ink sketch of a woman in a chair reading a book titled *WH*—it looks like me. But if so, it's a more elegant version, with my hair up and wearing a nineteenth-century dress. It's incredibly detailed and beautifully done. My pulse rate increases; he's spent a lot of time on this.

'Well, do you like it?' he asks, sounding unsure since I haven't spoken a word.

'I absolutely love it,' I tell him quickly. 'It's incredible, so detailed. I didn't know you could draw as well!'

Dain runs a hand through his hair and looks embarrassed. 'Another of my hobbies. I was looking at the one Charlotte did of Anne and got inspired. It's *Wuthering Heights*, by the way, the book. I couldn't fit the whole title in, so I put *WH*.'

I gulp, gingerly holding the card between my index fingers. The book reference and knowing that he spent a lot of effort on it are enough to start me welling up. Shit, I can't start crying all over it—the ink will smudge! Hastily, I pop it back into the envelope for safe keeping.

'I love it,' I repeat. 'You're a man of *many* talents.'

I don't mean it to sound sexual, but Dain blushes anyway and pulls at his collar. He's wearing a white shirt buttoned up to the neck along with his black waistcoat and looks like a hot vicar.

'Can I keep it?'

'Of course, I drew it for you. It's Miss Lizzy,' he says. He's gazing at me with a fond look in his eye, and now *I'm* blushing, also feeling a little like I might swoon onto the red velvet couch in front of the fireplace and require smelling salts (knowing Dain, he probably has some on standby). So much for me not being a virginal young lady, he's making me feel like one.

I float off to bed that night with the envelope pressed to my chest and put it under my pillow, along with the first note he wrote me, so I can look at it again tomorrow morning.

I'm starting to think Dain has been reading *The Victorian Man's Guide to Wooing a Woman* and is faithfully following it to the letter. There's definitely something to be said for the old-fashioned approach to winning a girl's heart.

But it's not only the thoughtful gifts and the drawing. It's him—I've been falling, in increments, ever since we met. His kindness, his intelligence, all his funny ideas and little ways. But I always knew this was going to happen. I knew it standing there on the landing in the parsonage when he was earnestly telling me about Emily Brontë's poetry. His aura is a powerful spell, dark as night and full of stars, and I'm powerless to resist.

Chapter 21

Do you think I can stay to become nothing to you?
Do you think I am an automaton?—a machine without feelings?

(Charlotte Brontë, *Jane Eyre*)

The smash on the flagstone startles me out of my reverie. I swivel at the noise and look down. My elbow has knocked a glass off the draining board. It's now in shards all over the floor.

Shit.

I've been fantasising about Dain, as per usual, and it's making me clumsy.

The object of my desire comes running in. 'What was that? Oh! Don't move, Lizzy. You might cut yourself.'

He crouches at my feet and starts sweeping up the fragments around my ankles with a dustpan and brush.

'Sorry, I'll buy you another one,' I say guiltily. I need to focus. I've been in a dreamworld the last couple of days, ever since he gave me that drawing.

Dain stands and puts the dustpan on the table.

'No bother,' he says softly. 'Are you hurt?'

He grabs my wet hand and inspects my pruney fingers closely, and I pull it away, laughing. 'It was my elbow, not my hand!'

'Do I need to put a plaster on that?'

'No, silly.'

I take a step sideways, but he's standing so close to me that I accidentally tread on his foot.

'Ow!'

'Sorry.' I pull an apologetic face.

'No, you're not.'

'I am.' Lazily, I flick watery suds at him; and they wet his round-collared shirt, which makes me want to giggle. He's always so formally dressed lately it's driving me to distraction. I want to ruffle his feathers, see him looking at me dazed with lust like he was in the alcove. Dain doesn't move, and I flick more water on his shirt around the nipple area, turning it a nice shade of see-through. Mmmm.

His eyes narrow, seeing me perv at his chest. 'Do you mind?'

'Not at all, Mr Vicar,' I say flirtatiously.

He snorts. 'Vicar!'

I grin. 'Well, if the cap fits.' I turn my back on him to continue washing up, thinking that's the end of it, but his arms go round me in a bear hug.

He mock growls in my ear, 'Don't call me that!'

I choke back a laugh, saying, 'But you are, Dain!' which seems to rile him up even more. His grip tightens, and I wiggle my butt against his hips, half-heartedly trying to escape. I'm thrilled to feel he's hard. Maybe I need to call him Mr Vicar more often!

He groans softly and leans into me so I'm bent forward over the washing-up sink. *Oh yeah, this is more like it.* I reach behind and touch his cock briefly, and he jerks back from me like he's been electrocuted. 'Sorry!' he exclaims.

I'm not sure why he's apologising when I'm the one who was fondling him.

I right myself and turn to face him, discovering the front of my T-shirt is wet through from where he's dipped me into the washing-up water. I pluck the sodden material away from my breasts, and it makes a suggestive sucking noise.

Dain averts his eyes like he is indeed an abashed vicar.

'It's OK, we were fooling around.'

'I-I'm sorry,' he repeats.

'Seriously, Dain ...'

But he's gone, disappearing as stealthily as a shadow.

I throw the sponge into the water in frustration. That was fun! We were actually having fun! And it could have led to more ... namely Dain stripping off my wet T-shirt and bra, laying me over the kitchen table and ... My nipples perk like soldiers on high alert as I play out the scene in my mind.

What is his actual problem?

My body is crying out for him to the point I feel like screaming. And he's not unaffected. His cock was as hard as steel—he wants me, I know it, as much as I want him.

Fuck this! Fuck him!

***

After storming around my bedroom, feeling like I want to punch a hole in the wall, I swap my wet T-shirt for a dry one, turn out my kerosene lamp, and crawl into bed, emotionally drained.

Why is he doing this? Why won't he let himself touch me?

I ask the question over and over, and eventually, there's only one abysmal conclusion: *he doesn't want to get involved because I'm not good enough for him.*

That's the truth, as I know it, laid out plain and simple. Pain lances my heart; and I curl into a ball, sobbing in the darkness, as the wind rattles the windowpane. *Oh, why did I move in here? I'm trapped in an unbearable situation!*

A flickering orange light appears on the wall and steadily grows larger. Great. That's all I need, a fire in my room. I bury my face into my sodden pillow. *I don't care. Let me burn.*

'Lizzy? Are you OK?'

Wiping my watery eyes, I roll over and see Dain outlined in the doorway, peering at me in a concerned manner. He's wearing a pair of blue-and-white-striped pyjama bottoms and grasping a metal holder with a guttering candle.

The sight of his bare chest and sexily mussed hair makes me angry again, like he's deliberately tempting me. I turn my head back and mumble 'Mmhmm' into the pillow.

He pads over and kneels by the bedside, placing the candleholder on the bedside table. Lifting my matted hair away from my wet cheek, he feels my forehead.

'Are you ill?'

'No,' I grunt as fresh tears well. *Only lovesick for you.*

'It feels like you have a fever.'

I huff and shift position irritably. 'I'm not ill. I'm upset. I think I should move out.'

He sighs disconsolately. 'But why, Lizzy?'

'B-because you don't want me. It's torture. I can't bear it any longer. I'm going to take my stuff and go back to Oxford,' I say piteously and start sobbing again.

Dain strokes my hot forehead with his cool hand.

'I do want you.'

'No, you don't.'

'I do. I've always wanted you,' he murmurs.

'You're only saying that so I'll stay and pay rent,' I whimper. I'm being pathetic now, but I can't help it. His determination to remain celibate is ruining me.

There's a pause. 'I've been thinking about our conversation, at the hotel.'

I look at him and sniff, wiping my nose with the back of my hand. 'Which part?'

'About solid boundaries. Maybe we could blur them a little. After all, we are two consenting adults who are attracted to each other, as you said.'

He stands up and tugs at one end of the tie of his pyjama bottoms. My breath catches in my throat. My eyes dart between his and the tie he's teasing out. Does this mean what I think it means?

Dain continues pulling at the tie, watching me. 'But if it's too soon, I understand. Klint—'

'I'm not interested in him. I only care about you.'

'Do you?' he says in low voice that makes my stomach flip.

I nod, unable to take my eyes off his fingers fiddling with the tie.

'I care about you too. That's why I was worried about doing anything. I don't want to hurt you after what you've been through.'

I shake my head. 'You won't.'

I'm not really concentrating on our conversation as I'm too busy watching eagerly as the tie comes undone and the cotton fabric shimmies down, hanging precariously on his hip bones.

'OK, well, if you're sure ...' he says teasingly.

My eyes fixate on his belly button and the trail of dark-brown hair leading down to the treasure I know is lurking beneath. If those pyjama bottoms drop, things are about to get interesting.

'I'm extremely sure.' Tears forgotten, I prop myself up on one elbow to get a better view.

Dain's pyjama bottoms fall, and he stands in the candlelight butt naked. The light flickers over his finely muscled arms, chest, and abs, turning his skin golden. His semi-erect cock bobs directly in front of me—just as long, pink, and glorious as I remember.

As my wide eyes rake over it, Dain clears his throat. 'Uh, I was also thinking about what happened in the kitchen. Hence ...' he says, nodding down at himself. His tone sounds defensive, as if daring me to reject him now that he's vulnerable and baring it all.

But, reader, he's gorgeous.

Wordlessly, I lift up the bedcovers, and he slips in beside me.

***

Dain caresses my thighs, then trails his hand over my stomach and up towards my breasts, and my pulse careens out of control. *Shit, this is happening.*

Suddenly, I'm paralysed by fear.

'You're not doing this because you feel sorry for me, are you?'

'Sorry for you? I think not,' he replies, moving closer. 'All I'm feeling right now is utmost affection and extreme arousal.' His hard length presses against my leg, and I can't help raising an eyebrow. He's definitely aroused! 'But I'm a Rochester, not a Huntingdon. You know that, don't you? I'd never take advantage of you,' he adds.

I can't help laughing a little at his earnestness. 'I never once thought you were a Huntingdon, and you're definitely better looking than Rochester.'

He grins at me, and I run my thumb lovingly along his high cheekbone and thread my fingers through his hair. 'And you're so pretty, Miss Lizzy,' he murmurs, tracing my lips with his tongue while sliding a hand up under my T-shirt to cup my breast. As we kiss and he feels my nipple, moulding it with his fingers, fireworks explode in my brain. Heat plumes down my body, a plumb line falling directly between my legs. I groan a little and reach down to touch his silky hardness.

'I wanted this on the moors,' he murmurs, emitting a small gasp and a moan as I stroke his full length with my hand. 'It was difficult ... to keep my hands off you, but you were with ...'

'*Don't* say his name!'

'All through the night, I couldn't stop thinking ... about what I wanted to do.'

'And what was that?' I kiss along his jawline, his sweet musky scent driving me wild. I want to consume him.

A pause as he sucks on my earlobe, then a whisper in my ear: 'To take off your top and your knickers. Can I now?'

'God. Yes. Please,' I groan and sit up. He lifts my T-shirt over my head and cups my breasts, kissing each reverently. I lie back; and he eases my lacy G-string knickers over my hips, down my legs, and off. I'm thoroughly aroused from his husky whispers and feeling his cock. So when his cool finger trails up my inner thigh and touches my hot, swollen clit, it's electric. I moan as he licks and blows on my neck and massages me lightly with his fingers, tears of relief rather than sorrow now collecting in my ducts. *Fuck, it feels so good, and I want him to feel good too.*

Dain groans in pleasure as I swirl my fist over his wet, slippery head and up and down his shaft.

'God.' He arches into me, and my legs fall open shamelessly as he rubs me harder. Moaning as heat spirals in my groin, I rut against his hand, unable to control myself, as he kisses my lips, my neck, my breasts and our hands stroke each other.

'Lizzy, oh yes, oh god,' he pants, along with several other choice expletives, as I fondle his tumescent cock. I have to laugh; there's definitely no chance of him being a vicar with that mouth!

He sucks on my nipple hard, and I start to unravel, groaning as two of his fingers play with my clit and stroke my entrance. 'I know you're not a Huntingdon,' I pant, opening my legs wider. 'But I give you permission to take full advantage of me now.'

Dain's fingers slip in and out of my wet pussy while he rubs my clit slowly with his thumb. 'Uuuuh, god, Jesus,' I moan, almost delirious, as electricity starts swirling up and down my limbs. My hips buck under his hand, seeking ultimate pleasure. My orgasm explodes from the epicentre of my core, waves of ecstasy fanning out all over my body. 'Oh yes, oh yes.' I grind my pussy into his hand, riding his fingers, begging him to keep going as I quickly stroke his cock. Moments later, he swears and cries out, his release flowing like honey over my hand.

Panting and shuddering in the aftermath, he holds me as

the wind howls and icy rain patters against the windowpane. All hell could be breaking loose outside, but I don't care. I'm where I've always wanted to be, lying in Dain's arms, sated—my inner tempest soothed.

Chapter 22

Oh! I saw a light, and I thought a ghost would come.

(Charlotte Brontë, *Jane Eyre*)

I wake alone in a cold room. There's no sign of Dain. Was last night a dream? The only signs that it wasn't are that I'm lying in bed naked and Dain's candle has burnt down lopsidedly and dripped a puddle of wax on the nightstand. But where is he? Hopefully, he isn't having regrets ...

To my relief, he appears, smiling beatifically in his pyjama bottoms while juggling mugs of tea and a dinner plate piled high with toast.

'Ey up chuck,' he says in a strong Yorkshire accent, and I laugh, pulling the sheet up so my boobs aren't on show. He deposits the plate of toast and cups of tea on the nightstand, shoving the candleholder out of the way. 'The heating's come on, but it's still freezing. So I thought we could have brekkie and stay in bed until the house warms up.'

'Good idea.' I'm loving the way he's acting like it's an

everyday occurrence to wake up together. I relax my tense shoulder muscles ... *Everything's OK.*

Dain hops back into bed and slyly tucks his cold feet under my warm calves, making my shoulders stiffen again. 'Flipping heck! Your feet are like blocks of ice!'

He hands me my Brontë mug and proffers the plate of toast. 'Hehe. Payback for the sleeping bag when I had to cradle your glacial body.'

I take a slurp of hot tea and a bite of strawberry-jam-laden toast. 'Well, if you hadn't, I probably wouldn't be here now, warming up your icy trotters,' I say, waving my slice of toast at him.

Dain's smile falters. 'I was scared to death I was going to lose you that night, so we probably shouldn't joke about it.' He shakes his head. 'I still have awful flashbacks.'

'OK, we won't talk about it,' I say hurriedly, feeling contrite. But I can't resist adding, 'Though I note my potential demise didn't stop you from wanting to get me naked!'

'Well, you'd warmed up by then ...'

After breakfast, Dain is in no hurry to leave; and we lie in each other's arms, cuddling and chatting about nothing. At some point, his pyjama bottoms come off again, and we can't seem to stop kissing or caressing each other.

'I should get up,' I groan, feeling too pleasantly full,

warm, and aroused to believe that I will.

Dain licks a speck of jam off the corner of my mouth. 'I'm well up,' he jokes. 'But yes, I know you've got an important meeting with your supervisor.' He sighs, playing with a lock of my hair. 'I also have to tackle a tricky scene with Azalea and Nathaniel.'

'Oh?' My interest piques. I'm looking forward to reading this book.

'Yes, they want each other badly. But there's a meddlesome brother that's cottoned on to what they're up to, and he's trying to put a stop to it to save her reputation.'

'Oh dear.'

'Yes, there's going to be an altercation at the family manor.' He frowns and narrows his eyes at me for dramatic effect.

I giggle. 'Well, good on him for trying. She sounds like she's got herself into a right pickle with that Nathaniel.'

Dain gazes down at me from his propped-elbow position. 'Hmm, I think she's too far gone. She's in love with Nathaniel and doesn't *want* to be saved.'

I reach up and gently rub my thumb across his bottom lip. 'I know the feeling.'

Dain's lip quivers under my thumb, and his dark-brown eyes soften. 'Is it silly to miss you when you're only going to be away for a few days?' he asks, referring to my impending trip to Oxford.

My chest pangs at his doleful expression. 'No, it's not silly …' I murmur. 'It's bloody ridiculous. I'll be back before you know it.'

He looks appeased; and we kiss tenderly, his fingers lightly stroking my bare back, sending shivers up and down my spine. His hand shifts down to cup my butt cheek, squeezing it, and I sigh against his lips. 'Sorry, I *really* have to get up. Can we take a rain check?'

Dain pulls back from me, looking hesitant.

A flicker of fear runs through me. 'What's wrong?'

'Nothing. But, um, I don't suppose you want to spend tonight in my room before you leave?'

My facial muscles constrict in shock, but I try not to show it. Up until now, I haven't been allowed to see his room, so I know this is a big deal.

I take his hand and kiss it. 'I'd be *honoured*, kind sir.'

Inwardly, I gulp. *Is this where I find out he has a dead bat collection—or something worse?*

***

On the train to Leeds, I'm away with the fairies, meditating on last night's tryst with Dain; from beginning to end—he was superb. Images float into my mind: the way he kissed my lips and neck in the candlelight, the deferential care and attention he paid to my breasts, the aching need when he caressed my clit. I'm throbbing just thinking about it. He's making me feel unhinged, like I'm floating across the fields in a dream. But a message from him reminds me it's all too real.

Dain: *Can't stop thinking about you. Hope your meeting goes well.*

Me: *Me too. I mean thinking about you. Not my meeting lol.*

Dain: *Haha, glad to hear it. I've been readying my room and imagining some of the delightful ways we can spend the evening. It's proving mightily distracting trying to write the altercation at the manor, so I'm writing the next spicy scene instead (winking face emoji).*

Readying his room? I'm not sure what he means by that. Hiding all the dead bats? Nevertheless, I like that he's getting all hot and horny thinking about me. I'm about to reply, but I get a more practical message from Klint.

Klint: *What time is your train arriving tomorrow?*

Me (sighing): *2.15pm.*

Klint: OK. *So you won't want lunch?*

Me: *No thanks.*

Klint: *See you then.*

Me: *(Thumbs-up emoji)*

Great. Thank you, Klint, for ruining my lovely sexting. With two message threads to two different men going on, I have to be careful not to send my next message to Klint when it's meant for Dain.

Me: *Glad to hear I'm inspiring your spicy scene lol. Can't wait to read that! Looking forward to spending the night with you xx*

Dain: *Me too xx*

I wish I didn't have to go to Oxford. I'm tempted to tell

Klint to give my stuff away. But I've paid for the train ticket now, and he's expecting me. Leaving Dain, even for two nights, is going to be excruciating, especially since I have a feeling tonight might be significantly more intimate. His 'delightful ways we can spend the evening' has set my expectation that he wants to take things further. Honestly, reader, with the way I'm on fire for him right now, I wouldn't say no.

* * *

It's early evening when, after having had a quick dinner in Leeds, I make my way through the cold gloom of Haworth, eagerly seeking the shelter of home and *him*. I've barely taken off my coat when Dain appears in the doorway with a lamp. 'You're back,' he says, sounding relieved.

I laugh, drinking in the sight of his gorgeous face. 'Of course! I'm hardly going to run away, am I? I've been dying to kiss you all day.'

He hooks the lamp on the coatrack, scoops me into his arms and kisses me in the glowing yellow light. I pretend to swoon but then actually do as the way he kisses is totally swoonworthy. My bag drops from my hand onto the floor, and everything falls out with a crash on the black-and-white-tiled floor. But I hardly notice, relishing the feel of his warm, soft lips moving over my cold ones.

He stands me upright again, and I wobble, seeing stars.

'Better?' he asks with a grin.

'Uh, yes, I think I'll live.'

He hugs me tightly and whispers, 'Have you eaten?'

I nod.

'Good. Let's go upstairs.'

I quickly tidy my stuff back into my bag but leave it where it is while he unhooks the kerosene lamp. He grabs my hand, and we walk up the stairs. We reach the top, and I see his closed door looming ahead. I freak out slightly, but I have to face my fear. *Lizzy, whatever is in there won't be as bad as what you're imagining—nothing ever is.* And the thought of spending the night with Dain is more than motivating me to get over myself. However, I wish he'd shown his room to me earlier so it wasn't such a big deal now.

He grabs the door handle and grins at me. 'Ready?' he asks.

I nod, my palms beginning to sweat. *I'm seriously going to scream if there's anything resembling a bat in there, and it'd better not be haunted.*

The door swings open, and he ushers me in. At first, I can't see anything but the orange glow of a fire burnt low in the grate. Then Dain holds his lamp aloft, and my mouth drops open. The walls and ceiling of the sizeable room are painted a rich ruby red to match the parlour downstairs, but that's not what I'm gaping at. There's an enormous dark mahogany four-poster bed hung with black velvet curtains, along with various other pieces of antique furniture. A woven oriental rug in an intricate pattern of scarlet and gold covers the floorboards.

'What do you think?' Dain asks.

'It's ... fantastic ...' I say, a little lost for words. An upstanding flat wooden contraption catches my eye. 'What's this?'

'It's a trouser press, in perfect working order. And look!' He gestures to the dresser, where there's a complete set of silver-backed gentleman's brushes. 'Horsehair. They were a real find and lovely to use.'

I puff out my cheeks. 'Why are you showing all this to me now?'

'After last night ... Well, I guess I feel closer to you. I know you won't judge me and think I'm nuts. I'm sure it must look a little eccentric.' He takes my hand and gazes at me expectantly, as if he's wanting me to say his exquisitely detailed libertine's bachelor pad *isn't* eccentric.

But at least I know what's in here now, and I can set my mind at ease. OK, so it's a bit strange. But what did I expect from a guy who's only recently come around to the idea of indoor plumbing?

'It's a little overwhelming, as is everything with you ...' I say slowly, and I see a flash of hurt in his eyes. 'Dain, I don't mean it in a bad way. I always need some time to adjust to your ... lifestyle. But it's really cool, very Byronic,' I say, and he brightens.

'Yes! That's the look I was going for.'

'I mean, this bed!' I shake my head and walk over and move aside one of the velvet curtains. It truly is a masterpiece, as high as my waist and super king-sized with thick carved wooden pillars at each end. It's made up with a black silk coverlet and has half a dozen plump black silk pillows. I push down on the mattress, and it springs back firmly.

'It's a memory foam mattress,' explains Dain. 'Offers great comfort and support.'

I press my lips together to keep from giggling. He sounds like a Victorian bed salesman.

'Aha, excellent,' I say seriously, giving it another quick push. 'So no chance of back issues?'

'Nope.' Dain grins at me roguishly and leans against one of the bedposts, folding his arms. He's wearing a white shirt with a ruffled neck and cuffs tucked into crotch-hugging skinny black jeans and looks rather like a lascivious Romantic poet. My pulse elevates. *Goodbye, Mr Vicar.*

Hello, Mr Romance ...

My glance happens to fall on the free-standing mahogany armoire to the side of the bed. It has three door sections, each with an ornate carved shell motif at the top. *Hah, I bet all his mood wear is stashed in that wardrobe—I'd love to have a poke around. I bet he's got some interesting bits and bobs in there ...*

I peer closer at the wardrobe as it looks vaguely familiar. I'm sure I've seen it somewhere before. Then it comes to me. It's depicted on the front cover of book 1 of Sophronia's Secret Life. *Come to think of it, the four-poster bed is too!* It's not random artwork from the imagination of a book cover designer—it's real. That book had me blushing hotter than spending fifteen minutes in a sauna. How much of it is drawn from real life?

Joelle's voice from the vintage shop flashes in my ears: 'Oo-er, looking for something to spice things up in the bedroom?'

My chest tightens, and I take a step back from the bed.

'Are you still happy to stay the night in here?' Dain says, a frown knitting his brow. 'We could go to your room instead if it's too much?' He looks so worried and unsure that my heart goes out to him.

I give my shoulders a firm mental shaking. *Don't be naive, Lizzy. He had a sex life before he met you, as you did with Klint, and he's not getting all het up over that. He wants* you *now, not Joelle, and that's all that matters.*

'No, no, it's fine. I'm just stressing about my thesis at the moment, worried that I'm not going to be able to do the topic justice. It's a heavy subject.' I give a short laugh and push my hair back from my face.

'Would a neck rub help?'

'It might.'

Dain places his lamp on the nightstand, and a sensual, cosy lit nook is created within the curtains. He crawls lithely across the bed, moves a few pillows, and leans against the black velvet studded headboard. 'Jump up,' he says, patting the space in front of his long spread legs.

He's not kidding. The bed is so high off the ground I have to do a kind of inelegant flying leap. I land in his lap, giggling, and come face to face with the Brontë sisters on his nightstand.

The three of them are posed in a black-and-white print in a small elegant silver frame. I should say, the *supposed* Brontë sisters. It's never been proven that the photo is of them because, as far as anyone knows, they never had any photos taken; and there's been no mention of this photo or any others in their letters or documents. But some people are adamant that it is for no other reason than they *feel* it's right. It's called *Les Soeurs Brontë* because the original photo had "Londres - Les Soeurs Brontë" written on the back.

'Do you think it's really them?' I whisper to Dain, as if they can hear me.'

'I *know* it's them ...' Something about the way he says it so decisively makes the hair on the back of my neck stand on end.

I gaze at the striking woman with the unusual sanpaku eyes who they say is Charlotte, and she stares back at me. *What isn't he telling me?*

But I know better than to ask. Dain is a closed book when it comes to spilling secrets of the past.

He gently lowers the photo so it's face down on the nightstand.

'Why did you do that?'

'There are going to be things happening in this bed that I'd rather the Brontës didn't see.'

Chapter 23

There is always a 'but' in this imperfect world.

(Anne Brontë, *The Tenant of Wildfell Hall*)

Naked and kneeling, I grasp one of the carved bedposts with sweaty hands as Dain, head nestled between my legs, licks lightly up and down my inner thighs. He's been teasing me, making me beg for his tongue ...

The evening has turned into a sexy game of cat and mouse to get the other person as close as possible to climax without them actually climaxing. Reader, it's delightfully delicious.

I especially enjoyed Dain's 'neck rub', sitting cross-legged between his thighs as he pressed sensual kisses along my hairline while one hand crept into my bra and the other craftily unzipped my jeans to finger me. He almost made me come but withdrew in the nick of time, with an evil chuckle, leaving me craving so much more.

Oh, so you want to play dirty?

Flushed and fully aroused, I turned and wrestled him back onto the pillows so I was lying on top, looking into his dark-brown eyes turned almost black with the pupils blown.

'Was that little game in your spicy scene, huh?' Tugging impatiently on the ruffled collar of his shirt, he helped me unbutton it, and I spread it wide to reveal his delectable muscled chest. Unable to resist, I repeatedly flicked his pink nipples with my tongue.

Dain grunted in pleasure and hardened against the top of my thigh. 'Yes. But Azalea was wearing a corset, and I had to stop writing as the scene got totally out of hand or, should I say, *in hand*.'

I grinned, imagining him writing with one inky-fingered hand while simultaneously jerking off with the other. 'Indeed. So what exactly was going on in that head of yours to make you lose it?'

'Um, I was imagining you on your knees under the table doing ... things ... to me.' He squirmed, and his bulging crotch jutted pleasantly into the apex of my thighs.

'Ah, so I'm guessing you'd like me to re-enact those *things*?' I murmured, slowly unzipping his jeans. Dain nodded, his eyes now black as night. As I exposed his erect cock, he gave a low guttural moan, watching as I wetted my lips with my tongue; and the game was on again.

The last laugh was on me, though, as I got him so

worked up he was in a right frenzy, his hands twisting the bedcover. With one last lingering suck, I sat back on my heels and watched as he hovered on the brink, his handsome face tense with frustration.

See how it feels, Mr Romance?

I couldn't hide my smirk, and it riled him so much that he unceremoniously stripped me and lavished his tongue over my nipples while teasing my slippery clit with his fingers, drawing out the pleasure but denying me release until I was nearly screaming.

Then, reader, I stripped and stalked him until he was backed up against one of the bedposts, gorgeous and grinning, his tempestuous eyes challenging me. I poised on all fours like a cat, ready to pounce, considering which bit of his luscious form to devour first.

Launching at his irresistible lips, we kissed open-mouthed, exploring tenderly with our tongues, as he slid a sly finger inside me, being careful to avoid my clit. Sneaky! But god, it felt good. I stroked my own fingers over his stiff cock, enjoying the feel of him wet and wanting, and he gave a deep throaty groan. 'Can you suck me again?'

I smiled to myself. 'Sure.'

But I took my time, kissing his chest and abs thoroughly, making him more and more agitated, before swirling my tongue around the tip of his salty, slick cock. Holding the back of my head firm, he eagerly slid into my open mouth, driving deeply—the sound of his moans and profanities filling the curtained space.

Goodbye, Rochester. Hello, Heathcliff ...

I let him fuck my mouth until his panting intensified, then inch by maddening inch withdrew, leaving his cock twitching and his eyes on fire. 'This could go on all night,' he said huskily.

'I'm up for that,' I answered, liking the way his half-lidded eyes browsed my breasts, lingered on my hard nipples, and dropped to my pussy.

'Swap places. I want to taste you.'

So here I am, naked, clutching a bedpost and begging for him to take me over the edge.

'Dain, *please*!'

He grasps my hips, then lowers me onto his warm waiting tongue, and I groan in relief as the flat of it rasps my throbbing clit. Wet, muffled noises of enjoyment sound from below, though by the way I'm moaning and rutting my hips, I think I'm the one who's enjoying it more.

His fingers explore my entrance as I ride his mouth. One of them drifts farther south. Caught up in the moment, I don't mind. Klint and I experimented, but he wasn't into anal, so it never went very far. *He was never really into any of it. Not like this.* But still, as Dain's wandering finger probes deeper, it's a bit too intimate.

'Hmm, maybe not,' I protest, and he instantly withdraws his finger and doesn't touch me there again. It makes me recall the graphic threesome scene in the Sophronia series, where our girl had a guy in front rubbing her breasts and clit and another underneath giving her oral and doing what Dain just did—which she enjoyed, of course. Sophronia seems to enjoy anything that's done to her, front and back.

Dain's attention changes focus; and as I expected from his books, he knows exactly what he's doing—licking, twirling, and sucking my clit greedily into his mouth. Heat pools low in my belly, then rages through my bloodstream. Gasping in pleasure, I hug the bedpost for dear life, succumbing fully to his expert tongue.

I'm on the verge of a soul-shattering orgasm when he scoots out from underneath, removes my hands from the post, and gently lays me down next to him. I'm quivering with desire and reverberating with frustration as he holds me.

'Hey, I'm sorry about doing *that*—you know, with my finger ...' he whispers.

'It's OK, I'm more pissed off you didn't let me come.'

Dain grins and, moving on top of me, strokes his hard cock over my highly sensitive pussy. 'Maybe this will help you out.'

I moan at the friction, thinking he's going to enter me, and I'm more than ready. But ever the gentleman, he waits to be asked to dip his quill into the inkpot. Just as I'm about to say he can, that I'm using protection, he pants, 'Oh, I'm close.' Then his hand rapidly strokes my aching clit. I'm lost in bliss, our hips writhing, when he cries, 'Lizzy, oh fuck yes!' And I'm right there too, his squeezing fingers sending me to heaven.

Afterwards, we lie with our limbs entangled, sweaty foreheads touching, breathing hard.

'You're amazing,' Dain whispers.

'You are too,' I whisper back.

He kisses me and peels off my body. I look down and see the sticky result of his orgasm covering my breasts and stomach.

'Stay there. I'll fetch a wet cloth.'

'Thanks.'

He gets down from the bed and heads to the bathroom, and I lie there, starfishing in a happy daze. I feel euphoric, like I've taken a heady drug. Dain appears again and wipes my body gently with a warm washcloth, which feels wonderful. Thank God for hot water. Clean-up is hardly romantic as it is, but it would be infinitely worse with ice-cold water. He takes off back to the bathroom again with the cloth, and feeling parched, I prop myself on one elbow to take a sip of water from the tumbler on his nightstand.

Righting *Les Soeurs Brontë*, I tell them, 'It's OK, you can look now.' Then I hop under the bedcover, black silk sheets sliding icily around my heated body. Nice!

Waiting for Dain to return from his ablutions or whatever he's doing, idly, I pick up a slim book of poetry from his nightstand lying next to the photo. It's a copy of *The Complete Poems of Emily Brontë*. I smile to myself; he loves her poems. I flick open the flyleaf and see something written there in light pencil.

The lamp has been turned down low, so I dial it up and peer at the handwriting closely. I can barely make it out.

To Dain,
All my love,
Gareth (p.166)

I stare, my gut twisting. What the fuck? With a shaking hand, I flip to page 166 and discover with dread it's the poem 'Stars'. The last stanza has been underlined with the same pencil.

Why did the morning dawn to break
So great, so pure, a spell;
And scorch with fire the tranquil cheek,

Where your cool radiance fell?

Footsteps pad along the corridor; and I hastily return the book to the nightstand, turn the lamp low, and lie there as stiff as a board with my heart thudding in my ears. Surely not, that's absurd—Dain and *Gareth*? But I'm having a visceral reaction, and somehow, I just know. This is the thing. *The thing he doesn't want me to find out about.*

Dain pops his head through the curtains and smiles at me. He's holding a plate with a peanut butter doorstep sandwich cut into halves and a large glass of milk.

'I got hungry. Thought you might be too.'

I nod mutely.

Shivering, he climbs into bed, holding the glass, and deposits the plate between us on the bed. 'Brrrr. Luckily, we've got an indoor toilet now, or we'd be freezing our arses off!'

I flinch at the word 'arses' and resolutely take a bite of peanut butter sandwich.

Maybe it's nothing ... a close friendship ... But 'all my love' isn't something you'd write to a guy friend, and I know there's friction there. I've seen Gareth's face shut down whenever Dain's name is mentioned. Does he have a crush on him? Is that why Dain didn't want to go into the hotel after he rescued me? There's another possibility, but my mind refuses to contemplate it.

I close my eyes, chew automatically, and swallow. But the lump of bread is like a bullet in my throat, and I gag.

'Shit.' Dain whacks me between the shoulder blades, and I cough as the lump disappears slowly.

'Here, have some milk.'

I swallow it down, cold and creamy, as he rubs circles on my back.

Dain takes the sandwich out of my hands. 'Maybe you shouldn't eat any more of that.'

I nod. But tears well, and another lump forms in my throat, one that won't be eased by drinking milk.

'Are you OK?' he asks, peering at me since I haven't spoken a word since he came into the room.

'Yes, I-I'm good, thanks. Just tired.' My voice sounds hoarse to my ears, and I feel so weird and out of it, like I've got shell shock.

'We should get some sleep. You'll feel better in the morning,' he says.

Reader, I don't think I will ...

Dain turns out the lamp, and we sink down under the black coverlet, as if into the bowels of the earth. Gathering me in his arms, he kisses me on the temple and whispers, 'Good night, my sweet Lizzy.' But I feel like I'm being held by a stranger.

He's off to dreamland in what seems like a matter of minutes, yet I can't sleep. It's pitch-black in the curtained space with no reassuring chinks of moonlight. Rain starts beating relentlessly against the windowpane.

Why oh bloody why, when I've found the man of my dreams, does there have to be a *huge fucking catch*?

Chapter 24

I am no bird; and no net ensnares me;
I am a free human being with an independent will,
which I now exert to leave you.

(Charlotte Brontë, *Jane Eyre*)

I wake in the grey gloom of morning, blinking groggily and wondering why I'm naked in a bed surrounded by black velvet curtains. My memory kicks in. *Oh yeah, the night of pleasure and pain.*

I run my hands through my birds' nest hair and over my dry cheeks, generally feeling like shit. My muscles are sore and achy since I've had only a few hours' sleep. I can't check the time either as my phone is in my bag downstairs and probably dead. Great. Of course, I, eager to spend the night with Dain, didn't think of the practicalities of charging it. And I need it since I'm heading to Oxford today.

Dain is nowhere to be seen, but I can hear clatter and the sound of running water in the bathroom next door. A hollow feeling resides in my stomach. I need to broach the subject of him and Gareth sensitively so I can get some clear answers.

I know him. If I don't handle this properly, he's likely to get defensive and shut me out. He's a private snail who peeps out of his shell only when it's safe; if it isn't, he's going to duck his little head back in and lock the door. I'm going to need calm and tact—traits I don't normally possess during a confrontation. This could get messy.

I must fall into a doze. When I open my eyes, Dain is standing by the side of the bed. He's wearing his blue-and-white-striped pyjama bottoms and smiling down at me.

'Hey, sleepyhead.'

'Urgh.' I sit up and wipe drool from the side of my mouth. 'What time is it?'

He hands me the glass of water from the nightstand, and I take a sip, studiously avoiding looking at the book of poetry.

'Just gone seven.'

I relax a little. Great, I've still got a couple of hours before I have to leave, so I can charge my phone.

Dain bounces on his toes, and I eye him as I take another swallow of water. He seems excited about something.

'What have you been up to?' I ask suspiciously.

He grins. 'Feel like a bath?'

I'm tugged—protesting lightly at the indignity of being naked, which he ignores—to the bathroom door. 'Hang on.' Dain puts a hand over my eyes and fiddles with the knob, nudging the door open with his knee. Foggy warmth envelops my body. His hand falls from my eyes, and I discover the room has morphed into a Turkish bath.

The copper tub is full of hot, steamy water topped with a meringue of bubbles; and there's a new copper wire tray attached to the side with a fresh cake of vanilla soap, a loofah, and my bottles of shampoo and conditioner, along with a small yellow rubber duck.

'My lady.' Dain takes my hand and helps me step into the water, which is exactly the right temperature. Mmm, lovely. I'm about to lie back and luxuriate alone, but Dain hops in behind me.

'Oh, here's trouble.'

'You know it.'

My resolve to talk to him about Gareth rears its ugly head but slips when I'm lying in his arms and he's soaping my stomach and breasts as well as lightly tweaking my nipples. My traitorous body responds, instantly wanting him and knowing, from his hard length floating beneath me, that he's feeling frisky too.

He fills the wash jug with warm water from the newly attached tap.

'I'll wash your hair for you.'

'Oh ... you don't have to.'

'You haven't seen it ...' he teases.

I touch my bed hair self-consciously, knowing how unruly it can get. 'Is it really puffy?'

He kisses my shoulder lightly. 'To be expected after last night. That was wild. Thought you might not want your ex asking questions.'

I sit forward and shut my eyes as he pours water over my hair, drenching it into a manageable state. But his words spark a notion in my brain. 'You didn't invite me to your room because I'm going to be seeing Klint today, did you?'

Dain doesn't reply as he's fiddling with the shampoo bottle, then says, 'I know it looks like I'm marking my territory. But my invite was based on me wanting to be with you and that alone. The timing was purely coincidental. Tilt.'

I lean my head back as he palms shampoo gently through my long wet hair, slowly massaging the pads of his fingers in tiny circles over my scalp. It feels delicious, tingly; and I sigh, relaxing back into his chest, thinking, *He seems open to talking about stuff. Maybe this is a good time to ask him about the inscription and get it out of the way. Hopefully, it's some silly nonsense of Gareth's, and I can forget about it.*

'Dain, can I ask you something?'

'Last night was wonderful, and yes, I'm going to be thinking about you every second you're away,' he murmurs in sultry tones, anticipating my question. He finishes shampooing and fills the jug with fresh water.

'I'm glad to hear that, but it's about something else.'

'Ask away, my sweet.'

I sit up again, and he pours the water over my head to rinse off the suds.

Oh god, I really don't want to talk about this, but it's going to suppurate like a sore if I don't.

Dain flips open the cap of the conditioner, and I turn my head slightly towards him. 'You know the book of Emily's poems, on your nightstand?'

He places a soft kiss on my cheek. 'Do you want me to recite one to you? I know most of them by heart.'

My heart twangs in my chest. *That would be lovely ... But no, Lizzy. Focus.*

'Um, I saw the message, written on the flyleaf. I'm sorry, I didn't mean to pry, but I read the underlined stanza too ... I'm kind of confused.'

A pause. Dain starts combing conditioner through the ends of my hair with his fingers. He tugs on the tangles, and it makes me wince. 'Why did it confuse you?' he asks and obviously knows what I'm referring to.

I can't tell from his even tone whether he's open to talking about it or about to shut me down at a moment's notice.

So I swallow and plough on, unable to stop the momentum of this conversation. 'Has ... has Gareth got a crush on you or something?'

Dain inhales deeply from behind me, and his hands drop away from my hair. When he speaks, his voice is low and careful, like he's feeling his way with the words.

'Gareth and I were ... lovers.'

The word 'lovers' hits my brain like a sledgehammer, but I have trouble comprehending it.

'What?'

'We were *lovers*,' he repeats, and I balk, fully getting his meaning.

'But ... are you gay?'

'I think after last night, you would know I'm not.'

I shake my head, feeling frustrated at what he's not saying. 'I don't understand!'

A pause. Then Dain says quietly, 'I like both sexes.'

The pieces of the puzzle click into place. Why he doesn't ever talk about Joelle and why he sounded all wistful when he said he'd had someone, but they'd parted ways. It was *Gareth*, not Joelle, he was talking about! The world tilts on its axis, and the bathroom becomes a suffocating steam prison.

I try to push myself out of the tub, but I'm not quick enough. Dain's wet arms embrace me tightly, and he talks in a fast moving stream. About how he and Joelle were in an on-again, off-again relationship and that *things got sexual* between him and Gareth on a hiking trip on the moors and that it felt right. But he still kept seeing Joelle too because he didn't want to stop, and he and Gareth were meeting up in secret at the hotel; and soon, *things became emotional.* How he confessed to Joelle, and she was angry but came around and that *things got experimental* when they tried to make it work between the three of them. But Gareth couldn't take it, and *things imploded ...*

It's too much to take in. 'No!' I gasp. 'I don't want to hear it!' I wriggle frantically, trying to escape from his arms. But he won't let me go.

My chest is heaving with the effort of trying to get away from him. Then much to my annoyance, I burst into tears, overcome from the lack of sleep and the shock of finding out the truth and being completely blindsided.

'Lizzy, this is why—this is why I was trying to protect you from me,' Dain says gently.

His caring, but pitying tone only makes me cry harder. It feels like he's saying, 'You should've tried to resist me, but you couldn't, and now look—it's your fault we're in this situation.'

With a superhuman effort, I throw off his arms, and he lets me climb out of the bath. Yanking my new white towel with embroidered flowers off the rail, I wrap it around my body. I still have conditioner in my hair. Fuck that. I'm shivering with cold rage.

'I can't believe I was about to give you my body. My heart. My soul. And all this time, you've been keeping this massive fucking secret from me!' I scream at him, my heart pounding in pain.

Dain's eyes open wide, and his hands white-knuckle grip the side of the tub. He's never seen me so angry before, and I know I'm supposed to be calm and tactful, but I'm spiralling out of control. I have no benchmark for this.

'Why the *fuck* didn't you tell me?' I yell, tears running down my face. Dain's eyes have gone all red and watery but I'm *not* going to feel sorry for him!

'I ... I wasn't sure you'd be comfortable with it. I thought you'd be put off if you knew.'

You thought right, buddy. 'Yeah, well, your butthole fingering now makes a lot more sense!' I say sarcastically.

Dain gulps. 'Can't we calm down and talk about this rationally? I can explain.'

'What's to explain? You fucked Gareth, and you fucked Joelle. Well, you're not going to fuck me!'

I storm out of the bathroom, clutching my towel, my hair leaving a trail of conditioner all over the floor.

***

'I *know* I should've told you. But as I said, there was a big chance you'd be put off, and I was afraid of getting rejected. So yes, I was avoiding having this conversation.'

Dain and I are sitting at the kitchen table. He hunted me down in my bedroom shortly after the altercation in the bathroom, insisting we talk. I made him wait until I'd dressed, sorted out my hair, and packed my tote bag. By that stage, my fury had dissipated somewhat. Feeling drained, I came out to the kitchen, feeling I owed him that much, though I'm not sure I'm in the kind of rational mind frame he requires.

'So what—you were going to wait until AFTER we'd had sex? Then drop the bombshell?'

'No! I almost said something when I came to your room. But you were upset because you'd decided I didn't want you, which wasn't the case at all. I thought if I could show you physically how I felt, you'd be more OK with it. And after we got together, well, I didn't want to ruin the moment. So I kept quiet.'

'You should've told me when I moved in—before we got

together!'

'I know, I know! But short of sending you online articles about bisexual relationships for no reason, I was in a quandary about how to approach it. What was I going to do, drop it casually into conversation? "Hey, Lizzy. By the way, in case you're thinking of getting it on with me, I'm bisexual. Does that bother you?" There was never a right moment, and maybe I didn't want to face it.' He drags his hand through his hair. 'But I was going to talk to you about it when you got back from Oxford.'

'Lucky me. That would've been fun to arrive back to after dealing with Klint,' I say, folding my arms and glaring at him. 'Anyway, I'm glad I know now, and I'm not in the dark about your sexual preferences.'

'God, you sound like my father. He said exactly the same thing after I told him, which is why I keep it to myself—so I don't get hurt when people act like this,' Dain says, his face souring.

'I'm not like your father!' I exclaim, annoyed that he's lumping me with him. 'I'm not some man who doesn't give a shit about you. I'm acting like this because I *do* give a shit about you.'

'Funny way of showing it,' Dain grumbles. He pushes the sleeves of his black long-sleeved T-shirt up his arms. It has a heavy metal band on the front. Huh, I've never ever seen him wear a T-shirt or listen to heavy metal. It must've been something he hastily grabbed out of his wardrobe. Unless it's Gareth's ... Perhaps they borrowed each other's clothes ... Aargh, don't think about it. My resolve hardens before it can break. Time for the tough questions.

I take a deep breath. 'Anyway, where do you see this going? Is it just sex for you, or is there an "us"?'

Dain leans across the table and grasps my hand, stroking his thumb across the back of it. 'Lizzy, you know there's an "us". It's always been there, from the time we first met. We're connected to each other. You must've felt it too?'

I know what he's talking about, but it seems like it's me from another lifetime—the Lizzy that couldn't stop thinking about him, yearning to be with him. Now that I know the whole situation, is it what I want?

'But how is this even going to work?' I ask.

'Like with any other couple.'

'No, I mean ... What if some cute gay guy strolls into town, and you like the look of him. Am I meant to turn a blind eye while you have sex with him and fall in love? I've seen *Brokeback Mountain*. I know how it works.'

Dain sighs. 'No, Lizzy, that's not how it works with me. If I'm in love with someone, there's nothing that can get in the way of that. Well, OK, I was in love with Gareth. I probably would still be with him if the whole thing hadn't gotten fucked up. It's my fault. I was greedy—I wanted both of them ... But that was two years ago, and I've moved on. I had to for my own sanity.'

'Has Gareth moved on?'

Dain looks uncomfortable. 'I can't speak for him. He doesn't want anything to do with me, which is fine. I get it—he got hurt. But so did I, and so did Joelle. At least she forgave me, and we're on speaking terms again, even if we're not the best of friends. I'm lucky I was able to salvage something out of the mess.'

Personally, I don't think Gareth has moved on, but I debate whether or not to give my opinion and decide not to.

He squeezes my hand. 'Anyway, it doesn't matter if he's moved on or not moved on. I have. And I've found someone amazing that I want to be with. It feels like a miracle after all I've been through. But it remains to be seen whether or not she wants to be with me.' His jaw works like he wants to expound on that statement, but he doesn't.

My feelings right now are a massive jumble of tangled wool, and I can't even begin to unravel them.

He said 'if I'm in love with someone'. So does that mean he loves me? Reader, I'm too scared to ask.

'Lizzy, are we going to be able to get through this?' he asks quietly as I'm still mulling over his words and haven't spoken.

'I honestly don't know. I need some time.'

'Take all the time you need,' Dain says resignedly. It sounds like he's already given up hope.

'I should go. Otherwise, I'm going to miss my train.'

He nods, releasing my hand, and smiles sadly at me. 'Yes, you'd better.'

I head back to my room to grab my bags, phone, and charger. I'm glad I'm getting out of here today, even if Klint is waiting for me at the other end. I look at my empty wheelie case. Should I take all my stuff with me? In case I decide not to come back? I'm torn straight down the middle with belongings in two houses.

There's a rustle by the door as a folded piece of paper is pushed underneath. I bend to pick it up. It says in curly Gothic script,

Lizzy,

I ask you to pass through life at my side—to be my second self, and best earthly companion.

Please come back to me.

Dain x

Tears spring to my eyes. It's what Rochester said to Jane when he was proposing and she was convinced that he didn't care about her. But Rochester was straight, not bi. And I can't quite believe that I'm special enough that Dain would forsake all others, women *and* men. I grab a pen and scrawl underneath,

Don't quote Jane Eyre. That's not fair!

I fold it and shove it under the door. There's scratching outside for a few minutes, and the note appears again.

It's how I feel. I don't want to lose you. This isn't your fault—it's mine. I should've told you. I'm so sorry. I hope you can forgive me. X

Time for more tough questions, ones that I don't want the answers to. Before I can change my mind, I write,

Did you have threesomes with Gareth and Joelle? Is the Sophronia series based on Joelle?

There's a silence outside the door after the note is received, ten agonising seconds of scratching, and the note is pushed back under.

Yes, but only a couple of times. It didn't really work. And yes, it is, but there was a lot of artistic license.

I crumple the note in my fist. The truth hurts. Lizzy Doyle, you are a naive fucking idiot.

Chapter 25

You are not so bewitched, ma'am, are you,
as to remain with him of your own accord?

(Emily Brontë, *Wuthering Heights*)

To say I'm struggling to process Dain's revelation is an understatement. I manage to ward it off with the hustle and bustle of getting to the station. But once I'm settled on the train, with nothing else to do but think, my mind is invaded with *the vision.*

Sophronia (Joelle) clutching the bedpost and moaning, with a guy (Dain) underneath licking her out and the guy in front rubbing her breasts and clit (Gareth). *Aarrrgh, the faceless lustful men that Tabitha Lavish was so good at* not *describing now have faces!*

It morphs into another worse vision: Dain having sex with Gareth at the hotel, maybe even in room 6 or 9. *Having a sixty-nine!* No wonder he didn't want to come in for breakfast when delivering me to the door!

The truth has now turned into a suppurating sore of a

different kind. Our two nights of passion and all our pretty words to each other now seem to be for nothing. I'm having to mentally adjust my whole notion of him starting from the day we met. Our 'Stars' conversation on the landing isn't special now because Gareth's always going to commandeer that poem for him. I feel deceived and betrayed by someone I thought I could trust.

A sob heaves in my chest. Who am I going to talk to about this? My mother is gone, and I don't talk to my father. No siblings. And Klint's driven away my friends. But one good thing about the digital age is that there are strangers, somewhere in the world, who have found themselves in the same situation and are willing to post about it.

Exhausted from reading through angsty online forums, none of which help, I curl up in the seat next to the window and attempt to catch up on some sleep. Maybe it's all the emotion coursing through my veins, but I have one of those vivid vision-type dreams I had at the hotel. It's raining, and I'm standing in front of an open grave with three women dressed in black stationed around it. I can't see their faces because they're wearing black veils. There's a feeling of extreme sadness in the air. I inch forward and attempt to peer into the grave. But the earth crumbles, and I fall forward, tumbling into nothingness.

I wake with a gasp, my heart thudding in fear. The train is still barrelling along. I look around. No one's staring at me strangely, so I don't think I screamed out loud or anything. I shake my head to clear it. What the hell was that about? Feeling completely weirded out, I check my phone to find out where we are and discover a message:

Dain: *I see you took your things and left my gifts. I guess that's my answer. Well, I can die happy now that I've known you. Tabby says goodbye.*

My heart constricts painfully. He's never sent me such a cold, unfeeling message before. But I guess I deserve it. Maybe I shouldn't have taken all my stuff with me. It does look a bit final. However, I was trying to be practical. I can't stay there when I'm feeling so confused and hurt. And I didn't want to take his gifts because I'd probably start crying every time I saw them, and it would make things more difficult.

I start typing a reply, saying I need time ... But I'm not sure what good that will do. Is time going to help anything? So I delete the words letter by letter.

Maybe it's the godawful dream I've had, but a strong sense of foreboding washes over me at his 'I can die happy now that I've known you'.

Don't be silly, Lizzy. He's being melodramatic. He's a writer. It's probably from one of his books. But I've read all of them, and I don't remember reading that line.

*****

As soon as I enter the flat, I can see Klint has let things slide. There are dirty dishes in the kitchen sink and empty wine bottles and books strewn everywhere. And there's a lingering stale smell in the lounge like he hasn't opened the windows in months. Klint emerges from the bedroom. And, reader, it's a bit of a shock. He looks rough.

His hair is scraggly and unwashed, his beard unkempt. He's wearing a baggy dark-blue Oxford T-shirt that's hanging on his skinny frame and grey jogger bottoms with a large tomato sauce stain on the crotch.

But there's nothing wrong with his mouth. Without even a hello, he starts giving me shit about Dain.

'How's the Brontësaurus? Has he told you he plays for both teams yet?' He smirks, and my heart sinks like a stone. Oh, so he knows. Klint's jeering message with the laughing face emoji makes perfect sense now. He's known about this for months and probably been giggling about it to himself.

'Hello to you too. Yes, I know,' I say through gritted teeth, wheeling my suitcase over to the bookcase. 'How did you find out?'

Klint flops onto the couch, kicks his dirty feet up on the coffee table, and starts cleaning his teeth with a used toothpick lying on the armrest. My senses recoil. He really does have some revolting habits.

'Gareth told me.'

'Why would Gareth have told you that?'

'Well, my girlfriend was stuck out on the moors, and Gareth asked me to ring Dain to go and help you. That struck me as being weird for a start. How did he know Dain had the necessary skills, and why couldn't *he* ring him? Since I was annoyed he was being involved, Gareth reassured me that Dain wouldn't hit on you. I was all like "What, so he's gay?" And Gareth got weird, and I kept probing, so to speak.' He chuckles at his own joke.

'And from what Gareth was saying about him breaking up with Joelle from the café, I surmised Dain was bi-confused. I also surmised from the way that he was going on about Dain that something had happened between them. It was like unplugging a dam—he couldn't stop raving about him.'

I start collecting my books from the shelf hurriedly and depositing them into the suitcase. 'Can we not talk about this?' The pain of finding out about Dain and Gareth is still fresh, and I don't think I can bear dragging my wounded heart over more gravel.

Klint doesn't hear me, or does, and refuses to comply. He tosses the salivary toothpick onto the floor and wiggles his bare toes like he's enjoying this. 'Anyway, I was getting pretty slammed from the free whisky top-ups, and Gareth was drinking wine and still rabbiting on about Dain and how great he was blah, blah, blah. But my suspicion about Gareth liking trousers was confirmed.' He smirks again.

'Why? What happened?'

'He stroked my hand and suggested we go up to room 9. I was shocked, as you can imagine, and shut that down immediately. I made some excuse about needing to sleep and scarpered.'

Gareth came on to Klint!

I stare at him. 'Wow, you kept that quiet.'

'Yeah, well, I had other things to worry about.'

'As I told you, Dain never once overstepped the mark when we were on the moors. He was caring and looked after me. If it wasn't for him, I wouldn't be here today,' I say. 'Not that you give a shit.'

Tears welling, I turn my back. But I can still feel Klint's eyes piercing through my shoulder blades as I put my last novel, *Little Women* by Louisa May Alcott, in the suitcase.

'I do give a shit,' he says with a sigh. 'I really hope for your sake that you're just flatmates. You don't want to be with a bi-confused person. He'll be on and off like a light switch, and you'll end up like Gareth—completely fucked in the head about him.'

'He's not bi-confused,' I say quietly. 'He knows he likes both sexes.' *And he doesn't have any light switches ...*

'Lizzy, please tell me you haven't done anything stupid like sleep with him?' Klint's tone sounds plaintive, but also half mocking, like he doesn't believe I'd get involved with someone like Dain. Beautiful, kind Dain.

I zip up the suitcase.

'Lizzy?'

'It's none of your fucking business!' I yell, rounding on him.

Klint's eyes widen, and his face goes mottled red. He gets up from the couch and runs his hands through his greasy hair aggressively. 'Oh fucking hell, you did!' he moans.

I'm not about to correct him on a technicality and get into the details of what we did last night.

Well, Klint, we played this sexy game ...

'Dain and I are living together, and we see each other on a daily basis—it's only natural that we've grown closer. What did you expect?'

Klint's jaw works like he's having trouble speaking.

'Some fucking self-control!' he spits. 'I haven't been with anyone out of respect for you.'

'We've been over for months, Klint!'

I lug the suitcase with the books over to the lounge door. It's going to be fun manoeuvring this on the train to wherever the heck I'm going. I have another bag in the bedroom I can use for clothes. I make a move to walk out, but Klint blocks my way.

'So what—you're his girlfriend now? Or his bi-bit on the side while he finds a man to fuck too?' he sneers.

I don't know. He gave me a note quoting Jane Eyre ... 'For God's sake, Klint, get out of my face. It's no concern of yours what I do.'

But what am I going to do now? I had two homes. Now I have exactly zero. I'm so confused, and Klint is shining the torch on my vulnerability. And what about my thesis? I've written 12,000 words. Am I going to chuck it all away when it's something that I believe in so strongly?

'There's something else you should know. Dain is mentally unstable. He tried to top himself after Gareth broke up with him.'

I stare at Klint. 'What?'

'It's true. Ask Gareth! It's why he doesn't go near him now. Joelle found out and told him. Dain swallowed a bottle of pills and was rushed to hospital. He had his stomach pumped.'

All the air in the room is sucked out. 'Are ... are you

sure?' I ask, my brain refusing to believe it. *Oh no, Dain!*

'Positive. Gareth was in vino veritas. He was telling me all sorts of things. Sounds like it was a bad time all round.' Klint shakes his head, but I can tell by his matter-of-fact tone that he doesn't give a damn about Dain.

He's building up to making a point, which, sure enough, comes straight after.

'With your history, you shouldn't be with someone like that.'

My knees start quaking. 'Don't you dare bring up my mother.'

'Lizzy, I'm just saying—'

'Even if it is true about Dain', I interrupt shakily, 'you should know how it would be for me to hear that and have some compassion.' *Oh god, Dain!*

He sighs. 'Fine. I won't say anything else. But you know it's not healthy for you.'

I guess I shouldn't mention I'm writing a thesis on depression ...

'I stayed with you and dealt with your issues, didn't I?' I state curtly.

'That's different. Sometimes I get down when I'm stressed, but I've been good at taking my medication lately. I feel like I'm on top of things.'

Really? You look like a dog's dinner.

'Can't we work things out, Lizzy?' he wheedles and looks at me with sad eyes.

But I'm too busy worrying about Dain to deal with Klint's emotional blackmail. I check my phone, but there's been no further messages from him—only that awful one: 'I can die happy now that I've known you' ... Shit! I need to get back to Haworth.

'No, we can't work things out,' I say, pushing past him and running to the bathroom. 'You can give my clothes to charity,' I toss over my shoulder. I haven't got time to sift through them. But my large toiletry bag is easily collected as I keep it in the cupboard under the sink. Then I'm out of here.

I bend down to collect the bag and see a distinctive gold tube standing on the shelf above next to a stack of toilet rolls. I pick it up and look at the end of it: Pink Pucker.

Reader, this isn't mine. I can't afford to buy £25 Elizabeth Arden lipsticks. Klint's claim that he hasn't been with anyone out of respect for me is looking a little dubious. My spine starts quivering in fury. He comes in as I've finished writing 'L I A R' on the mirror with Pink Pucker.

'What the fuck are you doing?'

I brandish the lipstick in his face. 'Whose is this?' I demand. 'A one-night stand?'

Klint looks at the floor, guilt written over his face.

'No one's.'

'Don't play dumb. You're such a fucking holier-than-thou hypocrite.'

'Fine, it's Susan's.'

I gape. 'Your supervisor? The old married one?'

'She's not that old.'

'She's 60!'

'Fifty-eight actually,' he retorts, his face an unattractive beetroot colour. 'I got lonely, OK? It was stupid. She was coming on to me, and it was over before it started. I'm not seeing her anymore. God, imagine.'

I shake my head slowly. 'Klint, when you do have another relationship, hopefully with someone who isn't married, please be a good person to them. Treat them well. This conversation is over.'

I walk past him. But he grabs me, pushes me up against the sink, and tries to kiss me. His breath smells foul, like wet, mouldy gym socks. I turn my head, nearly gagging, but he grips my jaw and twists it to meet his fleshy spittle-flecked lips.

No! Grabbing his wrist, I manage to lever one of his hands away from my jaw and chomp down hard, tasting blood. He yells in shock and springs away, clutching his hand to his chest, as I gnash my teeth at him like a feral dog.

'If you ever fucking touch me again, I swear to God I'll

kill you!' I howl. 'I don't want you! I want Dain! I don't care if he's bisexual. Whatever our souls are made of, his and mine are the same!'

Goodbye, Lizzy Doyle. Hello, Catherine Earnshaw ...

Chapter 26

The sharp iron tang of Klint's blood invades my mouth, making me feel queasy. I cease from running down the street, take a pull from my water bottle, and promptly vomit a stream of pink water onto the grass. He shouldn't have backed me into a corner. I'm a wounded dog, likely to attack without warning.

I try calling Dain—my third attempt since leaving the flat—while juggling my bulging tote along with two unwieldy suitcases. But there's no reply. It goes straight to voice message again. By this time, my anxiety is through the roof. Reader, as you know, I'm not a religious person, yet I'm praying fervently: *Dear God, please keep him safe.* But there's a dark void in my soul, and his silence is damning me; it feels like he's left the planet.

Nevertheless, I'm relieved I have a fully charged phone. If Dain's taught me anything about being prepared when there's a storm on the horizon, it's that.

Maybe he's at the parsonage; that's why he's not answering. At the train station, I call the Brontës' home and have a weird hopeful feeling that the fabric of time might stretch beyond all bounds of understanding and Charlotte will answer. Because I need her to tell me, 'He's not over here with us, Lizzy. He's fine.'

Charlotte doesn't answer. Instead, a man says in a clipped tone, 'Brontë Parsonage Museum. How may I help?'

'Hi, is your guide Dain Whitmore on today?'

'I'm not sure. I haven't seen him anyway.'

I think quickly. 'Can I speak to Bridget then? Sorry, I don't have her mobile number. It's a bit urgent.'

The man pauses before answering, 'I'll have to hunt her down and get her to call you back. What's your name and number?'

Relieved he's being helpful and not brushing me off, I give him my name and number and make him repeat it back to me. I'm not going to chance fate on a mistaken digit.

Bridget rings as I'm halfway to Leeds. I'm trying not to lose it, but each time I ring Dain and it goes to voicemail, my anxiety spikes.

'Hi, Lizzy. You left a message for me to call you?'

'Bridget ...' I'm so relieved to hear her voice I choke up and have to cough to clear my throat. 'Bridget, can you please go round to Dain's and check on him?' She knows we're flatmates, but I'm not sure what else Dain has told her.

'Why? What's wrong?' she asks, concern creeping into her tone.

'Nothing. But I'm out of town, and he's not answering his mobile, and I'm ...' I take a deep breath. 'Slightly worried. It's not like him.'

'OK, I'm sure he's fine, but I'll check. I needed to pop round anyway.'

'How's the editing going?' I ask. Dain's told her I know about him being Tabitha Lavish since she comes round to collect his pages.

'Good! This latest one is my favourite.' Her voice lowers. 'Very racy ...'

I smile to myself. You wouldn't know it looking at her, but Bridget is definitely an undercover spicy reader. My mind flashes back to when I first met her and how I thought she and Dain were having trysts on the moors. Ironically, I'm the one that's been having a secret affair with him.

Bridget promises to call me as soon as she's seen Dain, and my anxiety eases. At least I'll find out second-hand that he's all right, even if he doesn't want to reply to my messages. A plan of action is underway, but I still have one further train change and a bus ride before I reach Haworth.

***

What the hell is she doing? Washing her hair before she goes round there? Maybe I should've emphasised the urgency.

It's been an hour, but still nothing from Bridget, and my heart constantly rises and dips like a roller coaster whenever I check my phone. *Hello, someone? Anyone!*

***

It's early evening; and I'm on the Brontë bus, almost in Haworth, when Bridget finally calls back.

'Sorry it took me so long. I had to sort out some stuff at home before I went round.' Seriously? I really should've told her it was urgent! 'I knocked quite a few times,' she continues. 'But there was no answer. The house was dark, but that's not unusual since he doesn't have lighting. Maybe he's writing upstairs and turned his phone off?'

'Maybe.'

But he never writes upstairs, and I still can't shake this apprehensive feeling in my lower gut.

'He could also be at the Black Bull. Do you want me to check?'

Is Dain drowning his sorrows in whisky and crying over me in the corner like Branwell? God, I hope not.

'No, no, I'm ten minutes away from Haworth. I'll be there shortly anyway. But thank you.'

'No problem. Let me know if you do need anything. I'll stay up for a bit.'

'Thanks.'

I feel grateful that Bridget is involved. The next option is calling Gareth, and I really don't want to do that.

My footsteps slow as I near the house, my suitcases reverberating on the dimly lit pavement of the cold empty street. I think I've convinced myself that whatever I'm going to find inside is going to be bad, and I don't want to face it. But my feelings for Dain are spurring me on and making me brave enough to put my key in the lock. This isn't the same as my mother, and he might need help.

The house is in complete darkness.

And as silent as the grave.

'Dain!' I call out sharply, but there's no answer. *Shit.* Forgoing the kerosene lamp because my hand is shaking too badly to light a match, I switch my phone torch on instead. As I point it up the stairs, someone looms in front of me. 'Jesus Christ!' I gasp and shrink back but then realise it's just my phone casting a shadow on the wall. Trying to calm my nerves, I ascend, keeping the light focused on the stairs. *One step at a time, Lizzy. You can do it.*

I reach the landing and shine the light on Dain's door. It's closed. 'Dain?' I call, edging closer to it. 'Are you in there?' I knock softly. Still no reply. My heart is banging like a bass drum. I don't want to open the door, but I give myself a stern talking-to. *Whatever's in there might not be as bad you're imagining. Remember there were no dead bats. Just do it!*

Taking a deep shuddering breath, I grasp the handle, twist, and slowly open the door. Poking my phone torch into the cold, dark room, Dain's four-poster bed is illuminated—and the black velvet curtains are tightly closed. Uttering a low moan and feeling like I'm in a Gothic horror movie, I shuffle forward with my hand outstretched until I touch the edge of a curtain. Tears well in my eyes. *He's gone, I know it. Let's get it over with.*

Tentatively, I pull back the curtain and shine my torch in. My breath catches in my throat. Dain is stretched out on the bed in his ruffled shirt, his face pale and his hands crossed over his chest. Next to him on the bed is an open packet of pills.

I stare in horror.

I'm too late.

'Oh no, *Dain*!' I cry and burst into violent, racking sobs loud enough to wake the dead.

And maybe I do because Dain's eyes fly open.

'Lizzy!' he exclaims and smiles at me. Uncrossing his arms from his chest, he sits up.

Reader, am I seeing things? Do I want him to be alive so badly that I've conjured this? But his hand is holding mine, and I squeeze it to find it's solid and warm. Oh my god, it's real. He's alive.

Happiness like I've never known surges through me, and I start sobbing joyful tears instead of ones of grief. 'I couldn't get hold of you, and I thought ... I thought ...' I gasp.

Dain puts an arm round me, and I slump into him, still not quite believing he's in the land of the living.

'I've been writing all day! Azalea and Nathaniel broke up, and what with you leaving, it was a difficult chapter to write ... It gave me a headache, so I was having a little lie-down to recover ...'

Then he sees I'm still crying hard against his chest and grasps both my shoulders, peering at my face.

'Lizzy, what's going on?'

I gulp, trying to form sentences. 'Klint said after Gareth broke up with you ... I came back as soon as I could. But you weren't answering your phone. And when I saw you.

Like that. And with these pills!' I pick up the packet and thrust it at him.

Dain's hands fall from my shoulders, and he sinks back down onto the bed and puts an arm across his eyes as if to shield himself from me.

'Is it true? Did you ... did you take a whole lot of pills, after Gareth ... ?'

'I was desperate and alone. I needed my dad, but he rejected me when I told him about me and Gareth. It was like a double whammy. So I took a few pills I'd been prescribed for depression to numb the pain, then some more as they weren't working. I may have gone over the limit. I wasn't feeling great, so I rang 111, and they overreacted a bit.'

'And now?' I say, opening the packet.

'It's paracetamol. I had two,' he says defensively. I check, and most of them are there.

I bury my wet face in my hands and squeeze my eyes shut.

'You scared the bejesus out of me,' I say, my voice wobbling all over the place. 'I thought it was going to be a repeat of my mother.'

'What do you mean?'

'She killed herself when I was 16.'

Dain shoots up into a sitting position. 'Oh no. Don't tell

me you found her?'

I nod. 'In the bedroom after school. Pretty much like this.'

I start crying again as he rocks me in his arms, murmuring 'Oh, Lizzy, I'm so sorry. Oh, my darling girl' over and over.

After I'm all cried out, Dain leans over and lights a kerosene lamp, and I wipe my eyes with a stray tissue I find in my jacket pocket. It comes away blackened. At first, I think it's mascara. But there's a lot of it, and it's all over my cheek too. Ink seems to be leaking from his chest like black blood; the front of his shirt is covered in it.

'Have you got a quill in your pocket or something?'

Dain looks down. 'Damn.' He takes out the now rather bedraggled drawing of Miss Lizzy that he drew for me. My tears have soaked through his pocket and made the ink run.

'Oh no!' My eyes water again.

'Don't worry about it. I'll draw you another one,' he says quickly, patting my arm. 'I was feeling pretty rough after you left, so I had her in my pocket to keep me strong. Charlotte's been looking after me too. She's been on at me all day. "Don't do anything silly, Dain. Lizzy will be back. Just wait. Write and keep busy." So I waited, and I wrote like she said.'

I smile at him. 'She talks to me too.'

'She's quite bossy, isn't she?'

I laugh. 'She is! But usually right ... about matters of the heart.'

Dain takes my hand and kisses it. He puts my palm on his inky chest, and I can feel the reassuring thump of his heartbeat. 'I know you probably see the future with me as an unknown,' he says softly, 'and quite frankly, I can understand why you might be terrified after what you told me. I'm scared too, scared that you might decide you're better off without me. But I'm willing to risk heartbreak because I love you and I can't imagine life without you.'

I let go of the breath I've been holding. 'I love you too, so much. There's nothing I want more than to be with you.'

Dain grins. 'You've just made Mr Rochester very happy,' he says and kisses me with an intensity that takes my breath away. 'You bewitched me the moment I saw you on the parsonage landing. I thought all my Christmases had come at once.'

Reader, it's the truth. We've loved each other from the second our souls first met, even if it's taken a while for us to get our shit together.

Chapter 27

My soul is awakened, my spirit is soaring
And carried aloft on the wings of the breeze;
For above and around me the wild wind is roaring,
Arousing to rapture the earth and the seas.

(Anne Brontë, 'Lines Composed in a Wood on a Windy Day')

A few days after we declare our love for each other, an article appears in my inbox without warning. Dain is at the parsonage at the time, and I'm at home working on my thesis. The article is titled 'How to Date a Bisexual Person: 13 Steps (with Pictures)'.

Bemused, I read it, and it's along the lines of what I know already: he's attracted to both sexes, but he's chosen to be with me, and I have nothing to worry about. Even though I trust him implicitly, I suppose it does ease my mind further that he's not going to dump me for a hot guy.

I reply with: *Thanks for that, an interesting read!* and get *You're welcome!* in return. We don't talk about it when he gets home.

The next day, another one appears: '10 Things to Know before Dating Bisexual Men'. It pretty much repeats the other article but adds that I shouldn't ask him if he's secretly gay or for make-up tips. Noted. Now I'm more curious than bemused.

Me: *Are you pleading your case with these articles? I appreciate you sending them, but not sure why you are. I thought we were OK?*

Dain: *We are. I just wanted to make sure you know it's about the person. I'm attracted to both sexes, but it's the person I love—ie. YOU.*

Me: *I love you too. And I trust you. I know you're not going to run off with the first piece of juicy man arse that walks into town.*

Dain: *Well, if it's a juicy man arse that reads Jane Eyre, who can say what I'll do ... (that's a joke btw, I wouldn't even look twice at said man's arse!)*

Me: *Haha, very funny. I don't mind if you look, just not touch.*

Dain: *Good to know (winking face emoji). Anyway, why are we so focused on me? I'm sure you've had a little dabble.*

Me: *No, I haven't. I'm strictly straight.*

Dain: *Oh. OK. Well, I'll leave you to it. See you this afternoon. X*

I get back to my work, and a short while later, another article appears: 'Why More Women Identify as Sexually Fluid Than Men'. I sigh and roll my eyes. That one can wait.

* * *

Along with making sure I'm clued up on his sexual preferences, Dain has taken it upon himself to interpret my dreams since they're so vivid lately. He's even bought a dream symbol book at a local store with a black cover and silver swirls. So when I casually mention the one I had about falling into the open grave, his eyebrows shoot up to his hairline. 'Fantastic,' he breathes. 'That's a good omen.'

'Really? It seems kind of ominous.'

'Uh-uh. Dreams of death don't usually mean dying in

real life.' He practically runs to grab his dream symbol book from the parlour bookshelf and flicks through the pages excitedly. 'Aha, just as I thought. It represents rebirth. Your soul is recovering from mental trauma, and you're breaking old habits and behaviours that hurt you. It also signifies a new beginning and a spiritual transformation.'

'Interesting,' I say, knowing exactly what he's getting at. 'So that means ...?'

He taps a finger on the page impatiently. 'It means your toxic relationship with Klint is over, and you're embarking on a brand new and much healthier one with me, of course.'

'Ah, right. What about falling into the grave?'

'Well, it's unfortunate,' he says in a serious tone. 'But sometimes you have to fall into darkness before you can step into the light.'

'So Klint was the darkness?'

'I hate to say it, but to borrow your phrase, "if the cap fits",' says Dain sagely and returns to his book.

I know that's all I'll get out of him on the subject of my ex-boyfriend. He keeps his opinions to himself as he's never one to talk ill of people. But I know he despises Klint; his face scrunches up in distaste whenever his name is mentioned, like he's being forced to eat Brussels sprouts.

*****

Dain's also being very careful with me as we navigate through the aftermath of our 'false break-up', as he calls it, and all the revelations about our pasts. I tell him about how my mother struggled with depression for years, trying different medications, but nothing worked. In the end, it was easier for her to stop trying. My thesis is as much for her as it is for the Brontës.

Dain cradles me in his warm arms as I cry, and his loving words and soft kisses to my forehead give me the emotional healing I crave; he's like Tiger Balm to my soul.

Around this time, Emily's poetry is replaced by a slim volume of Anne's on his nightstand, and he enjoys reading her poems aloud to me by lamplight. There's a particularly lovely one that transports me to the moors and makes me think of my blustery walk to Top Withens. I'm aching to be outside and striding around in the fresh air, but winter has us in her icy grip, and the countryside is covered in snow. Dain promises that he'll take me for a hike 'as soon as the weather improves'. For now, I'm content to snuggle up with him in the four-poster, listening to his resonant voice as restless high winds keen round the house.

But, reader, a red-blooded woman can't live on poetry alone, no matter how beautiful it is. My physical need for him grows stronger with every passing day that we're officially together, and I know that when I catch Dain looking at me longingly, he's remembering our hot night of sexy fun before it all turned to custard.

Even though he's been wearing his vicar outfit lately, it's a ruse. He's testing me, seeing if he can get me to crack, but I'm determined to hold out and make him crack first. However, the thought of Dain on his knees, begging me to pleasure him, is definitely a daydream that's causing my resolve to crumble.

One cold, wet, grey afternoon, we're in the parlour, sitting at opposite ends of the couch with our legs stretched out in front of a blazing fire. I'm reading through the latest chapter of my thesis when Dain says, 'Would you mind having a look at this?'

Glancing up, I see he's proffering a book with a midnight-blue cover, and I smile upon reading the swirling gold title: *Forbidden Love on the Moors*.

It's book 1 of his Azalea's Awakening series.

'Oh my god, finally!' Carefully, I take it from him and check out the cover. It's the lower face and torso of a woman with pouting red lips and long wavy chestnut hair in a strapless blue corset. She has her hands on her hips. A dark-haired man is behind her, but you can see only his bent head kissing her shoulder, his fingers interlacing with hers.

'Wow, it's amazing. Your cover designer did a great job.'

Dain nods, looking pleased. 'Yes, she did.'

'Eeek, I'm going to start reading now!' I place my laptop on the floor and flip to the first page excitedly.

'OK, enjoy, my love,' he says and goes back to his own book with a small smile playing across his lips.

A few pages in, I realise it's a set-up. After Nathaniel removes Azalea's corset, the book gets *very* steamy. But Dain is watching me, so I can't react. I blink, cough, and turn the page.

'Are you all right, my love?'

'Yes, fine,' I say in a strangled tone. Dain's thigh muscle flexes next to my shin, and he undoes the top button of his round-collared shirt. Then another. But I ignore him and keep reading. Nathaniel has now affixed clamps to Azalea's nipples and is busy licking and nibbling her clit with gusto while tugging lightly on the nipple chain, causing her to moan in pleasure. Phew-weee! I lower the book, feeling hot and bothered as a steady throb starts up between my legs.

'Did they even *have* nipple clamps in the 1800s?'

Dain grins. 'Ah, you're up to that bit. Yes, you'd be surprised. The Victorians were totally into it. Nipple piercings too. I've done my research.'

I hate to think what his browser history is like on his laptop. Yes, he now has one after I pointed out that Bridget would be able to edit a lot faster if she didn't have to type up his handwritten manuscripts first. He seems to be coping OK, and his fingers are a lot less inky. Wi-Fi is his latest concession to the twenty-first century, and it's coming next week. Speaking of coming ... My eyes flick ahead to anticipate what might happen in this book so I can control my pounding pulse.

'Don't skim, Lizzy. You have to read it properly,' Dain urges.

So I read a few more paragraphs, but soon, I have to close it as my blood pressure spikes again. I blow out a breath, my cheeks flushing. 'God, it's really spicy! How do you write this stuff?'

He shrugs. 'I'm simply a vessel supplying what my readers want.' His dark eyes twinkle mischievously. 'Good though, isn't it?'

I put the book to one side, trying to calm down. No wonder Bridget liked it. Racy indeed ...

'Yes, but I can't read any more, not while you're watching me.'

'OK, sorry.' His lips twitch.

'I'll carry on later.'

'Sure.'

I put the book on the floor and consider picking up my laptop, but I'm so turned on I can't think straight; working is out of the question. Dain keeps reading with a knowing smile. After a few minutes, he undoes yet another button on his vicar shirt; and it gapes open, exposing his smooth chest and strawberry-pink nipples. I gulp. The crafty devil. He's weakened my defences with his book on purpose. *I'm in so much trouble* ... Ignoring him, I close my eyes and pretend to rest.

Another few minutes later, he comments, 'Gosh, it's hot in here.' I open my eyes to find Dain is now shirtless and has loosened his trousers. He stretches his arms above his head, and heat flows over me in waves as I gaze at his half-naked body and the tip of his glistening cock poking out of his pants. Fuck, he's so sexy. My mouth waters. I want him. Correction: I *need* him. What's left of my wall of resolve crumbles in a puff of masonry, and I fall upon his crotch, licking what I can see and tugging down his trousers until he's properly out and I can take him fully into my mouth.

Caught by surprise at my fervour, Dain quickly recovers and arches his hips, driving deeply into my mouth and letting out a long low moan of appreciation as I suck him hard.

After a few minutes, I reluctantly abandon his cock because I don't want him to come yet. I kiss my way up his chest to his neck, keeping one hand lightly stroking his shaft. He eases my leggings down and slips a hand into my knickers.

'Wow, you're really wet,' he whispers as I nuzzle his cheek.

'I wonder why,' I mutter. 'If your fans are as sexually deprived as I am, that book is going to be a bestseller.'

'Sexually deprived? Oh no, how terrible. We need to remedy that.' He squeezes my clit, and I gasp as heated electricity swirls around my groin. Then I mewl in pleasure as he starts fucking me with his fingers.

'So do you want to go upstairs or make love by the fire, oh, sexually deprived one?' he enquires in a husky whisper.

'Fire, please, fire,' I pant. I'm burning up anyway.

Possessed by a feral need I can't even begin to understand, I don't bother wasting time by taking off my leggings. Pulling them halfway down my thighs, I clamber on top of him, groaning as he inserts his slick length into my wet, needy pussy, adjusting my hips until he's all the way in.

'Ohh, Lizzy, yessss, oh, my love,' he moans. The feeling of his hard cock moving inside me is exquisite; and soon, I'm a sweaty, wild-haired mess, rutting and rotating my hips. I can't get enough. But we're too turned on for it to last long. Dain's breathing shallows, and his lovely lust-soaked eyes lock on mine as our bucking hips reach a crescendo, and we crest the wave of ecstasy together. My lips part in silent rapture, and he thrusts harder, crying out in pleasure as his orgasm hits; warmth gushes into me, and my shuddering core opens, welcoming all of him.

I collapse onto his chest, breathing hard enough to burst and to be honest, reader, slightly scared. 'What the hell was that?' I utter.

Dain kisses the top of my head and smooths down the back of my ruched-up T-shirt.

'Don't be afraid, my darling. It's love and passion,' he says, then pauses thoughtfully and murmurs, almost to himself, 'Yes ... love and unbridled passion on the moors ...'

Hmm, why do I get the feeling this could be the title of his next novel?

Chapter 28

It will be well, we wish it to be so.

(Emily Brontë, diary paper)

Sure enough, a couple of days later, Dain is furiously typing in a blaze of excited energy, which is rubbing off on me. He tells me book 2 is a second chance romance, where Azalea and Nathaniel discover they can't live without each other. Apparently, it's even spicier than the first. I'm not quite sure how that will be possible, but he's the raunchy romance writer, not me.

I suppose our antics could be inspiring him. Yesterday, he bent me over the sink into the washing-up water and took me from behind—twice! Once in the morning, fully clothed; the other in the evening, half naked, with my bare breasts dipping into the warm water and him fingering my slippery nipples and clit to heighten the pleasure. It was pretty fantastic. But when I came, gasping, I almost choked on a mouthful of suds, which wasn't so pleasant.

He said that he'd been fantasising about our encounter in

the kitchen for a while and needed to play it out as it should have gone. Glad to know I wasn't alone in that one.

But sex with Dain is not always fast and frantic. Tonight, the curtains of our four-poster bed are drawn back; and he's making love to me in the moonlight—slow, gentle, and achingly tender. The pleasure is intense, and I can't do anything but lie here moaning and arching my hips to meet his as he caresses my breasts and explores every inch of my mouth with his searching tongue.

When I'm lying in his arms, spent from an orgasm that quite literally blew my mind, I trail a hand over his damp chest languidly and sigh. 'I love you.'

Dain kisses my forehead. 'I love you too.' After a beat, he murmurs against my hair, 'I want to spend forever with you.'

My pulse elevates as his meaning sinks in.

'Forever is a long time ...'

He shakes his head. 'It's not long enough.'

My heart is a glowing coal. Tears welling, I bury my head in his chest, inhaling the comforting vanilla scent of his skin. He strokes my back lightly and lets me have my moment.

After a few minutes, he caresses my cheek; and I sniff and raise my head to find half his face lit by moonlight, the other in deep shadow. Light, dark, strong, soft—my Brontë lover is a man of many moods and ever-changing faces.

But forever *is* a long time. I brush my thumb over his wrist and press on his pulse point. 'Dain ...'

His eyes lock on mine. 'Yes, my darling?'

I take a deep breath and steel myself. 'Is there anything else I should know about ... before we spend forever together?'

His sculpted lips curve in a wide smile, and I feel his pulse rate increase beneath my thumb.

'No, my love, there's nothing else.' He draws me down to seal our fate with a kiss, but as he does, I see one of his eyelids twitch. Reader, it's so subtle I can't be totally sure it happened. I'm hoping it was a trick of the moonlight.

***

One day, a month or so later, I'm rootling through a jewellery box of his aunt's in the bottom drawer of the armoire. Dain gave it to me because he thought there might be something in there I might like. I haven't had a chance to look at it until now. The box is an ugly old thing: chunky black wood inlaid with purple velvet. Inside is a tangled clump of costume jewellery: necklaces, earrings, brooches, and such, which I'm thinking the vintage shop might want. Bridget is coming over tomorrow for a coffee and a natter, so we can sit at the kitchen table and detangle it. She won't mind, and she's got nimble fingers.

I extract the clump of jewellery, and there's a rattle at the bottom of the box as a ring falls out. A slim gold band. I pick it up to inspect more closely and see an engraving: 'Love, honour, cherish'. OK, there's something creepy about holding a dead woman's wedding ring!

I'm about to put it back in the box, but my hand jerks of its own accord, and the ring flies into the side of the drawer and slips down a gap in the edge. A prickling sensation runs across the back of my neck. OK, weird. Perhaps his aunt didn't like me touching it?

I prod at the ring with my finger but only succeed in jamming it in further. Damn! I need something to insert down the side and lever it out. Maybe a knife or perhaps the fireplace poker—that would work better.

I head downstairs to the parlour, where Dain is ensconced at the table, busily tapping away on his laptop, brow furrowed in concentration. Apparently, he's nearing a tricky section where he has to decide whether Azalea and Nathaniel should get married or live in sin. With all the kinky shit that those two get up to, my money's on living in sin. I can't see them having a normal life. It must be causing him stress, though, as I note he's steadily munching his way through a pile of my home-made chocolate chip biscuits.

Stealing around behind the table, I manage to grab the

poker without disturbing him. Back in the room, I carefully lift out the jewellery box, stick the edge of the poker in the gap, and apply gradual pressure to get the ring to pop out. But the glue affixing the bottom of the drawer to the side must be old or non-existent as there's a cracking noise, and the whole board comes up. Damn, I'll have to superglue it back in without Dain knowing. I reach down to grab the ring, and my fingers come in contact with something soft that yields to my touch.

Curious, I yank up the board completely and discover a flattish, bulky parcel wrapped in brown wax paper lying underneath. What's this? His aunt's personal documents? I pick it up and feel a stack of papers move beneath, and somehow, I. Just. Know ...

Quickly, I drop it back in the drawer as if it's burning metal. *Oh my god!* Leaping to my feet, I pace around, wringing my hands and stealing glances at the drawer with my heart pumping wildly. Surely not? Is it? Eventually, I can't keep my emotions inside any longer. 'DAIN, GET UP HERE!' I scream at the top of my lungs.

There's a pounding on the stairs, and Dain comes racing in, panting. 'What's the matter? Have you hurt yourself?'

All I can do is point at the drawer speechlessly, and his face drains of all colour. Then I know I'm right.

'Lizzy,' he says in a low steady tone, which he uses when

he's about to enter an argument. 'You need to forget you ever saw that.'

But now I'm bouncing around the room like I've got springs in my legs. 'I can't believe I've been sleeping with it right next to me all this time. No wonder she was getting antsy! She probably made me drop the ring. In fact, I *know* she did.'

Dain lifts the wooden board to put it back in the drawer, which I now know has a false bottom.

I tug on his arm. 'What are you doing?'

'I have to.'

'Are you crazy? Don't shut it up again. Why are you keeping it in there? *And why the hell didn't you tell me?*'

He sighs. 'I wasn't ever going to tell you.'

I gape at him. 'Never? Did you seriously think you could keep *Emily Brontë's lost novel from me?*'

He doesn't say anything.

'Fine, play dumb. But I need to look after it from now on.'

Before he can stop me, I pluck the parcel from the drawer and crawl onto the bed, holding it to my chest protectively like it's a newborn child.

'Lizzy ...'

'No, I almost died trying to find this, and you never said a word, *and* you said there was nothing else you were keeping from me!' I exclaim. 'Spill, buddy!'

Dain puts down the board and chews his bottom lip. 'I didn't lie. There is nothing else—nothing that will affect us. This is different. I'm sorry I didn't tell you, but it's for a good reason.'

'There had better be,' I say accusingly. 'Well?'

'There's ... there's a curse on it.'

I scoff at that. 'Curse? Who from?'

'Charlotte.'

'Oh.' Actually, I can quite believe that. 'OK, you'd better start from the beginning.'

'Can I sit?' Dain asks. I nod, and he gingerly perches on the edge of the bed, as if he's trying not to startle a nervous deer. 'You were on the right track when you went digging on the moors,' he says quietly. 'I thought the same thing after reading *Villette*, that she'd buried it. But those trees by Top Withens are sycamores. Remember what you said? About her burying the jar in a hollow beneath a pear tree?'

I nod. 'I remember.'

'Well, I knew there were ancient pear trees at Ponden Hall. One of the sons who lived there planted them because he liked Emily. It's an Airbnb now, so I stayed there and did a little secret digging in the garden one night and discovered the manuscript. It was buried quite deeply in a lead-sealed casket ...'

Dammit, trust Dain to get it right. Being a local, he

knows background stuff like this.

'And there was a letter from Charlotte included with it,' he continues. 'She said she didn't want the manuscript published. But she hadn't been able to destroy her sister's hard work either, even though she'd "pruned" a few of her poems. She was in a moral dilemma and had decided this was the best solution. Yet her restless conscience wouldn't let it go, and a version of the truth came out in her writing. She said that if anyone pieced together the clues, found it, and published it, she'd heap ill will on them and come back to haunt them.'

'Surely, she was joking?'

'Maybe. But she also said her motivation wasn't jealousy or selfishness—it was purely an effort to keep the family's reputation intact, or words to that effect.'

'Ooh, she must've thought Emily's book was quite scandalous. But surely, it can't be any worse than what you write.' Dain pulls a face at me. 'You know what I mean,' I say hurriedly. 'I doubt it's that bad, and Charlotte's letter is 175 years out of date! No one would care if it's a little bit spicy or something. They'd probably enjoy it more because Emily was ahead of her time.'

Dain shakes his head. 'I can't go against her wish, Lizzy. Emily must've written about things in there that were too close to the bone. I can understand why Charlotte did it. Some secrets are better kept hidden.'

Wow, that's nuts. Dain is more superstitious than I thought he would be. He's really spooked that she's going to haunt him from beyond the grave. But I can't fault him for having a strong loyalty to Charlotte—that's him all over. My heart sinks. I can't believe this. We have Emily's lost novel, and we can't publish it or even tell anyone. The Brontë fans would be screaming if they knew.

I touch the package reverently. 'Have you read it?'

He shakes his head. 'No. Of course it's going to be fantastic. I don't trust myself not to get it published if I do.'

'So if I read it, I'd be the first person since Charlotte and Anne?'

Dain nods. I feel hot, cold, and hot again. I stare at him with pleading eyes.

He sighs. 'Go on then. I guess the curse doesn't apply to reading it, but it doesn't change anything. It's still not being published. Look at what happened when you went digging around for it. I'm not taking the risk in case something happens to you.' He reaches for my hand and squeezes it tightly.

'OK,' I say, feeling disappointed. Isn't he *burning* to read it like I am?

'You'll have to wear white gloves so you don't smudge the ink. I'll fetch a pair for you.'

He kisses my hand and goes off while I sit there clutching

the package, feeling like I'm the chosen one. This is the best thing that's happened to me in my entire life—apart from meeting Dain, of course.

He returns shortly and gives me the white gloves. 'I thought you might like some sustenance as well.' He proffers a replenished plate of chocolate chip biscuits, and I see he's also clutching another pair of white gloves.

'Are they a spare?' I ask.

'No, they're for me. I changed my mind. If you read it without me, I'm going to have major FOMO.'

His eyes are bright, and he's flushed in the cheeks. *Ah, this is the Dain I know and love.*

The biscuits rattle around on the plate like a mini earthquake is taking place inside him.

'Careful, love.' I pry his fingers off the plate and gently lower it to the bed. Handing him a biscuit, I take one for myself, stuffing it in my mouth; we pull on our white gloves, grinning at each other like idiots.

'Shall we begin?' He sits next to me on the bed. 'You do the honours.'

I lay the parcel in front of us and start unwrapping it with my heart pounding. It's got several layers. Charlotte's bound it up well. I reach a blank sheet of yellowed brittle paper. Flipping heck, this is it. My brain feels like it's going to burst with the enormity of it.

Well, here we go, Emily Jane. Whatever's in here is going

to be strictly hush-hush between the three of us.

I gently lift off the blank page; and underneath, there's the title and her pen name, Ellis Bell, which she was using at the time. Dain's breathing quickens. 'There she is,' he says, and my eyes sting with tears. I'm getting emotional, and we haven't even started reading!

Carefully setting that page aside, underneath is a page that says 'Chapter One' at the top and is covered in Emily's familiar inky scrawl. I know it as well as my own from all the hours I've spent poring over what's left of her letters and diary papers. So little, really, for such a famous literary figure.

White-gloved fingers laced together, we settle with the manuscript, ready to devour and adore like the Brontë lovers we are.

Half a chapter in, I pause, feeling agitated. 'Dain, there's pertinent stuff in here that I can use in my thesis. Am I going to have to ignore it?'

Dain rubs his gloved thumb over mine. 'I don't know. Maybe we can publish it if we sacrifice something to appease Charlotte ...'

'What, like our firstborn?' I scoff.

'Well, that's another conversation entirely,' he replies, glancing at me hesitantly. 'Lizzy, I suspect now's not the time for it, but since we're on the subject of firstborns ... What do you think of Ellis for a baby name? It's gender-neutral. But if it's a girl, we'd have to have Charlotte, Emily, *and* Anne for the middle names so no one gets offended. And then there's the question of the surname. What sounds better, Doyle-Whitmore or Whitmore-Doyle?'

I stifle a giggle; he's so funny. As always, his deliberations catch me by surprise. But this time, I'm right there on the same page. A feeling of contented happiness washes over me. I definitely want to start a family with this wonderful man—when I've finished my thesis and after we've figured out what to do about Emily's book, but that's another story.

Now that I know what the future holds, I don't need to be afraid anymore; our love is meant to last—it's written in the stars. I squeeze his hand and say with a smile, 'I think Ellis *Doyle*-Whitmore sounds absolutely perfect.'

The End

Keep Reading

If you like historical fiction and contemporary romance, check out my dual timeline rom-com *POX*.

If you like contemporary romance and historical fiction then you'll love this funny, heartwarming dual timeline rom-com. Expect secret crushes, comedy-drama, fake dating, spice, self-discovery and a cast of entertaining characters. Grab your copy today!

Available on Amazon and Kindle Unlimited

Books by Angela

FANGED AND FLIRTY SERIES

Flossed In Love
Enthralled By You
Biting My Knight

MISS AUSTEN SERIES

Trusting Miss Austen
Visiting Miss Austen
Amusing Miss Austen

STANDALONES

POX
Brontë Lovers
The Holly Project
You Had Me at Ice Cream
I'll Meet You in Florence
The House of Dating Disasters
My Double Life
Travel & Mayhem

COLLECTIONS

3 Book Rom-Com Collection
Miss Austen Series Box Set

All books available on Amazon and Kindle Unlimited

Acknowledgements

Dear reader, I hope you enjoyed *Brontë Lovers* and Lizzy and Dain's story. If so, I'd be thrilled if you left a review or star rating on Amazon and/or Goodreads.

It takes a small village to publish an indie novel. Thank you to my beta readers, Lauryn Lambert, Katie Griffin, Katy Hristova, Lauren Kent and Ryan Thornton for their honest feedback and encouragement. Big thanks to my diligent copy editor, Peachy Yap, who corrects all my wayward commas; and my wonderful cover art designer My Lan Khuc Valle for her gorgeous cover art featuring the Brontë Parsonage. Thank you also to my partner Chris Lambert for his love and support!

For mood music, check out the *Brontë Lovers* playlist:
angelapearse.pub/book-spotify-playlists

To receive alerts on upcoming releases,
sign up to my newsletter at

➜ angelapearse.pub

About the Author

ANGELA PEARSE writes contemporary, historical, and paranormal romances. Known for her quirky humour, Angela's books are often described as 'page-turners', ranging from light-hearted escapades to darker satire.

A freelance editor with an MA in English, Angela is originally from New Zealand but now calls Edinburgh home, finding endless inspiration in its rich history and atmospheric streets. Visit angelapearse.pub for more information or to join her mailing list.